DRAWING CONCLUSIONS

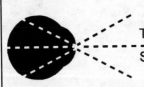

This Large Print Book carries the
Seal of Approval of N.A.V.H.

A SKETCH IN CRIME MYSTERY

DRAWING CONCLUSIONS

DEIRDRE VERNE

THORNDIKE PRESS
A part of Gale, Cengage Learning

GALE
CENGAGE Learning·

Farmington Hills, Mich • San Francisco • New York • Waterville, Maine
Meriden, Conn • Mason, Ohio • Chicago

GALE
CENGAGE Learning®

LIBRARY OF CONGRESS CATALOGING-IN-PUBLICATION DATA

Verne, Deirdre, 1965–
    Drawing conclusions / by Deirdre Verne. — Large print edition.
        pages cm. — (Thorndike Press large print mystery) (A sketch in crime mystery)
    ISBN 978-1-4104-7877-1 (hardcover) — ISBN 1-4104-7877-7 (hardcover)
    1. Women detectives—Fiction. 2. Environmentalists—Fiction. 3. Dumpster diving—Fiction. 4. Twins—Crimes against—Fiction. 5. Brothers and sisters—Fiction. 6. Murder—Investigation—Fiction. 7. Large type books.
I. Title.
PS3622.E7465D73 2015b
813'.6—dc23   2015004955

Published in 2015 by arrangement with Midnight Ink, an imprint of Llewellyn Publications, Woodbury, MN 55125-2989 USA

Printed in Mexico
1 2 3 4 5 6 7 19 18 17 16 15

For Peter and Mats.
Whatever it is, stick with it.

ACKNOWLEDGMENTS

After reading my umpteenth mystery novel, I was convinced I could write my own. Come to find out, I had a long way to go. Thankfully, my moment of inspiration led me to a wonderful group of supporters who educated and guided me through the process.

To Gay Walley, my first literary friend: I never had more energy than climbing the stairs of your fourth floor walk-up. It was worth every step.

To Terrie Farley Moran and my pals at the New York Chapter of Sisters in Crime: if not for the monthly meetings, my manuscript would still be in a drawer.

To Victoria Skurnick and the team at Levine Greenberg Rostan Literary Agency: thank you for taking a chance on a newcomer to the industry.

To Terri Bischoff, Beth Hanson, Nicole Nugent, and my fellow writers at Midnight

Ink Publishing: what a wonderful introduction to the world of publishing.

To Sue and Bob, my first fans, and my patient family: thank you for giving me the time and support to write through to "The End."

ONE

Charlie balanced the ladder at the base of the first Dumpster and yanked open the lid with a crowbar. He jammed a wooden wedge into the joint. Then he gave the metal lid a hardy slap to ensure it wouldn't accidentally slip and decapitate us.

"Okay, coast is clear," I said. "Let's suit up." I pushed up the sleeves of my hoodie and handed Charlie a box of surgical gloves, snapping on a pair for myself.

"You're up for the first dive, CeCe," he said. "Let me hear the Freegan motto."

"If it moves, stop, drop, and run," I said, placing my foot on the first rung of the ladder.

"That's what she said."

"You're a pig. Hand me the flashlight."

I steadied the ladder and swung one leg over the edge. Then I clipped the flashlight to the corner of the bin for a quick look-see.

"Good stuff," I said, passing a drippy egg carton to Charlie. "A few are broken but I can scramble and freeze them raw." A surge of adrenalin pumped toward my heart as I reached down into a pile of nearly fresh vegetables. It amazed me that after all these years of foraging for discarded food, I still got a high out of the hunt. This was a quality I shared with others in the Freegan movement. Freegans aren't necessarily poor or destitute; they simply dislike waste. I was willing to ignore the seeping smell of rot accelerated by the warming spring weather if the food could be put to good use.

"There's got to be ten pounds of bacon still in the wrapper. Prep the cooler."

"Trina and Jonathan asked for bagels and lox," Charlie reminded me. "See what you can do."

"Easy pickings," I replied. "There must have been at least three bar mitzvahs today." I threw a bag of bagels over the edge and shoved an industrial-sized carton of cream cheese into my sack. I pointed my flashlight toward the back of the Dumpster. It was full to the brim.

"Tomorrow I'll call the catering manager and connect him with the food pantry. This is a shame."

"We have room in the Gremlin," Charlie

said. "Let's do a drop at the pantry in the morning."

I looked at the Gremlin. The car was older than me. I'd rescued it from the town dump and was determined to drive it until it stopped. I wasn't sure I would make a great impression chugging up to the food pantry with a hatchback full of discarded food.

"They'll never take it. It's been sitting around too long, and we're not the original source."

"Too bad," Charlie said. "Keep digging."

I had my hand on a half-eaten aluminum tray of baked ziti when my ears perked up.

"Shit," I said as I popped my head over the rim of the Dumpster. "I hear something."

"Me too. Kill the light," Charlie said. He scrambled up the ladder and jumped into the bin for cover.

"Sounded like the bleep right before a siren," I whispered, my feet sinking into the moist refuse. I reached for Charlie's gloved hand.

"Do you think someone reported us?" he said as he squeezed my palm. The hum of a car engine reverberated along the walls of the metal Dumpster. With the lid open only a few inches, the sour stench became oppressive. I ran my hand under my nose to diffuse the odors.

"I think it stopped," I said and then added, "The police probably aren't interested in arresting two peace-loving Freegans repurposing day-old bread. What would they book us on?"

"How about 'willful consumption of post-dated food'?"

"Funny. What about 'premeditated attempt to lower the carbon footprint'?"

"Nice, CeCe."

With our eyes peering over the edge of the Dumpster, we watched the tail end of a police car cruise by. "Wonder where he's headed?" I said as I searched out Charlie's face in the dark. "I'm a little freaked."

Charlie exhaled slowly. "Why does this always feel so wrong when all we're taking is something no one else wants?"

"Because we've been conditioned to purchase food from a shelf in a store."

"There's something appealing about that scenario," Charlie laughed.

"I know," I said looking down at my shoes. "I've ruined more sneakers this way."

"Let's go barefoot next time."

"I'd rather convert to consumerism," I said, climbing out of the Dumpster. "Let's get out of here."

"My thoughts exactly," Charlie agreed.

"Grab the ziti. I'm starving." We hurriedly packed the food and drove out of the catering hall's parking lot with our lights off as an extra precaution.

"I'm sticking to main roads," I said. "The street lights make me feel safe. Is that lame?"

"Not to the guy who invented the night-light," Charlie replied.

"I never had a night-light."

"That's because you had Teddy," Charlie answered. "How many little girls have the convenience of a fraternal twin in the upper bunk?"

It was true. My brother had a way of making people feel safe even as a kid. It was no surprise he became a doctor.

"We did share a room for a frighteningly long time," I said. "If I remember correctly, you spent a fair share of nights in your Elmo sleeping bag on our floor to be close to your best friend."

"I loved that fuzzy red dude."

"I'm talking about Teddy not Elmo," I corrected Charlie.

"I love that dude too."

Charlie and I drove slowly back to the hamlet of Cold Spring Harbor, only a few miles northwest of the catering hall we had just pillaged. The moon hung low in the sky, illuminating the fan of interconnecting

13

inlets that littered the North Shore of Long Island. The narrow roads were crowded by early-blooming forsythia bushes, the gaps in foliage indicating the understated entrances to the old monied estates. With the windows rolled down, the clean scent cleared my nostrils and any hint of our Dumpster diving was contained in well-secured plastic bags. Like a beacon of safety, a light shone in the widow's peak of the harbor master's home. My home. Charlie, Trina, Jonathan, and Becky's home, as well as a smattering of cats, dogs, goats, chickens, and the random hiker. As luck would have it, the first settler in my family's long lineage was the original harbor master on the North Shore of Long Island. For well over a century, generations of my family skillfully guided schooners and barges toward the isle of Manhattan to exchange their goods.

 I inherited the defunct Harbor House with its oddball layout, rotting sills, and dirt-floor basement at the age of twenty-one. My family considered it the throwaway component of my much larger trust. I saw it as an opportunity to live an unconventional life off the grid with my equally committed green friends. It was an ideal existence for five twenty-somethings experimenting with organic farming and subsistence living.

14

"Hey, all the lights are on," I said. "Every damn one. That's going to cost us some money."

"Maybe they were hungry enough to wait up for us," Charlie said.

We turned onto Shore Road and were welcomed by two cars in the driveway. Now I knew where the police were headed.

"Crap." Charlie was halfway out of the car before I put it into park. "CeCe, are all the farming permits in place?"

"The permits are fine. It's the alternative farming I'm concerned about."

Charlie came to a complete halt, turned 180 degrees, and made a beeline for the car. I grabbed his arm for an awkward do-si-do.

"Chill," I said. "I'm pretty sure you smoked the evidence last night." I couldn't actually say it *wasn't* a drug bust. However, this seemed to be missing the element of surprise and the pack of hyped-up dogs that can sniff out an aspirin wedged under a car seat.

"We should call Teddy," Charlie said, his eyes darting desperately from side to side.

"Come on," I urged Charlie as we headed toward the house.

Trina, Jonathan, and Becky were sitting at the kitchen farm table. In the various corners and cubbies of the room, cops filled

15

in spaces like spare furniture. The room murmured with a sea of coughs and grumbles.

"Constance Prentice?" A broad-shouldered man reached out to shake my hand. He had thick dark hair like my brother and the same commanding presence. "I need a moment in private."

Charlie was glued to my back, a second skin. I rotated my head and mouthed what he and I were both thinking. There was only one person we both knew with enough clout to upend the local police department in the middle of the night: my father.

The venerable Dr. William Prentice was the founder and lead scientist of Sound View Laboratories, the central clearing house for all things DNA in the United States and around the globe. It was the home of the double helix, the national genome project, and a slew of other international scientific studies. In the world of hardcore science, it was hard to get bigger than Dr. William Prentice, a man who had devoted nearly fifty years to searching for the cure. Which cure? Who cares. Take your pick. From what little I understood (or wanted to) about DNA, once those elusive little genomes were trapped and mapped, the answer would tumble out and wrap itself around a prescription bottle with a child-safety lid fully intact.

I turned to the officer and considered his face. Familiar, serious, concerned. For a second I thought maybe we had already met, and then I realized he wore a mask of compassion. A face practiced in delivering bad news. If he assessed my face, I'm sure he was confused. Indifference usually does not precede the announcement of a parent's death. I was, however, the black sheep of the family. My father despised my bohemian lifestyle, hence our decade-long estrangement.

"Officer, I'm assuming something has happened to my father." My tone was flat.

"No, but we need to speak to you and your housemates about your brother," he said pulling a chair out for me.

"Teddy?" I said, pushing the chair back in place.

"I'm sorry but I have some unfortunate news," he said, offering me a seat a second time.

My ears rung like a warped tuning rod, the pitch escalating until I could barely decipher the officer's words. "Your brother, Dr. Theodore Prentice, has passed away."

I looked helplessly at Trina and Jonathan, but I could tell by their grave expressions that I had heard the officer correctly.

My beloved twin brother, Teddy, was dead.

TWO

The weight on my back was unbearable. I caught a glimpse of Charlie's hand as it flopped lifelessly on my shoulder. As I pitched forward, floorboards rising to my face, the room came alive and a team of trained professionals scooped me up before impact. At the unexpected announcement, Charlie had passed out on top of me and promptly wet his pants. Within moments, Trina, Jonathan, and Becky swarmed over us like an enormous worn quilt. Charlie lay prone on the floor with a bit of spittle hanging pathetically off his lip. The only thing I could think was that Charlie should have taken the chair.

Trina pulled my face toward hers and mumbled a stream of incoherent condolences. As she spoke, I ran my fingers over my ears in an attempt to fan away the resonating din. Unlike Charlie, I was conscious but barely functioning.

"I'm fine guys," I heard myself say as I inched my way to a standing position. "Really. Get Charlie some water and a change of clothes." I felt like I had swallowed a handful of NoDoz and chased it with a Red Bull. I had the sensation that all the light bulbs had been swapped out and replaced with strobe lights. I studied my pulsating hands as I directed the police officer upstairs. The soles of my feet barely skimmed the stair treads; I was transported on an escalator of raw energy.

I flung open the door to my attic art studio, hoping that the comfort of my personal refuge would take me down a notch. I spotted my painting stool and perched atop it. It was like balancing on the head of a pin.

"Ms. Prentice," said the officer who had followed me upstairs.

"Just call me CeCe," I replied waving my hand dismissively. "I don't know your name."

"Detective Frank DeRosa," he said hunching his back as he looked for a place to stand. The studio attic had a sharply peaked ceiling with slanted walls that effectively skimmed off two or three feet of headroom. Between my painting supplies and canvases, there was little room for Detective DeRosa to conduct his interview. He lifted one leg, placing it on a gallon paint can. I found his gesture offensive, like stepping on a pile of books at a library.

"So is this for real?" I asked ignoring his awkward stance.

"I'm afraid so." Detective DeRosa fired up his iPad, resting it on his knee, and slid his index finger across the screen. "Dr. Theodore Prentice was found at eleven p.m. in his office at the Sound View labs on Friday. Cause undetermined; autopsy ordered."

"You mean Saturday," I corrected.

"No, I mean Friday," he replied, calmly looking up from his notes.

"This happened yesterday?" I said as if I had forgotten how many days there were in a week.

"Technically, the day before yesterday. It's now Sunday. The family asked us to keep the press out until some initial facts could be gathered. We promised twenty-four hours of silence."

"But I'm not the press. I'm his sister. His only sibling."

"You'll have to take that up with your father," Detective DeRosa answered without apology.

I took the detective's comment in stride.

21

What could I expect? I hadn't been on speaking terms with my father since I'd left for college. My rebellion started early, and by high school I was probably unbearable to even a liberal-minded parent. I remember packing my bags stuffed full of thrift shop finds and stomping defiantly past my father on my way to a new life at art school in the city.

I walked over to the window, if only for the chance to turn my back on Detective DeRosa. I hated him for succumbing to my father's omnipotence. I felt an unbridled compulsion to run at the detective headfirst and pummel him with my fists. Why I had stayed in Cold Spring Harbor at all was a mystery to me. I could have lived anywhere in the world, but I remained here, among a town of pod people entranced by a shaman. Dr. William Prentice and his bag of magic potions owned the town. The lab was a major employer in Cold Spring Harbor, a great resource for the school district, and a prominent national institution.

I looked out across the bay at the laboratory complex covering almost the entire twelve-acre peninsula called Cove Neck. At low tide I could literally walk across the inlet and up the hill to my brother's office. Every June on our birthday, I made a barefoot pilgrimage across the spongy bay where Teddy would meet me for a celebratory picnic. The campus, as it was called, was a collegial setting where top scientists shared ideas and innovations leading to groundbreaking discoveries. It was also a spectacular site for an outdoor picnic.

The darker side of the labs was experienced by anyone who dared to cross my father's path. Sound View Laboratories was my father's empire and the training ground for his beloved son to carry on his research. I could visit, but I'd never be part of it. And that was just fine by me.

"Ms. Prentice?"

"I don't answer to Ms. Prentice," I replied sharply, catching the detective's attention. As he looked up, I surveyed his face. He had shaved this morning but would need another swipe of the razor within a few hours. The heavy growth around the lower half of his face framed his eyes, which were filled with doubt and query. He turned one corner of his mouth downward, rethinking his approach. He wanted answers from me and realized a change of tone was in order.

"I'm sorry," he said after some deliberation. To emphasize a truce, he put his iPad aside, giving me his full attention before continuing. "If you wouldn't mind, could you provide me the names of the people who live in this house and their relationship to each other?"

"You didn't come here to tell me about my brother, did you? You came here to ask us questions."

"The more information, the better."

We had nothing to hide, so I offered a quick rundown of the residents of Harbor House. "I have four housemates. Trina and Jonathan handle most of the farming. Charlie and I are childhood friends. He's also my brother's best friend. Becky designs clothing from discarded fabrics."

Detective DeRosa's fingers, which seemed almost too bulky for the slim electronic device, pounded away at the touch pad as if I had just revealed a buried secret.

I spun on my heels, arms folded tightly across my chest. "I still don't understand what happened. Teddy and I aren't even thirty. Was it a heart attack?"

"What if it wasn't a heart attack?" he challenged.

I walked back to the detective. "*What if it wasn't a heart attack?* What the hell does that mean?" It was ever so slight, but I felt the pressure of Detective DeRosa's imposing frame as he leaned into me. Subtle aggression. I took a step forward and lessened the gap. Not so subtle on my part.

"I was hoping you could provide some answers. I understand you were very close to your brother." The detective handed me his card. "Come by the station at your convenience. Your brother's death has not been classified as a homicide just yet, but on the outside chance it is, I'd like to start investigating before any more time has passed."

Detective DeRosa glanced around my studio. There were over a hundred half-finished canvases, many of them nearly identical.

"What's with the faces?" he asked, downgrading my artwork to circles with eyes.

"Portraits, not faces."

"Okay, portraits. Why all the portraits?"

"It's what I do. I'm an artist," I said as I walked toward the staircase.

I led the detective out of my studio, down the stairs, and directly to the front door of Harbor House.

"Good night." I opened the front door and stood to the side, a signal that our conversation was over. I flicked on the porch light on the outside chance he did not get the hint. The eco-friendly bulb cast a dull glow, highlighting yet another visitor.

"Dad?" I gasped as my father made his way up the stairs.

THREE

A batch of gnats swarmed the porch light and tested my father's patience as he swatted them away with a linen handkerchief. The bags beneath his eyes were swollen with grief and the corners of his mouth were bent so far south I thought he might have lost the ability to smile. We both hesitated, unsure whether or not to embrace. Before I had a chance to react, my father reached out to shake the detective's hand.

"Detective DeRosa, you're on your way out. I see you've already spoken to Constance."

"Yes, he has," I said, acknowledging the fact that I was the last to learn of my brother's death.

"I'm sorry about that, I tried to get here earlier," my father replied, his voice scratchy from overuse. "If you don't mind, I need a minute with the detective and then I was hoping you'd invite me in."

I left the two men to talk privately on the porch. I used the extra minutes to take stock of the house, assessing where best to receive my father. When one is raised as the child of a wealthy doctor, there are expectations, a certain level of decorum, even in the event of a death. I found myself reacting out of a habit engrained by good upbringing. I chose the room we had designated as the library, a cramped but organized storage room for our collection of eclectic, second-hand books.

I listened as DeRosa's car backed down the driveway and quickly selected a chair for my father. "Dad, this one is more comfortable," I said pointing to the lesser worn of the chairs. My father seated himself, pulling down slightly on his pressed trousers.

"I have to be honest," I said swallowing hard. "I don't know if I can do this with you."

"You need to calm down." My father started with the words he'd directed at me over and over throughout my childhood, even when I was perfectly calm.

"Teddy is dead," I said ignoring his patronizing tone. "Am I to assume you think this makes sense? Guess what, it doesn't. This doesn't make sense."

My father sat with his back straight and his forearms stretched tautly along the sides of the chair, like an airplane passenger preparing for a bumpy landing. "No, it doesn't," he replied, "but we've lost a lot of time, and I am willing to put our differences aside. I came here to discuss your brother. I was hoping we could be civil."

"Then why didn't you come to me yesterday and tell me about Teddy? He's my twin, for God's sake," I said, shoving the small of my back into my chair.

My father's hesitation was interminable. This was not a question he wanted to answer. I lifted my head from my hand and faced him full on.

"Dad," I pushed, "Why didn't you and Mom come to me sooner?"

My father sighed, and I sensed his growing impatience. This was a man who spoke and others bowed in awe. He did not take kindly to opposition, but my question was fair and I deserved a response.

"Because Theodore was an integral part of the labs and whether he died of natural causes or not, his passing must be presented to the scientific community with care," my father said in defense of his delay. "Our funding, our partnerships and our relationship with the public are dependent upon our ability to deliver results with absolute consistency. Theodore was involved in a number of high-profile studies, and the board requested a short period of time to review his work and determine the impact of his absence. The police agreed because at this point there is no indication of foul play."

"But —" I tried to interject, only to be cut off.

"Constance, this is not the time to be naïve," he said, holding his palm flat as if I were a puppy learning to heel. "The world is significantly bigger and more complex than this idealistic commune you've created here."

As I suspected, it took all of three minutes for our conversation to dissolve into disrespect.

My father rose from the heavily cushioned chair, and I could see the effort was a strain for his aging body. He walked to the bookshelves, his left hip showing the pull of arthritis. I'd never thought of my father as old until this moment. His frailty made me nervous. My father was a grand man, a pillar of strength. Now, he seemed beaten.

He ran his finger along a row of books, giving himself time to collect his thoughts. "You must realize that in the last ten years your brother has matured into a prominent and well-respected research doctor. I know that you and Theodore and your childhood friend —" My father pointed into the air to retrieve the name.

"*Charlie,*" I reminded him. "Teddy's best friend is Charlie."

"Yes, of course," my father fumbled, trying to cover his oversight. "The three of you have socialized for years. But you must remember that every morning your brother returned to the labs, joining company with some of the medical profession's key figures. You need to give your brother his due. This delay was proportional to his contributions."

"Just once, could you put the labs aside?" I pleaded, remembering how the missed dinners and business trips ate away at our family's dynamic. I'd never understood how Teddy was able to remain neutral all these years. He loved my parents and he loved me, but he kept his worlds separate. Now I wasn't sure my father saw Teddy in the context of family at all. "He's your son first," I slurred as despair mangled my words, "and a scientist second."

My father pulled his chin to the ceiling as if he were using gravity to draw his tears back into their ducts. I sensed a softening.

"In all my years as a doctor, I never

31

thought I would attend the autopsy of my son," my father began. "I want to assure you that I stood shoulder to shoulder with the medical examiner through the initial work-up."

"And you found nothing?" I said, dragging my sleeve under my nose.

"On this first round, no," my father said and then cleared his throat. "A more intrusive examination occurred after I left, and it will take a few weeks to receive the blood and toxicology reports."

"Don't protect me," I said, recalling how my parents replaced my pet goldfish a dozen times rather than telling me the fish had died. "I'm okay with the truth."

"The truth is I have no idea how your brother died, but I have asked the police to open an official investigation. That was my discussion with Detective DeRosa a few minutes ago. I came as soon as I got word from the board to proceed, and I'm here tonight to ask for your full participation. You and your housemates were close to Teddy. It's important you speak freely with the police."

"That goes without saying," I answered, now wondering if my father had already tipped Detective DeRosa off to my challenging personality.

My father leaned toward me, and for a second I thought he had lost his footing. I reached out to steady him but was met by a cold, dry kiss on the side of my head. "Thank you, dear," he said.

FOUR

Typically, we rose at odd hours, but on this particular day, Trina, Jonathan, and Becky were gathered in the kitchen by 8 a.m.

"Where's Charlie?" I asked as I opened a window by the kitchen table and breathed deeply in the direction of the water. The news of Teddy's death was suffocating, and these small gestures were all I could do to alleviate my anxiety.

"We thought he was with you." Trina placed a plate of fresh scrambled eggs in front of me.

"I see you found the food," I said. "Thanks for unpacking the car last night."

Trina and Jonathan came around the table, bookending me before I had a chance to run. Becky sat across the table and reached out to hold my hands in place.

"The funeral is tomorrow," Becky said. "I have all day to design and sew a dress for you. It's going to be a magical dress, because it will let you disappear and reappear as you please. It will carry you and envelop you and protect you from the freaks."

"Becky, *you're* a freak."

"Yes I am, and I love you and I want to help and this is the only way I know how."

"Then put the pedal to the metal and start sewing." I let her kiss my palms before she released me and departed in a swirl of heavy damask hiding her tiny frame.

"Remind me how she came to live with us?" I asked. Becky's outpouring of love caught me off-guard — we were more roommates than close friends.

"Charlie thought she was cute," Jonathan said and then added, "apparently, she doesn't realize Charlie finds lots of women attractive."

I shrugged my shoulders. Charlie's philandering was nothing new to me. I had bigger problems.

Trina pushed the plate toward me. "CeCe, you need to eat. Don't make me give you a lecture on nutrients."

I spooned some eggs into my mouth.

"You also need to see that detective today." Trina buttered my toast and put it in my hand.

"I don't like him," I said as I force-fed myself the eggs.

"I agree," Trina said. "He's pompous."

I pushed the plate away from me in disgust. "He's an asshole, and my father already has him in his pocket. He probably moonlights as security at the labs."

Jonathan rose from the table and adjusted the ratty pair of suspenders holding up his work pants. "If you'll forgive me, I don't think my presence is necessary for this man-hating session." He gave us both a peck on the cheek. "I love you CeCe, and I'm going to miss Teddy."

"Thank you Jonathan." I winked at Trina, knowing full well Jonathan had just spanned the entire range of his emotions. He was a farmer at heart; I couldn't expect more than this stoic demeanor. Trina, our resident earth mother, had ample depth for both of them.

Trina waited for Jonathan to depart before drilling down on the detail. "Look CeCe, something is not right, and I think the police and your father are suspicious. Your dad is a doctor. He'd know immediately if Teddy's death was natural."

"Thanks for the update." The realization that my brother was dead was sickening, but the suggestion that foul play was at hand was not outrageous. Young men do not drop dead at their desks without some encouragement. My shoulders tightened as pressure filled the deepest pockets of my head.

"Should I come to the station with you?" Trina asked.

"It's okay, Trina." I fumbled for Detective DeRosa's card in my pocket. "I can do it myself."

"Your mom called," Trina said with a cringe.

"Was she drunk?"

"Shit-faced."

I folded myself into Trina's arms then and let the tears flow. Her hearty frame was warm and reassuring, yet I had never felt so alone in all my life. Teddy's and my birthday was only a month away. I stretched my hand out behind Trina's back and imagined Teddy pulling me up to the shore, flip-flops dripping at my side, ready for our birthday lunch. I wanted to hold onto the image, but I knew Detective DeRosa was waiting for me.

"You should go," Trina said, releasing me.

"I know," I replied as I grabbed my sweat-shirt and headed off to the station.

The Laurel Hollow Police Station was a hodgepodge of low-slung historical buildings connected by a series of ambling breezeways. The setting seemed more suited to misdemeanors involving hobbits and goblins than murder. It was unclear to me how anything of a serious nature could possibly be resolved under thatched roofs as thick as muffin tops. Detective DeRosa was waiting for me by the front door when I arrived.

"Thanks for coming in, Ms. Prentice."

"If you don't call me CeCe, I'm leaving."

"CeCe."

"Yes, Frank?"

"Have you ever been here before?" he asked as he held the door for me. My head barely met the top of his arm pit putting him easily over six-two.

"Check the row of shoeboxes in the back and I'm sure you'll find a hand-written index card with a list of ridiculous stunts Charlie and I pulled in high school."

"I did my research. Unfortunately your records were sealed. The underage loophole."

Detective DeRosa led me into a bright, open room with floor-to-ceiling windows that looked out over the harbor. A row of desks housed a police force of about twenty officers. The handful present appeared rather sedate as they sipped the last of their morning lattes.

"Jesus, it's almost worth getting arrested for this view."

"I'm sure there's an inch or two left on your index card."

I followed Detective DeRosa down a narrow hall to his office. Given the tight dimensions, the wall of leaded glass cabinetry, and the telltale sink, I guessed it was a converted butler's pantry.

"So this is where the help sits?"

"I'd like to be of help," DeRosa said with his arms open to suggestion.

"But?"

"From what I gather, vegans pride themselves on self-sufficiency."

"It's Freegan, not vegan," I said enunciating the words clearly. "Freegans take what they can get. Vegans are picky eaters, the divas of alternative living." The mention of food lifted my stomach in an unpleasant churn. I pursed my lips and bit back a bubble. The eggs and stress were not agreeing with me.

Detective DeRosa's phone trilled, interrupting our interview. I could hear a woman's voice rising in panic as he nodded with concern, but the drama was not enough to distract me from the uncomfortable gurgling in my stomach. I tried to remember if I had passed a bathroom on the way in.

"It's your housemate," DeRosa said, pointing to the phone. "Trina."

I nodded, afraid to open my mouth.

"She says there might be something wrong with the eggs."

I nodded again, pointing at DeRosa's garbage pail with one hand while the other covered my mouth. In one quick motion, he grabbed a plastic recycling bin and shoved it under my chin. His timing was impeccable. I tossed my breakfast directly into the pail. Between the gut stabbing pains and the panting heaves, I was able to blurt out a few sentences.

"Is it just me?"

"No, your housemates are sick too."

"I need to get to a hospital," I burped. "There could have been rat poison in the Dumpster."

No more than three fine hairs on my forearm were trapped mercilessly under an inch of adhesive tape holding my liquid lifeline in place. The pinching had an almost pleasant effect compared to the knife in my belly. Screw the Abs of Steel disc stuck in my third-hand DVD player. A mouthful of rat poison will make you feel the burn a whole lot longer than stomach crunches. I rolled my head sideways and drew my legs into a fetal position.

"Trina, is that you?"

She was laid out in the bed next to me.

"Hey, CeCe." Her mellow voice had a maternal quality that made me feel safe. "Your dad stopped by when you were sleeping, but he didn't say anything and he's gone now."

"Then let me take this time to inform you that your cooking sucks."

"Don't make me laugh," she moaned. "I don't have any stomach muscles left." With a Herculean effort, Trina rolled her hip forward so we were facing each other. "Since when does the catering hall contaminate their leftover food?"

"I don't know. This kind of shit happens in Manhattan all the time, and I know the major supermarket chains do it to discourage the homeless." I tried to sit up, but it was useless. "We probably woke up because the painkillers are wearing off," I said as I pressed the call button with the energy of a last-place marathoner crossing the finish line. "Let's see what drugs are on the menu today."

A worried nurse shuffled in, followed by Charlie and Detective DeRosa.

"Hey Charlie, before I forget, pack a doggie bag of scrambled eggs for the detective," I said.

Charlie hurried to my side, ignoring my sick-bed humor. "Something's wrong, CeCe. Really wrong."

I looked over at Trina and braced myself for news that I expected neither of us wanted to hear. I had read about restaurants and food stores using rat poison to deter Dumpster diving. It wasn't exactly uncommon. What I didn't know was the lasting effects of poison. If defecating into a bag attached to my hip was in my near future, I was not going to be happy.

Charlie shoved his hands deep into his jean pockets. "I ate some eggs last night after the police left and you guys went to bed." His confession was underwhelming, as if he had nabbed the last of the dessert.

"And you're not sick?" Trina probed.

"No, I'm fine," Charlie replied.

"So it must have been something else we ate. Big deal," I said.

Charlie nodded to Detective DeRosa, who had been fairly unobtrusive up to this point. "Charlie scrambled the eggs last night." DeRosa addressed the room. "Then he divided them into portions. He froze some and left the rest in the refrigerator. We sampled and tested both parts, and the

42

frozen portion is not contaminated. That's why Charlie is not sick. The other half contains traces of rat poisoning. You, Trina, and Jonathan ate the contaminated eggs. Jonathan, due to his size, processed the poison faster and was released an hour ago."

"Are you suggesting Trina and I put on fifty pounds to beef up our resistance?" I asked.

"CeCe, cut the shit and listen." Charlie rose from my bedside and positioned himself next to Detective DeRosa. I didn't need a body language expert to see whose side Charlie was on as he ran his hands through his hair in frustration and continued with his story. "After I ate the eggs, I turned off all the lights and reset the lights to nine a.m."

"But when I went to make breakfast, the kitchen light was on," Trina said. "I remember thinking that was odd."

Even the nurse who had busied herself with my saline bag fell silent as we waited for someone to drop the bomb. Detective DeRosa lit up his iPad and tapped the screen with his index finger.

"We believe someone entered the house between the hours of four and six a.m. and poisoned the eggs in the refrigerator," DeRosa said as he looked up from his device and stared straight into my eyes. For a brief second, I had a flutter of recognition, just as I had the first night we met. I considered the circumstance of our first meeting and decided that the intensity of the situation had created this déjà vu feeling. We had never met, yet when we did the impact was lasting. His glance distracted me, and I turned my head toward the window.

"Seriously, CeCe. This is important." Charlie's chiding brought me back into the conversation.

"We have very little to go on," Detective DeRosa continued, "but at this point, we think you were the target, CeCe."

"What about Trina and Jonathan?" I said. "They got sick too."

"Collateral damage," Detective DeRosa replied. His iPad dinged, and he said, "I'll take this outside. It's your father; he wants an update." He nodded to the group and stepped out of the room as we digested the knowledge that someone wanted me dead — or at least out of commission.

"Charlie, this is nuts. How can I be the target of anything?"

"I don't know CeCe, but someone killed Teddy and the police think you're next."

FIVE

Charlie drove us home from the hospital that afternoon. The car ride was dreadfully silent, and I was lost in wondering how the rest of the world was about to perceive me. Selfish, perhaps, but I was still feeling pretty low after hours of sickness. Within a day, I'd be surrounded by hundreds of mourners bowing to the awe of money and influence. There would be gawkers and curiosity seekers, opportunists and press hogs. I'm sure I would satisfy the paparazzi in my role as the underachieving, crackpot sister with an inheritance big enough to support a small nation. As word got out about the attempt on my lifestyle, there would be talk of self-involvement, as if I had somehow brought this on myself, a twisted form of Münchausen syndrome. Rejected sister fakes poisoning after the murder of her more popular twin brother.

"Hey," I said to break the silence. "How

bad will the funeral be for me?"

"It's going to suck for all of us," Charlie said as he leaned hard into the gas pedal. "I'm going to be an outsider at my best friend's funeral."

As if green living is somehow a direct threat to the establishment, I thought. I wondered if my brother's death and the threat on my life were somehow connected to my lifestyle. Freeganism was alien to most, and I had often been accused of being overly idealistic. What drove me was a sense of logic. Why buy food, clothes, hell, even computers, when you can get them all for free? I'll admit, the Dumpster diving "ick" factor is high, but the rewards are enormous.

"Maybe I've gone too far in the past," I conceded, now worried that either my link to my brother or my actions had compromised the safety of my housemates.

"The video didn't help," Charlie said, referring to my how-to video on Dumpster diving, strategically filmed behind the cafeteria at the Sound View labs. It's amazing how much steak a medical grant can buy. Doctors, it turns out, eat pretty well.

"God, that was years ago. And you held the camera," I said, reminding Charlie of his role. "Anyway, that video went viral faster than an outbreak of H1N1. Teddy thought it was hilarious."

"Yes, but it embarrassed your dad at work," Trina said. "You'll forever be positioned as the rebellious sister, despite Teddy covering for you."

I didn't feel very rebellious at the moment. My stomach was sore to the touch, and I had to hold the seatbelt about an inch off my waist as Charlie took a tight turn. I grimaced and bit through a pain sharp enough to remind me of my resilience. It was this part of my personality that held back the torrent of tears and allowed me to focus on the horror of the situation without losing my mind.

Like me, both Trina and Charlie were deep in thought. I studied Charlie's face, a face I'd known since childhood. I had memorized every dip and pucker in his skin, the shape of his hairline as it fell over his ears, and the length of his nose in proportion to the width of his cheekbones. We spent the majority of our high school years in the back seat of his dad's car in full reproductive glory. We would kiss for so long that I could feel the pressure of his lips on mine hours later. By graduation, we had burnt out, realizing our strongest bond was Teddy. Teddy was Charlie's best friend and my rock.

Faces had always intrigued me, and I'm convinced the root of my obsession began with the glaring physical differences between me and my twin. Technically, we were merely roommates for nine months. Our conception involved two separate eggs, two separate sperm, and two separate sacs. Our dissimilarities, therefore, were not unusual and in fact quite common among fraternal twins. And as one pediatrician explained it to me, "Try to think of him as a brother who happened to be born on the same day." Regardless, our differences irked me. I had no attachment to my parents; I'd spent the better part of my life avoiding my father and mixing my mother yet another cocktail. From the day I sensed the presence of a life form next to me, I wanted nothing more than to capture our brother/sister connection through a tangible feature. A hooked pinky, an attached earlobe, a cleft chin, bow legs, knocked knees. Really, I'd take anything.

And yet there was my brother Teddy with his mountain-man physique and thick mane of dark hair. He had more body hair than Bigfoot and hands that could crush a bag of walnuts. His Roman nose led an observer's eyes straight down to a full set of lips and the warmest smile this side of the East River. I, on the other hand, was five-three on a good day. I often wondered if my growth potential was compromised by sharing space with my larger twin. With my dirty blond hair and Nordic looks, I could pass in a crowd of WASPy North Shore girls. That Charlie dug my tomboy gig in high school was a compliment considering he could have bagged any girl in town. It was my fascination with similarities and differences that led me to paint portraits. I am a self-proclaimed expert in the human body from the neck up. I would let my father and brother analyze DNA under the power of a laser microscope; my interpretation of DNA flowed from the tips of my fingers through the end of my paintbrush, spilling out across a canvas. I knew faces, and at this moment, I could tell from my housemates' expressions that doubt and fear were overtaking rational thought.

"Hey guys, I think this is getting blown out of proportion." I shifted in the front seat and addressed Charlie and Trina, although neither seemed to be on the same wavelength.

"I'm going to swing by the electronics store later and see if I can hustle up some used security equipment. I'm rigging the entire house with cameras," Charlie muttered to himself, eyes glued to the road.

"I'll guess I'll have to throw out the entire contents of the kitchen," Trina added, mentally cleaning out the kitchen cabinets.

"Please, can we focus on the facts?" I pleaded. "At this point, Teddy's cause of death is undetermined and there was no obvious evidence of a break-in. Am I right?"

Charlie nodded reluctantly.

"The rat poisoning is a little unnerving," I said, "but it didn't kill any of us, and we still don't know that it wasn't the catering hall that sprinkled the poison. Maybe they had a rat problem?"

"Maybe someone just wanted to scare you," Charlie offered.

"Okay, let's run with that."

"Maybe your father didn't want you at the funeral," Trina blurted. As soon as the words left her mouth, her face broadcast the fact that she regretted every syllable. "Oh my God, I can't believe I just said that. I am so, so sorry."

Charlie restated the obvious. "The rift with your father *is* local lore at this point. You have to expect that people will be talking about it."

"I realize that, but my father and I are trying to mend the past," I said reflecting on the meeting with him the prior evening and that unexpected show of affection. "Look, he made the effort to come by the house and I'm grateful."

"So you don't hate me?" Trina asked.

I reached into the back seat and felt for her hand. "It's okay, I'm not offended in the least. I expect to go back to being a persona non grata tomorrow."

"You're going to be a persona con spectacle in the get-up Becky's been sewing," Charlie said as he backed the ancient Gremlin, our only car, into Harbor House's driveway.

"Can you dial it back, Charlie?" Trina squeezed my hand. "CeCe, how are you not scared? Teddy's gone and you have no relationship with your family."

"Remember when we started up Harbor House and my father stopped by unannounced?" I said.

"That was some serious daddy rage," Charlie replied. "I think he called me a Commie."

"He called Jonathan a Commie," Trina corrected. "He called you a punk."

"Anyway, Teddy came by later that day and said something that gave me the strength to continue with our plans for Harbor House. He encouraged me to create

51

something bigger than us. He wanted me to live it, not just preach it." I could feel Teddy's presence in the car. I looked up at Harbor House and the rolling expanse of farmland behind it. Ten years ago, creating a self-sufficient living arrangement had seemed daunting, but with the gardens blooming and the fields sprouting, the improbable had become my reality. And in part, it was thanks to a few words from my brother.

"Charlie, do you remember?" I asked.

"Yeah," Charlie replied as memories of Teddy flooded his head. "He said, 'CeCe, you can't fall off the floor'."

A genuine smile spread across my face for the first time in two days.

Six

When we piled out of the car, I headed straight for my studio with a gallon of water and a handful of pills prescribed to heal a nuclear meltdown of the stomach lining. Trina and Jonathan curled up on the couch in the living room, and Charlie made good on his promise to install a security system. I had peeked in on Becky managing a bolt of luminous pink fabric. I was not encouraged.

"Pink, huh?"

Becky had spit a straight pin out of her mouth onto the floor and smiled. "Trust me."

I dipped my brush in a dollop of brown oil paint. I mixed in a smidge of black and added tone with a hint of red. I painted for three solid hours with odd intervals of rest just to make the doctors happy. By the end, I was left with five canvases of a male's head from the crown to the brow. The mop of hair appeared in various stages of styling, from a Caesar to a middle part, left part, right part, and finally swept back like a Wall Street fund manager. I didn't know where these images were taking me, and I was too tired to care. I stretched out on an old futon in the corner of the studio and prayed for a solid eight.

The door to the attic studio was too old for a traditional doorknob, and the sound of the cast-iron latch was unmistakable even in my deep sleep. I struggled to draw my battered body from its well-deserved slumber. The creaking floorboards scratched my conscience. I sprung up like a jack-in-the-box. The motion was extreme given the condition of my abdomen, and I cried out in a jumble of pain and fear. I tumbled on to the floor and skittered on all fours toward my easel. The moon splashed just enough light ahead for me to locate my bucket of brushes soaking in turpentine. I stretched for the can and a defensive weapon, but not before a hand grabbed my wrist.

"Ce, it's me." Charlie knelt down and pried my fingers from the can. "Man, you are one tough bitch."

"I thought you wanted to kill me."

"I came close at the hospital today."

"And now?"

"Now that I've saved myself from permanent blindness?" Charlie pushed the can of turpentine safely under the easel. "Come on, let's sit."

We sat shoulder to shoulder on the bed and before long I could feel Charlie's chest heaving in an uneven rhythm.

"You can't cry or I'll lose it. I swear, don't fucking do this to me," I said.

He turned his head toward me, and I recognized the tilt as if it were the junior prom. He kissed me so hard I had to grab the back of the futon for support. I drew my thigh across his lap and straddled him before he could change his mind.

"This is a bad idea," I gasped between heated breaths.

"I was hoping for bad," Charlie responded, running his hands under my shirt.

"Is this going to piss off your girlfriends?"

"Becky's a fling."

"Who else?"

"The red-headed barista from Starbucks."

"How 'bout the bartender from Garvin's Pub?"

"She'll be livid."

I gave in to Charlie as easily as sliding into a favorite pair of jeans. I couldn't count the years clearly in my condition, but I guessed our near-decade dry spell was about to end.

I was pleasantly surprised we'd both learned a thing or two since our high school grope fests.

"Your boobs are bigger." Charlie yanked my shirt over my head and tossed it across the bed.

"Your dick isn't."

"I still love you, CeCe," he said, breathing hard on my neck.

It wasn't sincere the first time I'd heard him say it, either.

SEVEN

"It's today, Charlie." I rolled over and grabbed my shirt off the floor. The sun poured relentlessly through the dirty attic windows, and I caught myself wishing for rain to match my gloom. Charlie was a bit more upbeat.

"I've heard of make-up sex, but this funeral sex is seriously underrated," he said, wiping sleep from his eyes.

"I'm only laughing because Teddy would have appreciated your black humor." I reached for an errant sock and dug under the sheets for Charlie's boxers. "This isn't going to bring him back, you know."

"It was worth a try," he said as he rose and pulled his thrift-store Calvin's just up to the bottom rung on his six-pack.

"It might get him a nephew," I laughed half-heartedly.

"Shit. Do some jumping jacks or something." Charlie was just about to leave when he spotted the canvases drying along the wall. "Is it Teddy?" he asked.

"I'm not sure yet."

Charlie nodded, then slipped through the attic door and hopefully found his way back to his room unnoticed. I gave myself a few more minutes of hiding in bed before I could muster the mental stamina to confront my brother's funeral. I took a quick shower and prepared for my fitting with Becky.

"Beck?" I knocked on her door at the end of the hall on the second floor of the house. "You ready for me yet?"

"Absolutely." Becky kneeled at the base of a small platform Charlie and Jonathan had built to showcase her collection. "I'm just finishing the hem, but I'll stop here and make sure it's the right length for you."

The dress hanging on the headless mannequin was undeniably stunning. The pink fabric I had feared was more of a soft peach with a faint undertone of yellow. "Becky, this is incredible. It looks like the color of my skin and hair all rolled into one."

I stripped down to my underwear and pulled the dress carefully over my hips, letting Becky zip the last few inches. I glanced quickly in the full-length mirror, feeling a tinge of guilt as I admired my reflection.

The layers played nicely on my straight frame and for a passing second I envisioned myself going on actual date as opposed to having noncommittal sex on a futon in the attic. Becky tossed me a pair of strappy sandals from a local thrift shop that pulled the whole ensemble together. I left the room knowing it would be the one and only time I'd wear this dress, but I'd carry it with the respect it deserved.

Then the five of us gathered on the front porch of Harbor House. There were lots of hugs and kisses, and Becky started to choke up, causing an avalanche of contagious tears. We looked out across the bay in the direction of the Sound View labs campus and waved our final goodbye in the direction of Teddy's office.

"I don't think we'll all fit in the Gremlin." I fished my keys out of my bag.

"It appears your dad sent some transportation," Jonathan said as he walked me around to the side of the house to find a stretch limo idling in the driveway. "You take Charlie in the gas guzzler and we'll follow in the Gremlin. If you need to leave early, I can always take you home."

"You're a good man, Jonathan," I said. "Are you sure you don't want a ride?"

"I already called shotgun," Charlie said,

holding the door open for me as we stepped into the limo.

"So I guess I'm not good enough to ride in the *family* limo," I said, settling myself into the soft leather seats.

"Come on, CeCe. Cut your dad some slack. At least he sent the car," Charlie said in support of my father. I decided not to tell him my dad couldn't even remember his name the other night.

I flipped up the refrigerated compartment next to the seat to reveal a split of champagne. "There must have been a mix-up at the garage. This is a party boat not a funeral limo," I strained to make my voice heard over the driver's pounding music.

"So maybe this would be the wrong time to tell you how hot you look in that dress?" Charlie placed a hand on my knee.

I promptly removed it. "You think?" I leaned forward, banging on the retractable glass separating the passengers from the driver. Up to this point, our driver had been content to ignore us, garbling a few heavily accented words upon our departure. I had caught his name, Igor, and suspected he was Russian, but I was no expert. "Hey, Igor," I said. "I hate to be a pest, but can you turn your godawful music down?"

"You kiss your mother with that mouth?"

Charlie said.

"I kissed you last night and I don't re-member hearing any complaints." I opened another drawer built into the leather seating to find a stack of girly magazines. "Obvi-ously, my father did not tell the limo service the purpose of the excursion today. Do you think this driver knows we're headed to a church and not a nightclub?"

The limo had backed out of our narrow drive and drove west on 25A. A snaking line of cars filled the tiny parking lot at St. John's Episcopal Church. The lot at the fish hatch-ery next door was already packed to the gills as well, and a brigade of police officers were guiding mourners into the lots at the Sound View labs just a short walk from the church. In the thick of the crowds, I was able to pick out a handful of people I recognized.

"You better duck. Mr. Merrit, our seventh-grade science teacher is here. You may have been his worst student on record."

"Yeah, but he loved Teddy. I would have failed if Teddy wasn't my lab partner."

I was about to bang on the window again and demand door-to-door service when the limo driver made an unexpected turn around the corner.

"He must be as frustrated as we are," I said.

"Hey, there's the Gremlin." Charlie tried to open the window to wave, but the button was stuck. We ended up passing the Gremlin going in the opposite direction. I could see a look of confusion on my roommates' faces. As soon as the crowds broke, the limo picked up speed, barreling down Harbor Road in the direction of Lloyd Neck.

"Is there a back entrance to the church?" I asked.

"Got me."

"Charlie, this is not cool," I said. "We're headed in the opposite direction of the church."

Charlie released his seatbelt and scrambled around the limo trying the doors and windows, but we were locked in. I slammed the glass partition with the heel of my shoe, but it bounced back like a super ball. We passed a few cars, but the tinted windows only allowed for viewing out, not in.

"He's headed toward the Marshall Field Estate," Charlie said.

The path to the estate was curved like a Slinky and shrouded in trees. The original home of the Marshall Field family, a retail tycoon, had been converted to a state park over fifty years ago, and depending upon funding, the ground maintenance waffled between poor and absolute neglect. We sped past the unmanned ticket booth and down a pitted road toward the main house. The limo veered around the back of the mansion and up onto the stone esplanade. Off the patio, an expansive hill covering at least an acre rolled down to a freshwater pond that let out into the Long Island Sound. In any other circumstance, the setting would have been breathtaking, but with the nose of the limo pointed straight down the hill and the back tires balancing on the edge of the terrace, the landscape did not interest me.

"What the hell's going on?" I said. "Don't tell me he's lost. I swear I am not missing my brother's funeral."

The driver's side door opened. Igor pulled his stocky frame out and trudged toward the back of the car, lifting the trunk lid.

"Okay, maybe it's just a flat tire and he's using the patio as a jack," Charlie said, loosening the only necktie he owned. He signaled through the back window to catch Igor's attention before yelling, "Hey, open the door and I'll help with the tire."

Charlie and I waited a second for Igor to release the lock.

Nothing.

"Screw this," Charlie said. He grabbed a

set of keys from his pocket and yanked off the thin wire ring. "Can you see Igor?"

I scooted around the limo looking for our driver, but the open trunk lid blocked my view. Through the side window, I was able to see down the sloping hill to Long Island Sound. It was still the greatest sledding site in town, with a hair-raising drop-off just before the edge of the pond. When the pond was frozen over, a rider could skid another 100 yards across the surface. The only catch was stopping the sled before you plummeted into the sound. In fact, just mounting a sled safely without tumbling down the treacherous hill was half the thrill.

"You remember sledding here?" I asked Charlie. "Didn't you chip a tooth?"

He nodded, but his eyes were fixated on the key chain. I watched as he straightened the circular wire by flattening it between two keys. He examined the tip and then bent it in a 45-degree angle.

I caught a glimpse of Igor holding a hefty tree branch. I pressed my face against the window to see Igor wedging the branch under one of the rear tires. I was pretty sure this wasn't how you fixed a flat. I felt the car lift a few inches off the ground.

I thought about the Gremlin. The first week I owned it, the brakes had given out while it was parked outside Harbor House. A loose marble would have rolled a few feet down our driveway's gentle grade; a 2,000-pound car was another story. Once the Gremlin picked up speed, it accelerated across the street and landed in a ditch.

I didn't need a foot of snow underneath me to understand what would happen if the limo took this particular hill at top speed.

"Oh my god. It's not a flat. He's trying to push the car down the hill," I heard my voice rise in panic. "Do something, Charlie."

Charlie was busy snaking the wire into a keyhole next to the glass partition.

"Come on, dammit, catch," Charlie muttered.

"Faster," I screamed.

The back tires released, and the car began to inch forward. A memory of the Gremlin's shattered front window and mangled bumper came into my mind.

"We're moving," I yelled. I heard the trunk shut and watched as Igor heaved himself into the bumper.

"Charlie?"

"Don't talk to me." Charlie had one eye shut and the other was focused on the key hole.

I prepared myself to be submerged under

water. Wasn't there something about opening the windows a crack to let water in slowly? Too bad we couldn't open the windows.

"Here we go," Charlie said as the tinted partition separating the compartments of the limo moved three quarters of the way back into its sleeve. The car picked up speed. Charlie clamped down on my hand as I slipped off the seat.

It felt like a hayride gone awry as we bounced and toppled down the hill. "Quick, I won't fit," Charlie said as he took hold of my hips and forced my torso through the window to the front seat. "Grab the emergency brake."

I looked down at the empty space under the radio. "Where the hell is it?"

Charlie shoved my rear end forward and yanked my legs toward the right like a boat rutter. "It's not the fucking Gremlin. Look on the floor next to the door."

I located the brake and jammed the heel of my hand down as the car continued its forward plunge at an increasing speed. Charlie wedged my right leg through the opening and, using my thigh muscles and the seat for leverage, I pushed my hand on the brake again and felt it engage.

The tilt of the hill and the downward motion of the car forced the rear end of the vehicle to upend to a vertical position. In a near perfect pirouette, the car twisted around. We were left facing uphill but sliding backward.

"We're not stopping," I screeched. My entire body was now fully in the front seat. I threw the car in park and slammed my foot on the brake. The car kept rolling, but the pace had slowed down to a point where I was no longer praying for my life.

"We're still gonna hit the water, Ce. Turn the wheel left and aim the back bumper for that elm tree." With its last burst of energy, the limo plowed into the gracious tree, forcing me backward and then forward into the steering wheel. My head ricocheted, and I could feel a stab of pain rush down my spine. If it hadn't been for Charlie's arm wrapped across my shoulders like a seatbelt, the damage would have been much worse.

"Where's Igor?" I asked.

"I saw him running for the woods when the car spun around," Charlie answered.

The sound of sirens racing across the estate slowed my breathing. Trina or Jonathan must have realized something was off when they saw the limo headed away from the church. A row of police cars filed in and parked with military precision along the crest of the hill. Sure enough, I spotted the Gremlin in the distance. The front door of the limo opened easily. I exited the car and signaled to the officers. I spotted Detective DeRosa instantly and gave him a thumbs-up.

Out of the corner of my eye, I caught a flash of light that bounced off the hood of the limo. If I had to re-create the scene, I couldn't say whether I saw the spark first or heard the ping. Regardless, the combination led me to believe I was being shot at. My initial reaction was to suspect the police, and I raised my hands in protest. I'd come out of the driver's door, but I wasn't responsible for this!

Detective DeRosa swung his arms in a downward motion like a referee at a football game, but his shouts were drowned out by the distance. The band of officers shifted toward the woods and let loose a torrent of bullets in the direction Igor had apparently run. Whether it was poor planning or unbridled fear, the police force seemed to have forgotten the miles of trails snaking around the estate, which were frequented by day hikers and horseback riders.

As if on cue, two startled horses emerged from the woods galloping for dear life, their riders apparently tossed into midair. I dove back into the limo and ducked under the dashboard.

"Igor's trying to take DeRosa out," Charlie yelled from the rear. I could see he had his back against the side door. In the midst of the activity, Charlie had somehow grabbed the GPS off the dashboard and was tinkering with the back panel. "There's got to be a data card in the back that stores the location requests. I bet I can figure out Igor's starting point."

"Hey, unless that gadget can deflect a bullet, it's not going to help us right now!"

"I think we're off Igor's radar," Charlie said. "He took a couple of pot shots at you and now he's aiming for DeRosa."

I peeked out the windshield at the exact moment DeRosa went down like a bag of M&M's with a hole in the bottom.

EIGHT

Huntington Hospital was becoming an all-too-familiar place. A few of the nurses remembered my name, and I was practiced enough to ask for a size small hospital robe. Charlie had a slight concussion, I had two cracked ribs, and a bullet had grazed Detective DeRosa's shoulder. We were functioning, but we had been beaten, and the overall mood ranged from confusion to disbelief. Since it was evident at this point that a real threat against my life had taken place, the three of us were placed in a single room with round-the-clock surveillance.

Detective DeRosa pushed the remains of lunch away and grabbed for his ringing cell phone. He looked at the number and handed the phone to me mouthing the words *your father.*

"Hey Dad," I said into the phone, "about that limo you sent for me." I smiled weakly to DeRosa and Charlie, trying to make the best of a miserable situation. I listened quietly to my father and then held the phone against my chest to address DeRosa and Charlie. "He says he didn't send the limo," I whispered.

"I'm aware of that," DeRosa replied as I returned the phone to my ear.

"I'm a little banged up, Dad. My ribs are sore, but I'm okay," I said, thinking how strange it was that I needed a direct threat on my life to get my father's attention. "I think Charlie and Detective DeRosa took the worst of it." I listened to my father, who was clearly agitated at this bizarre turn of events. His voice took on a deep bellow, and I pulled the phone away from my ear as the volume increased.

"Absolutely not," I said to my father. "Thank you for the offer, but I don't want to go that route." I begged off the phone, hitting end while my father was still speaking. "He wants to hire a bodyguard for me," I said to Charlie. "Can you imagine?"

"It's not a bad idea," Charlie said. "Tell me you're not just a little bit freaked out."

I considered his comment. If the eggs were an isolated case, it would be easy enough to explain. Being hijacked by a rogue limo driver was another story. The coupling of these events was indeed disturbing and made me nervous in a way I had never experienced. Yet at the same time, I felt an urgent need to keep my head clear, as if reality had slapped me silly. If someone were after me, I'd need every advantage I could muster; keeping my head together was a priority.

"What do you think, detective?" I asked.

"It's not a great idea," DeRosa explained. "I spoke to your father about protection earlier. I'd prefer the police department be the sole provider of security. The more parties involved, the more screening for the department. Coordination is key, and an outside provider complicates the effort. That being said, these threats are real and you need coverage — but I'd still prefer the police provide the protection."

"Well, I guess I should take comfort knowing my life has some value," I said. "Of course this issue with the limo presents a conundrum. Should I be relieved my father didn't send a limo driven by a hit man or hurt that he didn't send a limo for my brother's funeral?"

"You should be racking your brain to find a link between you and your brother," DeRosa replied.

"Hey, Igor was shooting at you too. Successfully, may I add."

"That's because the county is paying me to protect you."

"So now it's you who's collateral damage?"

"Part of the job."

"What do we know about Igor the limo driver?" I asked.

"Only what you've told us, CeCe. Short, beefy guy with a Slavic look. The riders that got tossed from their horses reported something similar."

"Charlie, grab me that pencil and the lunch menu," I said.

He lowered the sound on the television and tossed the paper and pencil my way. "You can order for me, Ce."

"Forget food for a second." I flipped the menu over and grasped at the fleeting details dancing around my head. I sketched quickly with few erasure marks. "Here's your guy." I passed the drawing to DeRosa.

The detective's skepticism diffused within seconds. "Forgive me if I underestimated your talent. This sketch is excellent."

"She does caricatures too." Charlie made a goofy face. DeRosa chuckled and hit the nurses' call button. A cop materialized at the door.

"What's up boss?"

"Fax this picture to the station. Get it

scanned and run through the database for close matches. Have the station send the mugs over as soon as possible."

"Anything else?" the officer asked.

"You done with that newspaper?"

"Sure thing." The officer handed over the newspaper. Detective DeRosa perused the paper like a speed reader on crack, but I could tell one article intrigued him because he folded the paper inside itself a few times until it was as stiff as a board.

"CeCe, how'd you do that?" DeRosa asked. "The sketch?"

"That's what I do. I've been drawing and painting since I was a kid. I did go to art school, after all."

"No, I mean how did you remember the details of Igor's face so clearly?"

"I didn't. I don't have a photographic memory or anything like that, but when I paint I practice grouping common facial characteristics. Like Igor, there's a typical Russian nose and few variations of that feature." My explanation did not satisfy DeRosa. "Charlie, help me out," I said.

"What can I say? Everyone's got a thing. I'm into computers, she's into facial features."

"Charlie dropped out of MIT," I said to fill in the blanks for DeRosa. "Computer

Science major."

DeRosa looked at Charlie. "MIT?" he asked.

Charlie nodded.

DeRosa got out of bed, grabbed the remote from Charlie and turned off the television. With his good arm he swung a plastic chair into place between Charlie and my bed.

"The two of you need to cut the act." DeRosa slammed the wadded newspaper on my bed to reveal a single story dominating the front page.

"Read it out loud," he commanded, "and stop pretending you don't know anything."

I cleared my throat with a sip of water from a paper cup. That bought me just enough time to scan the article in front of me and prepare for the volcanic explosion bubbling up from DeRosa's chest cavity. I tried to breathe deeply in an effort to steady my voice, but my cracked ribs and still-healing stomach allowed only for a shallow huff.

"Bethesda, Maryland. National Institute of Health grant coordinator, Dr. Naomi Gupta, commits suicide." I eyed Charlie and watched as his features froze faster than a kid's tongue on a metal pole in December. I continued. "Dr. Gupta, a former researcher at Sound View Laboratories and current NIH employee, was found dead by hanging in her apartment. Sources assert that the recent NIH rejection of a twenty-million-dollar grant proposal submitted by Sound View Laboratories, Dr. Gupta's former employer, may have caused undue professional and personal stress."

DeRosa shoved the paper at me, his thumb pointed squarely at the photo of the deceased grant coordinator, Dr. Naomi Gupta. "I saw this woman in your studio the first night we met. In fact, I saw at least ten portraits of this exact face lined up on the wall of your attic."

I glanced over at Charlie, who was trying very hard to melt into the folds of his sheets. I broke the silence with the truth. "Naomi and Teddy were engaged."

"And?" DeRosa pushed.

"They ended it more than a year ago," I answered. "I was painting her as an engagement gift, but after Teddy and Naomi broke up, there wasn't much motivation to finish."

"Did she sit for the portraits? Was she at Harbor House at any time?" DeRosa grilled.

"She didn't need to sit. I knew her face and frankly I couldn't stand her long enough to entertain the idea of a sitting. I painted her for my brother. He asked."

"Were you jealous of her?" DeRosa probed.

"No, we were just different people. She was all about the purchases that come with making money."

"When were you two going to tell me that your brother was at the tail end of a break-up? If we're looking for suspects, the ex-fiancée would be a good place to start."

"Come on Frank. You're grasping on this one," Charlie said. "They dated, they got engaged, they broke up. Like CeCe said, Naomi was materialistic but not a killer."

"Who broke up with whom?" DeRosa asked.

"Teddy dumped her," Charlie said. "She fled to the NIH about six months ago. I think Teddy was relieved to have her off the campus."

"He was? How have we not talked about this, Charlie?" I remember being so thrilled the engagement had ended that I didn't even bother to pump my brother for details.

"Guy stuff," Charlie replied. "Anyway, something happened that made Teddy question her ethics and Teddy was all about doing the right thing. I think he started to see Naomi the way the rest of us saw her."

DeRosa turned to Charlie. "I need you to

clear one thing up relative to 'doing the right thing.' You ate the eggs after midnight and no one saw you until the next day, and you were the only resident who didn't get sick. I looked back at the report of the poisoning earlier. Trina said you weren't at breakfast. You caught up with me at the hospital that afternoon. I gave you the benefit of the doubt and figured you needed some time after finding out your best friend was dead. Now I may think otherwise. So I'm asking you, where were you from two a.m. until the next afternoon? Is there any chance you drove to Bethesda, Maryland, and back?"

Charlie fiddled with his bed sheet and readjusted his pillow to buy time.

"Charlie, I'm kind of curious myself, and I won't be hurt if you say you were with Becky," I said.

"I was Dumpster diving," Charlie admitted.

"That was earlier in the evening," DeRosa corrected.

"Yeh, and after the house quieted down and everyone went to sleep, I went to Teddy's place and rooted through his garbage."

"Why?" I asked.

"I don't know. I guess I thought I'd find something."

"Did you?"

"Not really. I sat in the barn until the sun came up with two bags of garbage, but I couldn't bring myself to go through them. The bags are still in the barn." Charlie adjusted the gauze pad on his head and directed his confession to DeRosa. "I swear I didn't know about Naomi, but I did go through Teddy's mail and noticed her return address on an envelope. It looked like a Hallmark card."

In one fluid motion, DeRosa commandeered every electronic device in the room. Calls were being made, buzzers were being buzzed, and stuff was starting to go down.

"Is there anything else you want to add?" DeRosa asked Charlie. He had a cell phone hanging off one ear and a hospital phone off the other. Charlie grabbed his torn jeans, which were hanging over a hospital chair, and tossed a set of keys over.

"These keys are for the large cupboard at the back of the barn. I threw Teddy's garbage in there." Charlie fished around his jeans once more and produced a thin wafer of metal no larger than a quarter. "And here's the data card from Igor's GPS."

NINE

DeRosa had us all released from the hospital within the hour. We were escorted back to Harbor House, where the police set up shop in one of the empty bedrooms on the second floor. The room offered a lovely view of the sound with a clear shot of our gardens and farm below but was quickly transformed into a makeshift headquarters — an extension of the Laurel Hollow Police Department on Shore Road. A truckload of computer equipment was carted in, and we did our best to dig up a conference table, a few desks, and at least six mismatched chairs. Trina cleaned out a small storage closet across the hall from the makeshift police office, and we shoved an old bed in the corner for DeRosa. Although unorthodox for the police department to establish camp in a private home, it did create a false sense of security that I was happy to indulge. Having the police on premise also defused my father's demands for increased security, thus reducing his incessant calls to DeRosa.

My life had been threatened twice, my twin brother was dead, and his ex-fiancée was cooling down in a morgue about three hundred miles south of this room. None of this sat well with me. Worse, I had missed my brother's funeral. Closure and safety had replaced mourning.

Information trickled in slowly, and piles of papers formed mountains on the Formica conference table. The official autopsy report appeared inconclusive, revealing only that Teddy suffered an extreme loss of oxygen in a short period of time. For lack of a more accurate label, the coroner used the term *asphyxiation,* although no external bruising was identified around the mouth or neck area. Residual bruising was discovered on Teddy's chest, but the coroner suspected my brother caused it by pounding on his own chest, as if he knew he was choking. Both of Teddy's hands were balled in tight fists, but nothing was found in his esophagus. The results were disappointing and if not for the attempts on my life, the case would probably have been shelved. In light of recent events, however, the autopsy report could not be disregarded. Something or someone had prevented Teddy from taking the hundreds of millions of additional breaths he deserved over a lifetime that would have easily spanned another fifty years.

"Let's take it from the top." DeRosa had gathered his team, including two cops from the station and me.

As he revisited the facts of the case, I picked up my pencil and started to doodle. I did a quick sketch of Officer Cheski and then started in on a profile of Officer Lamendola. The two turned out to be decent men. Sergeant Cheski hailed from Queens, an ex–New York City street cop who thought the tony suburbs of the North Shore would increase his chances of seeing his children grow up. That was until Igor unloaded a magazine in his direction. His partner, Lamendola, was a rookie who had just graduated at the top of his class from the academy.

"Are you paying attention?" DeRosa asked.

"Sure," I said.

He reached over and slid the pencil out of my hand. "You realize how unusual it is for the police to actively involve a citizen in a case."

"My fault," I apologized. "I'm just trying to get a handle on everyone in the room."

"What do you need to know?"

"Do you have a brother?"

DeRosa hesitated, though there was no right or wrong answer.

He tapped the pencil on the table before saying, "I'm an only child."

"That makes two only children in the room," I said, wanting my comment to make all of them uncomfortable. I rose from the table. "If it's okay with everyone, I need a break." Before I left the room, I gathered up a pile of my doodles. The incessant sketching had been with me for as long as I could hold a pencil. This current mass of swirls and curves gave way to yet another face. The same face littering my attic with paint still wet from recent brushstrokes. I felt close to this man filtering out of the tip of my brushes and pencils, but the more I drew, the less it looked like my brother. I let the papers slip from my hands and drop into the nearest waste-paper basket.

TEN

DeRosa came by my studio the next morning. He carted in a carafe of coffee, two mugs, and some pie as a peace offering. I laid my brushes down and made room on my sketch table for the food.

"I'm sorry I walked out yesterday." I reached for a steaming mug.

"I'm sorry I'm about to eat a piece of pie recovered from a Dumpster."

I lifted the piecrust with my fork and spotted chunks of apples and whole raspberries. "You're in luck. Looks like Trina made this one from scratch, although who knows where she got the fruit."

"I'm hoping you have some leftover stomach medicine." DeRosa balanced an enormous scoop on his fork, as if the size of the mouthful was correlated to the depth of his authenticity. He swallowed and carefully wiped his mouth with a napkin, then turned serious. "I'm not going to pretend I understand your grief, but we need to find some common ground if we are going to work together. Help me understand how we can do that."

"Frank, I like people who own up to something. I'm drawn to people who pick a life philosophy, stand by it, and consider their personal impact on society as they act out their choices. I don't get any vibe from you. There's something you're keeping from me. It's either something about you personally or something you know about my brother."

"It's not the first time I've been accused of playing it too close to the vest. Luckily for me, a detached persona is a good fit for a cop's life."

He didn't get it. "Look. Charlie and I are pretty smart. Same goes for Trina and Jonathan, although the jury is still out on Becky. You have to give us some credit. You can't entertain subsistence living without half a brain. I'm less concerned about my fate than understanding what happened to my brother. Not to be melodramatic, but Teddy was the most important person in the world to me. I want to help the investigation."

"I think you can."

"Then let's finish this slice and I'll help you get to know Teddy. I'll fill you in on everything I know about my family and the labs."

He took another bite of pie, and then, finally, nodded to seal our bargain.

I looked out the window and saw a gathering around the barn. A team of forensic specialists was sorting, examining, and labeling my brother's garbage on large metal tables. I consider myself an expert on garbage, but the sight of Teddy's final refuse now seemed a perverse intrusion. I'd be surprised if in the history of police investigations a recycled *People* magazine had ever cinched a big case.

"I can't watch this," I said. "Can we get out of here?"

"How about a drive?" DeRosa suggested.

"Where to?"

"You're in the driver's seat, CeCe."

"Where are you from?"

"Freeport."

"Tough town," I said. "Care to be my guide?"

ELEVEN

It took approximately ten miles of Long Island stop-and-go traffic, a quick gas refill, and about twenty-eight traffic lights for Detective DeRosa to defrost from frozen solid to lukewarm. Still on the defensive, he peppered me with questions about my family and childhood. I was honest, albeit slightly biased in my favor.

"So what's the great divide between you and your father?" he asked.

"Why? Did my father say something to you?" I asked.

"He said the two of you hadn't always seen eye to eye."

"That would be an understatement." I laughed, remembering the endless arguments I'd had with my father as a teenager.

DeRosa pointed to a small gap in the next lane and I darted in with inches to spare. I discovered it was impossible for him to sit passively in the passenger seat. I pretended to follow his driving suggestions, hoping a transfer of control would loosen him up.

"Give me one childhood memory that describes you," he said as he readjusted the passenger side mirror.

I continued to drive, moving the car to mimic DeRosa's hand signals. "I do remember once in kindergarten, my parents hired a seamstress who sewed her fingers to the bone making an elaborate replica of a Snow White costume. The day before Halloween, I hid it under my bed and begged an old white sheet off the cleaning staff. I poked two holes for eyes and used an old stocking to tie it around my neck."

"And the first Freegan ghost was born."

"A memorable day," I replied. "Then I hit my teens and my grades took a nosedive. Charlie and I went full throttle into a series of unforgivable teenage hijinks."

"The current police term is *antisocial personality disorder* or APD."

"Really? Well, here's the catch when it comes to *my* APD. My father is the guru of DNA. He's invested the better part of his career studying the impact of DNA on human development. In the nature versus nurture wars, my father is on a third team. His team believes DNA can be manipulated and reformed. Left alone, DNA is your destiny. With proper social and medical intervention, Dr. William Prentice believes entire generations of people can outsmart their DNA."

"How so?"

"One of the first studies my fathered pioneered was in the 1960s, and it concerned the effect of folic acid on prenatal brain development. Now, everyone takes prenatal vitamins. His study evened the playing field."

"I'm starting to like your father even more."

"You should. He's pretty amazing," I agreed. My credibility seemed to be slipping. "But family and work are two different things, and I don't think I interested him as much as his next scientific breakthrough."

"I'm on the edge of my seat," DeRosa deadpanned.

"Ever heard of epigenetics?" I asked.

"Nope."

"I'll tell it the way my brother explained it to me. He and my dad were entrenched in the study of changes in genetic code. Not the type of changes that occur over multiple millenniums — like fish to cave man to human. It's the study of DNA changes within a generation."

"I thought DNA couldn't change."

"Technically, it can't. But apparently super-scientists, like Teddy and my dad, have found a lever on the DNA that can be turned on or off, and that lever can be affected by external forces like nutrition, stress, and the environment."

"Give me an example."

"Let's say that your DNA has predetermined your ability to positively process stress," I said, finally swatting DeRosa's hand away from the dashboard. In the last minute, he had readjusted every dial on the Gremlin. I returned all the dials to their original position.

DeRosa opened and closed his window a few times while I continued.

"As I was saying, your stress control gene is turned on, and that's why you can take a bullet to the shoulder without running to a therapist. But imagine if you were raised in a low-income, crime-ridden area that overpowers your natural instinct to process stress positively. Your lever, also called an epigenome, could easily turn off. Your DNA combination hasn't changed, but the lever is off. Your kids will inherit your DNA, which is programmed for positive stress. However, given your crappy environment, you will now pass on good DNA with its levers turned off. The DeRosa rugrats, no matter how much love and attention you and your wife give them, will have a meltdown at the sound of a balloon popping."

"I'm assuming you used that particular example because I grew up in Freeport dodging drug addicts and random bullets. Should I schedule my vasectomy now?"

"I may have been a bit insensitive. My father's problem is that I've disappointed him on both the nature *and* nurture perspectives. In his eyes, I'll never live up to my inherited traits, which are a direct reflection of his own DNA. How embarrassing for an overachiever to raise a slacker. To make matters worse, I grew up in the lap of luxury with every opportunity handed to me on a silver platter, yet according to my father, the only thing royal is my ability to screw it up."

"You're his life's work gone bad," DeRosa summarized.

"I'm his outlier. If you can repeat a science experiment with ninety-nine percent confidence, it still means there's a one percent chance of failure. And that's me."

"And Teddy was his success."

"Teddy was the best son a parent could imagine."

Frank pointed to the next exit. "Get off at

Roosevelt and we'll head south toward the water. And lock your door."

"Is this excursion going to challenge my DNA?"

"CeCe, something tells me World War III couldn't put a dent in your constitution."

We drove aimlessly through Freeport, partly because I was out of my element. The north and south shores of Long Island are so distinctly different a tourist might half expect to pass through a passport control booth at the end of an exit ramp. The differences lie in the physical geography. A glacial slide from the last ice age deposited a pile of rocks in the northern half of the island, washing the remains southward to create miles of sandy shores, almost like a melting ice cream cone on its side. North Shore inhabitants travel south for the beaches and the airport, while those on the South Shore find little reason to travel north. Unlike the east/west parkways famous for their congested traffic, the north/south venues are virtually empty.

"It's so flat."

"Like a pancake," DeRosa responded. "Freeport literally spills out into the Great South Bay. There isn't even a land boundary to mark the end of the town. Let me guess: you've been to Jones Beach a million times but never stopped along the way."

"Guilty of day-tripping."

Frank thumbed left to a sign advertising the Nautical Mile, a tourist area nestled in one of Freeport's many canals. It was early in the season, but a few hearty beachgoers were dragging their aluminum chairs across the boardwalk to enjoy the surf close up. I turned into municipal parking, picked a spot, and scrounged around for quarters.

"I got this one." Frank pulled out a county police card and placed it under the windshield.

"Didn't know the good old boy network traveled this far south," I said squinting to see DeRosa's name on the card.

We exited the Gremlin and Frank gave a passing patrol car the thumbs up.

"I'm not a Cold Spring Harbor cop. I work for the county and got pulled in for the case."

"How so?" I asked.

"Two weeks ago, a row of ten potted hydrangeas was stolen from the plant nursery about a mile from the labs," DeRosa said.

"So the men in blue are searching for a thief concerned with curb appeal?"

"Cheski and Lamendola will solve the hydrangea case within the week, but their experience is limited and correlated directly to the amount and type of crimes in wealthy areas on the North Shore. It's common practice to bring in a county expert on bigger cases."

"And your expertise is?"

"Anything out of the ordinary," DeRosa said as he tapped his hand along the dock's railing. He pointed to a fleet of boats bouncing gently on the water. "Remember the senior couple from the South Shore found murdered in their leisure cruiser off the Bahamas?"

"Sure," I said, easily recalling the highly publicized case about a seemingly ordinary businessman who was covering up a lifetime of affairs and crooked business deals. "Didn't the wife hire a hit man to kill her husband and his lover only to be mistaken as the girlfriend herself?"

"Almost. The twist was that the wife was having an affair with the hit man. The hit man was trying to dump her and figured it would be easier just to kill her along with the husband. He farmed out the hit to some loser who couldn't swim. Apparently, the second hit man killed the wife and husband, fell off the boat, and then washed up in the Caribbean. Problem was, we couldn't make the connection between the first hit man, the second hit man, and the wife."

"How did you break the case?" I asked.

"Both men ate lunch at the restaurant across the street." DeRosa pointed with his chin to an unremarkable fish restaurant. "Every Tuesday for three straight weeks. The restaurant owner had credit card receipts. Then we found a bank envelope with a wad of cash in the second hit man's car. The envelope was from the wife's bank, and the fingerprints of all three were on the envelope, indicating that the money had been passed from the wife to each of the men."

"That's a good story," I said.

His face registered insult. "It's not a story. It's real. And it's interesting because it has layers."

"And Teddy's case has layers," I replied.

"You said it yourself: young men do not drop dead without a reason," he said, confirming my earlier suspicion.

"I guess my father is pleased the department brought in the big guns," I said as we walked along the boardwalk.

"Powerful men like him come to expect service and attention." He led me to a fishing shack with five small tables. He signaled the waiter and called for two beers and a plate of steaming oysters. "Unfortunately, people in your father's position also expect complete control, and in this case, he's just a civilian. He's in a tough spot because he still has a company to run and a board to answer to. The fact that your brother was an employee of the organization, and an important one, complicates your father's role."

"What's my father attempting to control?"

The waiter brought the drinks and oysters. I eyed the beer.

"Are you on duty?" I asked.

DeRosa looked at his watch and paused. "Not now."

I smiled. Maybe there was something real about Detective DeRosa.

"Your father has given us access to the labs, but only under his careful supervision. Teddy's death puts the labs under a microscope. The longer the case drags on, the more negative exposure there is." DeRosa took a swig of beer. "Your father wants this to come to an end quickly. On a personal level, however, he won't allow your mother to be interviewed. He insists there is nothing she can add that he hasn't already covered."

"My mother hasn't been sober since the early eighties," I said as I picked at the label on the ketchup bottle.

"That might explain his hesitance. And since she's not a suspect, technically she doesn't have to speak with us."

"Maybe." I felt the foam popping on my upper lip as I took a sip of beer so cold I could feel its tracks down to my stomach. "There may be layers there, too."

"How so?" he asked.

I tilted my head back and let an oyster slither along my tongue. I was hesitant to explore my relationship with my mother, but if it helped find Teddy's killer, it was worth it.

"My mother earned a master's degree in art. Before she married, she had built a following in Europe and traveled extensively."

"So your artistic talent comes from your mother."

"A direct DNA transfer. And by all accounts, she was as carefree as I am when she was young."

"I guess *carefree* is the new word for *rebellious*?" Frank tapped his beer mug and a waiter filled it instantaneously.

"I'm being generous in my descriptions." I rolled my eyes. "Anyway, something derailed her along the way, although the source of her troubles has always been a mystery to me. I can't tell you how many times I studied photos of her face from earlier periods of her life trying to recapture a moment from my youth when she appeared genuinely happy."

"What was she like when you and Teddy were growing up?" DeRosa asked.

"My mother wasn't hands-on," I replied, remembering the rare occasion she would tuck us in and kiss us goodnight. "The day-to-day care was provided by nannies and the house staff. She was reserved, somewhat distracted, as if she had lost her focus. In fact, as a child, I never saw her paint."

"It's odd she stopped painting. Is it possible she had a breakdown of some kind?" DeRosa barely gave me enough time to reflect on my youth. "Did she leave the home for any period of time?"

The truth was in my pause. My mother had in fact left the house, and more than once. Yet in all these years, I had never examined her absence out of the context it had been presented. "We were told she had chronic fatigue syndrome." My answer surprised even me.

"And you never questioned it?"

"I was seven years old, and my father is a doctor."

"Did Teddy ever mention your mother's illness after he received his medical degree?"

"Damn, Frank, you really are good at this."

"So he did?"

98

"About three months ago, he scheduled a round of blood tests for my mother. Honestly, I thought he was concerned with her liver. He told my mother he wanted to check up on her chronic fatigue."

"Interesting." I could see DeRosa falling deep in thought. He took out his iPad and jotted down some notes.

"Is this important?"

"I'll take anything I can get at this point," he responded.

I gave him a good once-over from the top of his head to the point where the table met his chest. He was broad, bordering on big, with a stillness that seemed practiced. His presence was appealing but at the same time impenetrable, possibly because his job was to evaluate evidence regardless of the outcome. I imagined how witnesses and criminals alike could be drawn in only to be caught off-guard by Detective Frank De-Rosa. I did not want to be on the wrong side of this man.

"My parents live down the street. I can walk from here." Frank motioned to a row of recently renovated buildings along the water. "One of the patrolmen will drive me back to Harbor House tomorrow."

"Sure," I said.

"Can I give you some advice?" he asked.

"If it helps the investigation."

"You've got this thing with faces. I can see the way you stare at people for an unnaturally long time. On the upside, you put your talent to work with the sketch of Igor. I liked that." Frank threw a twenty on the table. "But on a personal level, it's a little threatening."

"Get real," I said. "I eat food from strangers' garbage cans. Do you think I care that my lingering gaze makes others uncomfortable?" I tossed my head as if I'd let him get the last word. "Later, Frank."

I drove home from Freeport knowing full well that I'd given more to Frank DeRosa than I'd gotten. I bet the standard police handbook strictly advises against developing personal relationships with the players in a case. Conversely, the investigation required my participation, and I was feeling underappreciated. DeRosa would have to look long and hard to find someone closer to Teddy than me, and whether or not I liked Naomi, I was almost family with Teddy's now deceased ex-fiancée. In addition, I was still related to my mother, who was still married to my father.

And that's exactly where I was headed.

TWELVE

Two understated stone pillars punctuated the gravel drive, signaling an entrance lined with enormous birch trees. Although not visible from the street, the main house rose impressively from the grounds and could be spotted about a half-mile down the way at the end of a circular driveway. I'd always felt our driveway was pretentious since it's impossible to park efficiently in a circle. The message is, don't park; wait for the valet. As if a stationary car in full view of the front door is somehow offensive. I did my best to position the Gremlin smack dab in the middle of the cul-de-sac.

I let myself in but felt the hesitation of being unwanted in my own childhood home. It crossed my mind to knock on the front door but that would have been an outright admission of my disinheritance. Within a minute, a cleaning woman popped a head around the corner of a doorway.

"Is my mother home?" I asked.

She nodded toward the plant atrium, a beautifully designed indoor greenhouse off the kitchen. Even as a child, I remembered my mother soaking in the humidity of the glass enclosure. Charlie insisted it was an excellent remedy for sweating off alcohol toxins.

I found my mother resting on a summer lounge, a tall drink balanced on a side table, her lids fluttering in half sleep.

"Mom."

"Constance?" She turned her head, and I made note of the lines etched deeply around her eyes. Unless my father could find a gene linked to skin elasticity, I was looking at myself in forty years.

"Mom," I said again.

"Teddy's dead," she replied.

I have no idea where it came from and, despite all attempts to control my breathing, an enormous sob erupted from my mouth. The cleaning lady snuck a peek and then skittered off in haste. My mother held her drink out for me.

"Take a sip sweetheart," she said.

I reached for her glass without questioning its contents.

The shock stopped my tears faster than a shot of vodka. "This is just soda."

"You're disappointed?" my mother said.

"Did I miss something? Like a six-month stint at Betty Ford?"

"I'm doing it on my own. An attribute you may be familiar with."

"I recognize that streak of independence." I smiled at my mother and, for the first time in years, it was returned. "Trina said you called the other day. She thought you were inebriated."

"People hear what they want," my mother said. "I was sober."

"Congratulations. How long?"

"About two months," she replied. "Teddy ran some tests on me and suggested I start painting again. A therapy of sorts. I'm a good artist but not good enough to paint drunk." She patted her lounge chair, and I came forward to sit. "Your father doesn't know."

"What? Mom, that's insane. How could Dad not know?"

"I have the liquor delivered regularly. Norma, that's the woman you saw when you entered, pours the bottles out for me and we fill the recycling bin each week."

"But why?"

"Your father doesn't deserve my sobriety. He'd try to own it, but it's mine. Teddy helped me see that."

"That's pretty harsh," I said as I took another sip of the soda and rethought my primary purpose for coming here. I'd intended to quiz my mother about Teddy, but I wasn't prepared to deal with her newfound sobriety. I had very little experience dealing with my mother sober. Given our similarities, I chose a rational approach.

"I think there's more to Teddy's death than an accident or an underlying medical condition," I said, hoping my mother would follow my honest lead. But she remained silent. "Mom, is there anything you can tell the police?"

"I can't," she said, and I noticed a slight tremor gripped her hand. "Teddy was never mine. He belonged to your father. There's nothing I can tell the police except that he was a very special boy and an amazing man."

"What if it was me who died?" I asked without really wanting to hear the answer. "What would you tell the police?"

My mother's answer hung at the tip of her tongue, as if she had considered the question before. "I wouldn't have to tell them anything," she responded. "You're a survivor."

"Whom did I belong to?"

"Yourself," she said emphatically. "That's

the way I wanted to raise my daughter." She motioned for me to come closer and as if she were making up for decades of lost time, she ran her fingers through my blond locks.

"I guess I should say thank you, Mom," I said, "but I have a favor to ask first."

"You'd like to root through our garbage before you leave?" she said, giving me a quick pinch on the cheek before releasing me.

"Nice, Mom, but I'll pass. I'm stuck on a painting. I keep sketching the same head over and over without progress. Maybe you could stop by Harbor House and give me some advice now that you're back at the easel."

"I actually just started driving again, with Norma as my co-pilot. As of yesterday, I made it all the way to the main road and back without the shakes."

"I'm five miles away. Piece of cake in broad daylight. You can bring Norma if you want."

I gave my mother a peck on the cheek. Her skin felt cool and I recognized her smell: a mixture of expensive perfume and freshly washed hair. As I leaned in, I noticed her earlobes. Just a small, soft droplet, like mine.

Just before I let myself out, I caught

Norma's attention.

"Norma. I wanted to thank you for helping my mother."

"Yes, ma'am."

I grabbed a pad and pen from the front hall desk and jotted down my number. "Please call me if my mother needs anything."

"Yes, ma'am."

THIRTEEN

Activity at Harbor House started to wind down. The investigators had tagged and recorded each and every scrap of Teddy's garbage. Lamendola entered the information into an evidence database. Cheski handled background checks on the labs' employees both past and present. Coming up on the two-week anniversary of Teddy's death, I felt as if the investigation had stalled.

"Hey guys. When do you knock off for the day?" I pulled a chair up to the table and grabbed a handful of homemade chips.

"We'll probably put in another hour or so," Cheski said. "We want to make sure Frank has a preliminary report tonight, and then we'll meet bright and early tomorrow."

"I'm in," I said to show support.

"We're glad to have you, CeCe. It's actually pretty nice working here."

"Yeah, Becky brought us a great lunch,"

Lamendola added. "All this healthy stuff from your farm. Cheski might even drop a few."

Cheski patted his midsection in agreement. "You know, CeCe," he said, "your friend Charlie has turned out to be a real asset. We were having trouble accessing the national crime data, and he hacked through a police-grade firewall within minutes."

"Thank god he's not a terrorist," I said.

Lamendola's face lit up like a hazard flare.

"I'm kidding." I grabbed another chip. "Anyway, I just wanted to say thank you."

I headed up to my studio and found Charlie spread out on my futon, barefoot, bare chested, and sporting a pair of cargo pants that had seen better days.

"What are you reading?" I asked.

"An outdated *Maxim* from Teddy's garbage."

"Charlie, you stole evidence?"

"It's mine. I left it at Teddy's about six months ago. Like he'd ever read crap like this." Charlie spread the pages of the magazine to reveal an alluring photo of Jessica Alba looking like she had crawled out of a vat of grease.

"Is that supposed to turn me on?" I said.

"So you're turned on?"

"Let's see." I used my fingers for a count-

108

down. "I've been poisoned, shot at, and rolled down a hill in a two-ton car. If I was into sadomasochism, I'd be on the verge of ecstasy." I closed the magazine and slid it across the floor.

"See, I knew you were turned on," Charlie said.

I pretended to bang my head on the futon in utter frustration. "How is it possible you are still single?"

"I'm holding out for you, CeCe."

Against my better judgment, I reached out for Charlie, who was more than willing to scoop me up from the chaos of my life. I wanted to feel safe, even if it was fleeting.

"I'm exhausted, Charlie, and you are about to take advantage of me."

"Maybe it's me who needs the attention," Charlie whispered as his lips brushed past mine.

Charlie's stubble was rough against my cheek. The harder I kissed him, the deeper it dug into my skin. It was painful and cleansing at the same time, as if we could scrub off the anger and hurt that had accumulated since Teddy's death. Charlie lifted my hips with ease, and I followed his lead like a well-trained puppy.

This is better than last time, much better, I thought. The taboo had been broken, so we offered each other the patience and time we deserved. I fell asleep with Charlie's arm snug under my head. As I drifted off, I thought how bittersweet it was that Teddy's death had caused me to welcome Charlie and my mother back in my life.

FOURTEEN

The knock on the door was slightly less jarring than the buzz of an alarm clock. I swung my arm across the sheets and found an empty spot still warm from Charlie's presence.

"We're starting in five," DeRosa's voice rang out like a boot camp sergeant.

"How about ten?" I mumbled into my pillow.

"We found something. It's urgent."

In the time it could have taken me to answer, I was up and dressed. I flung the door open and covered my morning breath with the back of my hand.

"Pee and brush."

I scooted past DeRosa to the bathroom. I rinsed and spit more times than necessary to buy myself some time. DeRosa's expression was classic conflict, a mixture of discomfort and disappointment. With his eyebrows gathered like a pincushion and his head tilted to avoid looking directly at me, I sensed his discovery was divisive.

Within minutes the team formed. A pile of donuts sat untouched on the table. DeRosa started talking before I had time to snag a Boston cream.

"Cheski sorted through the list of employees provided by the labs. Without beating around the bush, it turns out the labs employed a Jonathan Randolph ten years ago from June 2000 until March 2001."

Charlie's shoulders rose, signaling his confusion, and he shot me a glance of complete bewilderment.

"Is that our Jonathan?" I asked.

To confirm the answer, Cheski slid a black-and-white photocopy of Jonathan's lab security photo across the table while he read his accompanying report.

"Jonathan G. Randolph, a medical student enrolled at Yale, was hired for a fellowship in the spring of 2000 to assist in a genetic study of fruit reproduction. The position required supervision of greenhouses two and three and resulted in a three-hundred-page report detailing the growing pattern in mutant fruit species."

"I did not know Jonathan had worked at the labs," I said emphatically. I sought Charlie out for confirmation, but his head was buried in his hands. "Charlie?" I implored. "Help me out here."

"Fuck," Charlie slammed his fist on the table.

"Come clean, Charlie." DeRosa's statement was more an order than a request.

"Dr. Prentice gave me and Teddy a summer job at the labs after sophomore year. It was grunt work. We cleaned out the greenhouses, carted soil around, maintained the watering system."

"Could Teddy and Jonathan have crossed paths?" DeRosa asked.

"Yeah. I mean, it's possible they met before we hooked up here at the house," Charlie answered.

DeRosa read the report, jotting down questions at the same time. "Charlie, do you remember Jonathan from that summer?"

"I don't remember Jonathan specifically because there were probably twenty medical students working in the greenhouses. But it was different for Teddy. He focused on learning. He followed the experiments and helped some of the students make observations and take notes. Teddy did anything to put him closer to the action."

"Big whoop," I said stunned by the direction of the conversation. "So Teddy and

Jonathan may have known each other. Who cares?"

Cheski responded to my statement by reading the remainder of his report. "After the fellowship, Jonathan G. Randolph dropped out of Yale medical and applied for a full-time job at the labs. His application was rejected."

I leaned backward and crossed my arms protectively over my chest. "And you assume the motive for Teddy's murder is that a disgruntled worker cracked after a decade of peaceful living and killed my brother out of pent-up professional jealousy?"

"Before we go down that route," DeRosa said, "tell me how you met Jonathan and how he came to live at Harbor House."

"He and Trina worked at a local organic food co-op. Trina and I made friends, and Jonathan's knowledge of farming intrigued me. They came out to visit me a few times when I renovated the house, and it all came together. It's as simple as that."

"Think hard," DeRosa pressured. "Did Jonathan approach you first? Did he suggest the living arrangements? Maybe farming in trade for lodgings?"

"Frank, do you have any idea what you are suggesting? That somehow Jonathan sought me out because for years he had harbored an inexplicable grudge against my brother after he dropped out of medical school and Teddy went on to become a success?"

"I dropped out of MIT and I haven't killed a single mathematician," Charlie said as he perked up at my reasoning.

"Well there you go," I responded. "Case closed."

"CeCe, be reasonable," DeRosa said. "Jonathan is the only link we have between you, Teddy, and the labs."

"Okay, Einstein. I'll make it easy for you. Ask Jonathan yourself." I pointed in the direction of the door. "And let me remind you that he's not the only link. Teddy's ex-fiancée Naomi, a former lab employee, is still dead. What happened to that?"

Cheski and Lamendola were collectively subdued. DeRosa rose abruptly from the conference table and stalked out in a huff. Cheski and Lamendola scurried off behind their leader, leaving me alone with Charlie.

"You held your ground."

"No thanks to you," I said with disappointment. "You practically locked the cuffs on Jonathan yourself."

With the dexterity of a circus performer, Charlie tipped backward in his chair, balancing precipitously on the two rear legs.

"I'm losing it," he said, letting the chair slam forward. "I can't handle Teddy's death."

"How crazy could we be if Teddy chose to hang with us?" I asked.

"Pathetic but true," Charlie responded and then paced the room, his fists shoved deep in his pockets. With a dejected grunt he rested his head on the windowsill. "Check it out. DeRosa, Cheski, and Lamendola are headed to the barn."

"I guess that would be my fault," I said as I joined Charlie and watched DeRosa enter the barn. "I just don't get why Jonathan didn't say anything to us about the working at the labs."

Charlie made a beeline for the computer, unscrambling a mess of cords and power strips. The screen lit up and he punched some buttons, allowing a stream of distant voices to fill up the room. The interior of the barn filled the monitor, revealing DeRosa's back and a very surprised Jonathan.

"Security camera." Charlie patted the screen like an old friend. "I rigged the property after the egg incident."

"Is this legal?"

"It's your property, CeCe. Technically, the cops are trespassing." Charlie redirected the camera and adjusted the sound. I had the impression we were eavesdropping from a hayloft.

"Jonathan, I'd like to keep this informal, but we have a few questions." DeRosa's voice rang clear.

"You know I worked at the labs," Jonathan offered.

"We do. Any reason it didn't come out sooner?"

Jonathan heaved a mixture of dirt and manure into a wheelbarrow. For a split second I worried his shovel might be repurposed as a weapon. If DeRosa's information was correct, then I really had no idea who I had invited to live in my home. Katrina and Jonathan had lived with me for ten years, but the friendship was through Katrina. That's the funny thing about couples; you tend to accept the significant other without question. Maybe I should have asked more questions, but Jonathan had always presented himself as a quiet and thoughtful man.

I wanted to believe I was right, but I assumed DeRosa was prepared for a confrontation. I noticed Cheski and Lamendola's strategic positions covering both exits. I exhaled with relief as Jonathan placed the tool carefully on the ground.

"Mind if we talk in the greenhouse?" Jonathan gestured toward the door blocked by Cheski.

DeRosa motioned to Cheski, and I slapped Charlie on the arm. "Can you change the picture? Is there a camera in the greenhouse?"

With a flip of a switch, we were in the greenhouse ahead of Jonathan and the police. We watched the foursome file in, and then we heard a knock on our door.

"CeCe, it's me and Becky," Trina's voice was as thin as a wire. "Something's up. Detective DeRosa asked for Jonathan, and neither of them looked happy."

I opened the door and waved them in. Trina and Becky gathered around the monitor, unaware of the drama about to unfold. I'd rather hear Jonathan confess to an affair with a barn animal than have him implicate himself in my brother's murder. Becky's hovering wasn't doing much for my mental state either. Although she and Charlie weren't an official item, I'd have a hard time explaining why I was wearing Charlie's t-shirt under my sweatshirt. If only we were in a *Three's Company* episode and Mr. Roper could bumble in to break the tension.

"Why is Jonathan in the greenhouse with the detective?" Becky asked innocently.

"Because Colonel Mustard was detained in the billiard room with the wrench," Charlie replied straight-faced.

I glared at Charlie and reminded myself that guys do not rank brains highly on their criteria for sex. As always, I was the anomaly on Charlie's lengthy resume. I turned my attention back to Jonathan and noted his relaxed appearance as he addressed the police.

"Come closer and look at these green pepper plants." Jonathan held out a leafy specimen for the men to examine. "Notice anything odd?"

Lamendola took a shot at it. "My Italian grandmother grows peppers. These plants are fuller than hers. Heartier."

"That's because there are three fruits per stem and a typical plant produces only one fruit per stem." Jonathan beamed with pride. "My study at the labs involved decoding the fruit-making process. At the time, I attended Yale medical with a specialization in genetics. I seriously considered making a jump to botany, which is why I pursued the fellowship at the labs."

Trina's mouth grew slack, and she reached backward for a chair. Jonathan's prior life was obviously news to her. I ran my arm around her shoulder in silent support and watched as a red flush crept up her neck to flood her face.

"Please tell me this is not happening," she murmured as Jonathan continued.

"At the time of my employment, the ability to increase a fruit's yield through genetic manipulation as opposed to the overuse of synthetic fertilizer fascinated me," Jonathan said. "The social value of doubling or tripling a harvest without losing the taste and nutrition of a fruit or vegetable is overpowering. A discovery of this magnitude has the potential to save starving communities in third-world countries." Jonathan fingered the plant gently. "The social and economic upside is magnificent."

"How does it work?" Lamendola asked.

I wondered if Lamendola wanted to grab a handful of Jonathan's bionic seeds for his grandmother.

"Ever crack an egg with two yolks?" Jonathan asked. "Double yolks are a chromosomal mishap or a mistake — but not to a botanist interested in genetic preening. Through careful collection and cross breeding of hyperactive seeds, the botanist is able to repeat the mishap and literally tease out the recessive mutation until the mistake becomes dominant."

"Like getting two dozen eggs each with

double yolks," Lamendola said in awe.

Jonathan was pleased with his new proselyte.

"And this is what you did at the labs?" DeRosa asked.

"Yes, but with tomatoes," Jonathan confirmed. "The problem is that Dr. Prentice was not impressed with feeding the poor. Actually, let me correct myself. Dr. Prentice is a genius, and he has done a tremendous amount of good in this world. However, given the size of the labs and the financial demands of running an operation of its size, Dr. Prentice needs to be mindful of cash flow. He financed the study for its commercial value — the ability to overproduce mountains of ripe red tomatoes for high-end supermarket chains."

"Sounds like dear old dad," I whispered to no one in particular.

"I can't say I'm an expert on patents or intellectual property, but are you allowed to replicate these studies at Harbor House without infringing on the labs' initial work?" DeRosa's question was spot on.

"That's the amazing part," Jonathan said. "To do this, a farmer needs only some seeds, dirt, manure, and sun. However, identifying mutant seeds takes the patience of a gold miner. When I worked at the food co-op, we sourced fruits and vegetables from organic farmers all over the country. I built my own network of growers that is much deeper and, dare I say, more fruitful than anything the labs could reproduce."

"How so?" DeRosa was skeptical. "The labs have millions of dollars for these studies."

"But they don't care about farming with the same passion," Jonathan replied. "My network is people like me. A grassroots, back-to-the-soil movement of farmers with a long-term perspective on social change through agricultural engineering."

"But you applied for a full-time position and got turned down," Cheski pointed out.

"That's incorrect," Jonathan said without a hint of defiance. "I withdrew my application when I realized that I'd be working for the DNA mafia." Jonathan's eyes scanned the ground with discomfort. "Please don't tell CeCe I said that."

Our room of Jonathan supporters burst into laughter at his slip-up.

"So you knew Teddy from the summer you worked at the labs?" DeRosa asked. "And Charlie, for that matter?"

"Of course I knew Teddy, but I can't say I remembered Charlie."

"Story of my life," Charlie mumbled.

"Teddy helped me transcribe notes and take photos of the plants," Jonathan said.

DeRosa's shoulders lowered a mere centimeter, and I could see that Jonathan's sincerity defused the doubt in the room. "Why doesn't anyone else in Harbor House know you had a connection to Teddy and the labs?" DeRosa asked.

Jonathan took his time gathering his thoughts. He was a reflective man, and I knew his next response would be as genuine as his earlier explanation.

"Dropping out of Yale medical school is highly embarrassing. My whole life was geared toward achievement. My parents were horrified, and my girlfriend dumped me because she thought she was going to marry a doctor."

Trina started at the mention of a girlfriend, but she remained seated with her attention on Jonathan's confession.

"I felt awkward staying in the area," Jonathan admitted as he kicked a ball of dirt with his foot. "But I enjoyed having access to the scientific community. I remained friends with some of the other scientists, at least for awhile. At some point, I had an epiphany. I didn't need millions to plant seeds. I just needed access to land. Meeting CeCe was happenstance or maybe kismet. I was already dating Trina when they became friends. Everyone saw me as the organic farmer, the guru. I guess I didn't want to disappoint them with my history."

"And Teddy never mentioned anything?" DeRosa asked.

"I asked him not to," Jonathan said. "I started making real progress here at Harbor House. I wanted to be recognized on my own merit. Teddy honored that request."

"Explain."

"The labs are a scientific machine spitting out achievements like an assembly line. Even if my discovery becomes world renowned, the labs could attempt to ride along my success. Their public relations people would find a way to label me as a scientist with a former association to the labs. Accumulating recognition is the route to future funding, after all." The corners of Jonathan's mouth turned up slightly. "I think Teddy secretly liked the idea that an independent researcher could triumph."

His last comment received a round of applause from the Harbor House inhabitants. In the greenhouse, the men shook hands and parted ways. I gave Trina and Becky a hug, closing another chapter on Teddy's death. Trina and Jonathan's relationship might require some mending, but I had faith in both of them.

But then I realized that this was the first lead we'd had in days, and it had just dried up. I hoped Cheski and Lamendola had dug something up on Naomi Gupta, my brother's deceased fiancée. There was also the matter of Teddy's garbage slowly rotting in organized piles; maybe there was something to be had there?

FIFTEEN

I came upon DeRosa wandering the rows of neatly planted corn. In late spring, the baby stalks were barely visible but gaining traction for the long growing season ahead. The farm was impressive even to an experienced grower. With Jonathan's direction, Charlie had built a complex irrigation system with pumps fueled by the power of the sun. Every inch of tubing and hardware was salvaged from a junk yard, giving the operation a Rube Goldberg machine appearance. I imagined DeRosa's opinion of the Harbor House clan was shifting quickly from distrust to respect as he observed the rewards of our labor.

"You seem absorbed," I said to DeRosa.

"I just got a message from a beat cop in Freeport." DeRosa turned his cell phone over and held up the text for me to read.

"Holy shit. Your condo was ransacked?"

"Evidently so," DeRosa replied, his voice

tinged with disgust.

"What are you thinking?"

"I've worked a lot of cases. Could be retribution. The department will do a rundown of recently released felons I've collared."

"But it could also be connected to Teddy."

"I'm thinking it's that too."

"Did they take anything?"

"I had a two-drawer file cabinet with personal items. I'll have to drive home today and confirm, but according to the guys there was a square spot free of dust next to my desk exactly where I kept the cabinet."

"And the contents of the cabinet?" I asked.

"The usual," DeRosa replied, as he turned off his cell phone. "Mortgage papers, police academy records, birth certificate, release papers from the army."

"Sounds like someone, maybe Igor, is interested in getting to know you better," I said.

"Or find a weak spot." DeRosa turned his phone over a few times and then pointed to a bench with expansive views of Long Island Sound and the Sound View labs. A band of seagulls circled overhead, no doubt planning their farm-fresh meals for the next two months. Seagulls are the Freegans of the bird community, and as much as I hated the damage they caused our crops, I had to admire their ingenuity. No matter how many times we reengineered our compost bin, the seagulls always found a way in. DeRosa and I walked over to the bench. I let DeRosa lead the conversation.

"Let's take it from the top one more time," he sighed.

"Okay," I agreed, eager to please. "The police came to Harbor House one week ago Sunday after midnight."

"Back up." DeRosa rolled his hand counter clockwise. "Your brother died on Friday. The coroner timed the death between eight and nine p.m. His body was discovered by a cleaning person at eleven that night. What were you doing on Friday afternoon?"

"Cripes, Frank. I am not a suspect."

"Poor wording. Let me rephrase." DeRosa's gaze was locked on the horizon. Deep in thought, I could see his mind fight to cut through the mounting clutter of the case. "Describe the days leading up to your brother's death."

"That's unfair, like a trick question," I said taking offense. "You're asking me to relive normal only to be confronted with Teddy's death again."

"It's important." DeRosa's eyes were still frozen in their sockets. If he didn't blink soon, I'd have to snap my fingers.

"Give me a second. It seems like a lifetime ago." Our lives at Harbor House were relatively fluid. No one had a smartphone or kept a calendar, and since I was not employed, my presence was never required anywhere on any specific day. Thinking in terms of dates did not come easily to me, so conditioned was I to come and go as I pleased. "I guess that Tuesday I reorganized my studio and purged a bunch of older paintings."

DeRosa popped out of his trance. "So what I saw on Sunday is considered clean?"

"You're just like Teddy. Disarray made his heart palpitate."

"Why did you keep the unfinished paintings of Naomi?"

I shrugged. "I don't know." Why did I keep Naomi's portraits? I tried to think of a more suitable answer. "I think I couldn't capture her, and it bothered me. She seemed elusive somehow."

"You might be on to something there," DeRosa said. "Keep going."

"I went to the food co-op with Jonathan and Trina on both Wednesday and Thursday," I continued. "The beginning of the growing season is a bit like a farmer's kick-off party."

"How about Friday?"

"I painted most of the day. In the afternoon, Charlie and I took a bike ride."

"Did you speak with your brother during the week?"

DeRosa's question caught me off-guard.

"I didn't. Not once."

DeRosa made to continue, but I interrupted him.

"That's a problem. I usually spoke to Teddy all the time." The revelation disturbed me. I struggled now to recapture the exact time line of events. "I called Teddy on Tuesday, but his secretary said he was busy. Same thing the next day. If I'm remembering correctly, we hadn't spoken since the prior week."

"Did you have a regular pattern?"

"Teddy checked in almost every day. He usually called me in the morning. Nothing big, just a quick hello. Sometimes Charlie would get on the phone too to confirm their racquetball game. The labs have an indoor court and they played regularly." I grabbed DeRosa's phone and dialed the house phone. Charlie picked up on the first ring.

"Detective DeRosa, how may I be of help?" Charlie mocked.

"It's me, you halfwit. I have an important question: Did you play racquetball with

130

Teddy the week he died?"

"Uh, no. He cancelled on me," Charlie replied. "I won the week before, though. I bet he's rolling over in his grave knowing I got the last point."

I pressed the button to end the call and felt my hand go limp. DeRosa caught his phone as it slipped to the ground.

"Oh my God," I cried. "Teddy must have known something."

I turned to DeRosa. My body begged to cry, but my tear ducts were dehydrated. It was almost as if my internal clock for mourning had timed out, forcing me to deal with the case. I buried my head in DeRosa's chest, my hand resting firmly on his shoulder. I felt his heart pick up speed and his chest tighten. A new fact had surfaced now, and we both knew it. Teddy was not caught unaware in his office the night of his death. He was involved in something that led to his death, and he was not oblivious to the threat, hence the canceled appointments and cut-off communication with friends and family.

DeRosa pried my hands from his body. "We're not working fast enough," he warned. "Forget offense, we're not even playing solid defense."

"You're supposed to be the expert."

131

He punched away at his phone. "I'm going to try and book a flight. I'd be more comfortable if you were with me."

"Where to?" I asked knowing full well the Caribbean was a long shot.

"National Airport. Washington, D.C." DeRosa spoke into the phone, dictating flight instructions to a desk officer on the other end. "Just see what you can do," he said as he clicked off his phone and marched down the dirt path.

"I'll call you with the details," he yelled over his shoulder.

Sixteen

DeRosa slammed his plastic tray on the wobbly cafeteria table overlooking the runway at LaGuardia Airport.

"Excuse me," I said, as I inched along the wall past a family with five kids, all of whom required a heavy dose of Ritalin and a solid spanking. Four of the five kids sported the family's upturned nose with a sprinkling of freckles across the bridge. I eyed the youngest boy with suspicion and gave the parents the once-over. The boy's dark hair and hooked nose seemed glaringly out of place. I let my imagination wander, coming to the quick conclusion that the mother must have had an affair and in her fried state had lost interest in all things disciplinarian. With my luck in the gutter, I fully expected to see at least two of the kids seated in my row at takeoff.

Cafeteria patrons aside, the flickering fluorescent lights and mauve décor ensured that the Gateway Café would never make the pages of a Zagat's food guide.

"How did you get through the line so fast?" DeRosa squeezed into a chair and eyed my plate full of food. "It's like the entire borough of Queens chose tonight to eat out at the airport. It's not even a Friday night."

I looked at DeRosa. It was Thursday. Tomorrow was Friday, and Teddy would be dead exactly fifteen days.

"I didn't go through the line." I bit into one half of a cleanly sliced triple-decker club while I reached for DeRosa's food receipt. "You paid $8.50 for the hamburger, $3.00 for the oversized chocolate chip cookie, and $5.50 for the bottled beer." I crumpled the slip of paper and tossed it over my shoulder. "Total damage: $17. My bill: zero."

DeRosa's bottom lip pursed like a fussy baby refusing a bottle. "Please tell me you paid for the food, CeCe."

"I didn't pay for the food, Frank. You know damn well I snagged leftovers."

"Leftovers?" DeRosa took a swig of beer. "Well, that's rich. You're actually referring to half-eaten food headed down the conveyor belt as your personal doggie bag."

"It's all about perception," I said as I

134

savored a hunk of ham wrapped in bacon and marinated in mayonnaise. "Here's a riddle for you. You work a full day and return home in the evening. You change out of your clothing and stuff your underwear in the hamper."

"That's overly personal."

"I take that as a yes." I sipped my water fountain water from a free paper cup and continued with my inquiry. "The next day you don a pair of fresh underwear and head back to the station. Within minutes of arriving, the chief assigns you to a stake-out where you stew in an unmarked car for forty-eight hours waiting for a tattooed perp to limp out of a drug den."

"You watch too much television." DeRosa broke his cookie in half and handed me the bigger piece. I continued with my riddle.

"You return home and, similar to a regular work day, you undress and put your underwear in the hamper."

"My mother trained me well."

"Your future wife will thank Mama DeRosa. Anyway, here's my question." I leaned across the table and in a serious voice asked, "When is your underwear dirty?"

"When I take it off," Frank replied without missing a beat.

"So, ladies and gentlemen of the jury," I

said as I raised my hands, palms open in astonishment. "The defendant claims that underwear, regardless of how long it is worn, be it ten minutes or ten days, is clean until it is removed. The defendant claims the concept of dirty is a matter of perception."

DeRosa swallowed his cookie as if it was rotting spinach. He didn't take kindly to a trap that easily caught him. I ignored his displeasure and forged on with my analogy.

"A man with plastic gloves and a hair net prepares a club sandwich." I took another satisfying bite of my free meal and wiped my mouth politely. "He cuts the sandwich in half and wraps it in cling-wrap. I eat one half and a stranger eats the other half. Does it really matter if I pick my half up at the counter or on the conveyer belt? Food ownership is a matter of perception."

"The conveyor belt doesn't have a spit guard," DeRosa countered.

"And your underwear is still dirty," I replied.

"CeCe." His face relaxed, and he seemed to drift off to a place that preceded his overuse of the word *interesting*. "What if we are making too many assumptions about the facts of the case?" he posed. "If it's all about perception, what if we looked at the facts from another point of view?"

"How about the killer's point of view?" I suggested.

"We'll get there, but we need to go through this exercise first. Work with me," DeRosa said. "We believe Teddy knew he was in danger. We suspect that Naomi was involved in something per Charlie's feedback about their break-up. We think Naomi's suicide and Teddy's death are linked." DeRosa rustled in his tote bag and located an evidence baggie holding a greeting card. "I brought this because I wanted to match Naomi's handwriting, stamps, and pen color to anything we find in her apartment."

DeRosa wiped the table down, unzipped the baggie, and presented the card. We read Naomi's inscription in tandem. *"Teddy, I did what you said, but it's not what you promised."* Naomi's crisp lettering was confident yet tired. Her signature seemed rushed, and I sensed from the card that her resolve had faded.

"How do you read this?" Frank asked.

I had a slight advantage over him because I knew Naomi when she was alive. The *it's not what you promised* part definitely sounded like Naomi. She had a way of getting what she wanted. I had a distinct and unpleasant memory from the first summer

Naomi and Teddy dated. In an effort to establish her power position, she purposely made elaborate plans for Teddy's birthday, refusing to recognize our birthday picnic tradition on the shores of the labs. Through gritted teeth, I even went so far as to invite her along — an honor not even bestowed upon Charlie. With her high heels sinking into the mossy grass and a stern finger wagging at Teddy, it appeared her tantrum was in vain. I watched as my brother marched resolutely away from Naomi and down to the water toward me.

"I think Teddy wanted something from Naomi," I said tentatively. "Naomi gave him whatever he requested, but he did not deliver on his promise."

"He purposely screwed her," DeRosa said.

"Yes." I felt my grasp on the facts getting fuzzier. "In fact, she was so angry that she found a way to renege on the NIH grant." I searched for a plausible ending. "Teddy's denial of her was so overwhelming, she hung herself?" My voice rose with uncertainty.

"Does that sound like Teddy?"

"Actually, it doesn't," I said. "He was a stickler for following through. Especially when it had to do with promises he made."

"What if Naomi wanted something from

138

Teddy," Frank said, reworking the scenario.

"Like what?"

"I don't know," Frank confessed. "What is the goal of a medical researcher?"

"Recognition." Having listened to years of my father and his cronies discuss the merits of authorship and publication, I was sure of that answer. "Scientists want their names to be associated or assigned to a particular discovery or breakthrough. Recognition would be a definite motivator for Naomi. She needed to be noticed."

Frank tried a new angle. "Okay, so what if Naomi participated in one of Teddy's studies, but he refused to give her credit?"

"If she deserved it, Teddy would have been happy to recognize her, but maybe she didn't deserve credit."

"Because her results were incorrect, a case of bad science," DeRosa said. "That must be professional suicide for a scientist. Is it possible that Teddy helped her undo her mess, but the problem snowballed? Maybe that's why he didn't communicate in his final days."

I nodded my head slowly and let the snippets of logic fall into place. "Let me try something else. Maybe Teddy didn't want something from her," I offered a reverse scenario. "Maybe he wanted to stop her from doing something."

"Interesting." He used that word again. "Is it possible Teddy wanted Naomi to deny the grant because the application was based on something false that she had provided?"

"Now that sounds like Teddy," I said with glee. DeRosa's realistic portrayal of Teddy brought back positive memories of my brother. "But why did she *kill* herself?"

"Do you think Teddy led her to believe he'd take her back if she resolved the issue?"

"I'm going to have to give Naomi some credit here. I don't remember her as a wilting flower, and I don't think a break-up would drive her to suicide. If she hung herself, then the professional stress threatened her reputation. Whatever she did wrong was about to be revealed and it was linked to the labs. Teddy asked her to extricate herself from the issue, and he promised to control the negative backlash but whatever it was, it caught up with him too."

An indistinct female voice pumped through a speaker announcing the boarding call for our flight to Washington. DeRosa grabbed my hand and yanked me from my chair. "We're late, CeCe, but your sophomoric underwear example got us to think out of the box. I think we're on to something. Tell me this: How and when did Naomi come into your brother's life?" DeRosa asked this as he kicked off his shoes for security. He used his badge to signal a security guard, who provided a sealed bag for his gun. I placed my worn Keds in the plastic bin next to his shoes and gun and watched our mismatched assortment of personal items roll down the line. A TSA agent motioned me through the detector. I located my sneakers and slid them on.

"How'd they meet?" Frank asked again as he replaced his gun in his holster.

"I don't remember," I said with some discomfort, as I bent over to tie my shoes. "One day Teddy was single and the next he wasn't."

Seventeen

The family of five did indeed plop two of their nastier brood in the seats next to me. Because we booked late, DeRosa had a seat a row in front between two more of the kids. He tried valiantly to negotiate a swap, as if I were a hostage, but my pint-sized kidnappers wanted nothing to do with the trade. We suffered in silence for the fifty-minute flight and landed without incident. That is if you don't count the four crayons I cracked in half out of sheer frustration.

We left the airport only to find a line for cabs deeper than an *American Idol* open audition. I tugged on Frank's shoulder and begged him to show his brass.

"Come on, Frank. You didn't get that badge for nothing and we *are* working on an active murder case here." He gave me a look but caved to my whining and flashed his badge. He gave the cabbie an address in the northwest section of Washington, D.C.

"How about it's my turn for a riddle?" he asked.

"Hit me," I responded, and I noticed a sly smile sneak across DeRosa's mouth.

His competitive edge came to the forefront and unlike our previous interactions, I saw now that he did not like to lose. Up to this point, DeRosa the cop had presented himself as controlled and composed, a collector of facts and evidence. This new DeRosa liked a puzzle. If he were anything like my brother, he would be motivated by the frustration of not knowing the answer, almost as if failure were the trigger. With my brother, it was the race to solve the human genome. Teddy's brain engaged when an answer seemed elusive. He loved to ruminate on the endless iterations of possible solutions. Frank DeRosa got going with the challenge of an impossible case, a case with too many loose ends and no solid suspects.

"I'm serious, Frank. Bring it on."

"Okay," he said as pulled his pant legs at the knees and got comfortable in the back of the cab. "Let's say the Freegan lifestyle catches on similar to the green movement. Slowly but surely, the idea of reusing and repurposing food, materials, and other resources becomes a mainstream concept.

Even large corporations get in on the act."

"I'm with you."

"However, within half a century, the word *Freegan* dies out as quickly as it was accepted and eating from Dumpsters becomes as foreign as living on the moon." Frank laid out his scenario, and I waited for the punch line. "How did a popular movement with positive social impact become obsolete?" he said.

"Because we won," I answered. "That's the end game."

"So you're not as naïve as I thought."

"Bingo," I said. "I'm also not so naïve that I think your scenario will actually play out. But, let me congratulate you on getting from point A to point Z at the speed of light. Most Freegans, even the ardent ones, can't get their heads around the fact that popularizing our philosophy will eventually put us out of business."

"So then," DeRosa said. I could tell by the way he rubbed his hands together that I'd found his soft spot. He loved puzzles just like Teddy. "As new converts join the ranks of established Freegans, the ability to find leftovers becomes more and more difficult. The fast rate of Freegan acceptance creates a severe scarcity of garbage, and the rejection of consumerism forces hordes of

Freegans to become even more economical and efficient. Before long, society at large — now a massive anti-consumerism machine — is so good at *not* overproducing that there's nothing leftover to scavenge."

"Bravo, Frank." I put my hands around my mouth and breathed out to mimic the sound of the roaring crowd. He had indeed worked his way through the enigma of the Freegan philosophy. We Freegans can only fill our stomachs if the majority of the world is wasteful. If our ranks swell, there'd be more of *us* than *them;* much as we disliked *them,* they were a necessary part of our equation.

The cab let us out at a bed-and-breakfast on Calvert Street, about a block off the main drag in Adams Morgan. The town was lit up like Mardi Gras and a hip crowd of young people bounced in and out of the hottest restaurants and bars. I remembered that DeRosa and I were both young, and I felt a twinge of jealousy watching the revelers enjoy a night on the town.

"So what's our plan?"

He checked his watch. "It's ten p.m. Naomi owned an apartment on this street. We're meeting the cop who found her body at her apartment tomorrow morning. He'll show us her place and go over his report.

Then we have an appointment at the NIH with her supervisor."

"What are the sleeping arrangements?"

"We're in adjoining rooms with a shared bath. I'm sorry for the proximity, but for safety reasons, you need to be within screaming distance."

"I can live with that."

"Then let's get some sleep and we'll see what tomorrow brings."

We entered our suite through DeRosa's room. He made a swift sweep of the place, and I thought it was a joke as he moved from room to room checking for a hidden assailant. As he closed the closet door he said, "Looks good to me. If you don't mind, I'd like to keep the pass-through door about an inch open."

"Okay, but I want first dibs on the bathroom."

"All yours," he replied.

I don't have a nighttime routine. As a Freegan, I never bought into the idea of make-up or face creams. As a result, it takes me about three seconds to prepare for bed. This was always a fact that astonished men who are used to the time-consuming effort it takes the average female to scrub, powder, and perfume. DeRosa was no exception.

"Are Freegans against water?" I heard

from the other side of the door.

"I'll shower in the morning. It's not like you have to share a bed with me."

I heard DeRosa mumble sarcastically under his breath.

Turning off my light, I gave in to the fact that I was very, very tired. It had been a long day, starting with the accusations against Jonathan and ending with the troubling realization that Teddy had probably been aware of something sinister. Between the trip to the airport, the flight, and the mental exercises with DeRosa, I was beat. As I drifted off to sleep, a soft tap sounded at the interior door.

"CeCe?" DeRosa's voice seeped through the crack in the door. I considered the situation and feigned sleep although my eyes were now wide open and staring anxiously at the ceiling. I'd drawn my legs up in the bed, piled high with lacy sheets and puffy pillows. The whole damn setting screamed romance, and I certainly wasn't stubborn enough to ignore his good looks. Unlike Charlie's lanky frame, DeRosa was big, but I understood husky in a comfortable way since Teddy had also been a larger guy. I knew what it felt like to reach up on my tippy toes and hug a man with horizontal girth. Teddy's growth spurts came at avalanche speed, and I was no more than twelve before I had to climb up to his shoulder to whisper a secret in his ear. I weighed my options and chose the path of least resistance. I remained silent.

"CeCe?" DeRosa's tone rose past a whisper. He tapped on the door just in case I didn't recognize my first name.

"Yes, Frank."

"I need to ask you something."

"All right." I stretched out the syllables at a snail's space. I tried not to think about where this could go. Would I be embarrassed to hear how he would phrase his proposition?

"Ready?"

"As I'll ever be," I responded.

"What happens when the human genome is deciphered?"

An exceptionally long, uneven sigh released from my lungs, a relief similar to being passed over by an angry teacher expecting the answers to a homework assignment. "You mean what's their end game?" I answered.

"Yeah."

I'd bet his question had been discussed at length by a committee of medical ethicists. Somewhere, someone with a Ph.D. was probably producing a hefty dissertation on this topic. But without the ability to reference academic texts, I relied on my own common sense.

"When the human genome is deciphered, all diseases can be identified in gestation. Prenatal genetic manipulation will wipe out diseases before they start."

"Who does that put out of business?"

"The pharmaceutical companies."

"Interesting," he responded.

I closed my eyes knowing DeRosa was now wide-awake. I finally figured out what made him tick — a good puzzle. Before I drifted off, I gave him something else to think about.

"Don't forget about your break-in, Frank. You need to figure out how you fit into this mess."

He met my comment with a grunt.

EIGHTEEN

For a split second I thought I had been swept off for a weekend of fine dining and sightseeing. The bed covers smelled like fresh lavender and appeared impossibly white, as if they had just been selected off the shelf of a department store. My eyes adjusted to the morning rays streaming through the wooden shutters, now tilted to allow for maximum sun exposure. The shadowy figure looming by the window snapped me out of my fugue. When I found my vocal chords, they begged for my protector.

"Teddy," I screeched with raw fear. The features of a man came into focus and I was less than pleased as the apparition took on a fully human form. I yanked the alarm clock out of its socket and flung it like a grenade. "Fuck you, DeRosa."

His reflexes were primed, and he caught the clock with ease. In fact, he was so swift

I could almost imagine him catching a bullet at a short distance.

"Sleep well?" He ignored my outburst.

"You're only supposed to enter my room if you hear me screaming." I jumped out of bed and reached for my jeans. "You're not supposed to be the *cause* of my screaming."

"Why are you getting dressed?" he asked.

With my pants mid-thigh, I found it difficult to interpret his question. I froze like a lawn ornament waiting for him to make his next move.

"You promised to shower this morning," he said and then tossed me my door key. "Meet me downstairs in the dining room in ten and be sure to lock up."

The heavy brass door key hit the floor with a thud as he sauntered off. Clearly, my mental meddling caused DeRosa's tossing and turning. Lack of sleep can bring out the worst in people. I understood his cranky disposition, but I wasn't entirely willing to take one for the team. I grabbed the complimentary fluffy white robe and checked my watch. If I timed it correctly, it would take me exactly twelve minutes to appear in the dining room — an additional two minutes of aggravation for Frank DeRosa.

Normally, I'd linger in the shower suffocating myself in plumes of steam. However, wasting hot water at the bed-and-breakfast concerned me. Harbor House had ample hot water because we had a highly efficient, nearly cost-free geosolar system — a complex setup combining solar panels and geothermal plumbing to provide hot water throughout all three floors of the house as well as the outer buildings. Once Harbor House residents got the alternative energy bug, we were hooked. There's a wonderful feeling of empowerment when you see your energy bills plummet faster than a parachute with a broken release. On this particular morning, I sacrificed my lengthy shower, shaving minutes off my normal soak time, and popped out as soon as the soap was out of my hair.

I towel-dried my head, thankful that my homespun haircut needed no more than a few brush strokes to be public ready. My blunt bob had been my trademark since childhood for the simple reason that it worked. My cheeks and nose showed the rosy effects of the late-spring sun and with a good night's sleep behind me, my blue eyes sparkled with hope that today we'd get a break.

I stared intently at myself, wondering what DeRosa thought about me. My standard uniform consisted of jeans, t-shirts, and sneakers, and I was often mistaken for someone younger. I abandoned the concept of a bra before I was even old enough to be offered one, adding to the tomboy effect. Luckily, my anatomy never required excessive amounts of support. If I guessed DeRosa's type, I'd pick a voluptuous maven with dark, flowing hair. He'd want someone to soften his brawn without overpowering his stature. I imagined a damsel in distress with a hint of Sophia Loren's curves. Our adjoining bedrooms did not tempt him. I was more dame than damsel, and usually the direct cause of the distress.

"Sorry I'm late," I said with indifference when I reached his table in the dining room. "Let me grab a scone and a cup of coffee."

"The breakfast is included so you can eat with the rest of us paying patrons instead of at the Dumpster."

I poured myself a cup of coffee and tossed a few extra rolls in my bag.

"You just can't help yourself, can you?"

"You'll be thanking me later." I buttered my scone and selected a dab of homemade orange marmalade with a silver teaspoon so worn the handle felt like a slip of paper. "When are we meeting up at Naomi's place?"

"We've got a few minutes." He powered up his iPad and tapped an icon. The beeping noise seemed horribly out of place in the eighteenth-century bed-and-breakfast. Even DeRosa glanced around nervously, as if he had broken with etiquette.

"Any updates from the home front?" I asked.

"Your father calls every few hours, but I can manage that," he said as he ran his finger across a screen of icons. "He's not thrilled I took you to D.C., but as I explained to him, it's actually safer having you within arm's reach."

"The two of you are making me feel embarrassingly helpless, and I don't like it."

"You have a better solution?" he asked not waiting for a reply. "Charlie left a message for you to call later. More importantly, it looks like we've got a departure point for Igor's GPS."

"No way." I was genuinely surprised, as pertinent clues seemed few and far between.

"Don't get your hopes up. It's not exactly the lead we were looking for." DeRosa swung the pad around for me to see. A map of Brooklyn filled the screen with a red marker on a side street. "Based on the GPS configuration, the limo's starting location is this building in Brighton Beach, Brooklyn.

That's the heart of the Russian immigrant community. It's also a black hole for police investigations. There's no chance of getting anyone to talk in that neighborhood."

"Is it a language gap?"

"No, there's a heavy mob influence in Brighton. Makes residents hesitant to talk."

"Do you think the *Russian mob* is involved?" My breakfast roll swelled in my mouth.

"Hard to say. All we know is that a limo left from this neighborhood, and the man driving the limo seemed to look Slavic."

"Can't you show my sketch around?"

"We can and we will, but I doubt anyone will come forward. At this point, I don't see a connection between your brother and the Russian mafia. However, my guess is the job was contracted out and Igor was just low man on the totem pole. We'll shop the sketch around, residents will recognize him as a street criminal, but no one will be willing to risk their safety to report him."

"So that's it?"

"CeCe, we're not giving up on Igor. We ran the sketch through a national database with no matches. We showed the photo at the Sound View labs to see if Igor was on the campus, and we checked footage of the labs' security cameras. No luck there.

Cheski and Lamendola also went through mug shots by hand, hoping for an ID. I mean, for all we know this guy just got off a plane and he botched his first job — your hit. Now that I think of it, his inability to complete his mission may have earned him a pair of cement boots."

"Can you show my sketch around Freeport?" I asked. "You know, like near your apartment? Maybe Igor was the one who broke in."

"Actually, that's not a bad idea." DeRosa fired off an email to Cheski and Lamendola. "Igor would, in fact, be noticeable in Freeport, and if we could get a description of his vehicle — assuming it's not another limo — at least we'd have something to track. It's possible he's been cruising around Cold Spring Harbor undetected."

The thought sent shivers down my arms. Much as I relished the image of Igor burping up bubbles at the bottom of the East River, I knew better. If Igor was alive, he was waiting patiently to strike again. Unfortunately, I was his primary target and DeRosa an added bonus.

NINETEEN

Naomi had lived in an apartment in a brownstone about two hundred yards from our bed-and-breakfast. Calvert Street was a tony address with fully renovated buildings painted in a palate of historical colors. Four stories including the basement apartments, the brownstones harkened back to an era of cobblestones and horse-drawn wagons. We met Officer McDonald on the apartment's stoop.

"So, y'all partners?" McDonald asked me.

"Me?" I said with surprise. "A cop?" I looked at DeRosa and laughed.

He rolled his eyes, leaving McDonald feeling awkward.

"Sorry 'bout that," McDonald said. "I just figured, 'cause you two seem like you've known each other awhile."

"Just since Teddy's death." I wondered what type of vibe DeRosa and I gave off. True, I felt comfortable with DeRosa, and now it appeared others had started to take notice.

"I see. So are you related to the doctor in New York?" McDonald asked me.

"He's my brother."

"I'm sorry for your loss," McDonald said, showing his accent wasn't just for show: he was a true Southern gentleman.

"Thank you," I shook his hand. "My brother was engaged to Dr. Gupta, but the engagement broke off before her suicide."

"And the lady doctor is not a suspect in the case?" McDonald asked.

"She's not a direct suspect," DeRosa answered. "However, given the timing of her suicide and Dr. Prentice's death, we suspect she was aware of a threat against Dr. Prentice."

"But she's not a suspect," McDonald persisted. "I'm only asking because I can't let just anyone upstairs if you think this is anything more than the site of a suicide."

"We're not ruling out Dr. Gupta's knowledge of a crime, but there's no reason to think a crime has been committed here," DeRosa answered as he gave Naomi's building the once-over.

"I'll have to take your word on that," McDonald replied.

"So what's with this building?" DeRosa

asked. "It doesn't seem to fit with the rest of the block. In fact, it's an eyesore."

Peeling paint hung off the building, and the dome-shaped cupola leaned precariously toward the street. That surprised me because I knew Naomi was a stickler for appearances.

McDonald put his hand firmly on the iron railing leading up the brick stairs to the heavily carved French doors. The doors, however impressive, were in desperate need of a good oiling. If I had a rag and a pair of rubber gloves, I would have done it myself. Officer McDonald gave the railing a good shake, and it swayed easily under the pressure. "Be mighty surprised if the building hasn't been hit with code violations. Especially in neighborhoods like this, pressure from local community groups forces owners to make changes. Wait till you see inside, there's something may get your brain a-turnin'."

The exterior lack of curb appeal extended to the building's interior. The neglected lobby was poorly lit and smelled like a basement. The labeled mailboxes indicated only one other resident besides Naomi.

"What's rent go for on this block?" DeRosa asked.

"Most of the block is owner occupied. A

one bedroom co-op runs about three fifty, and a well done two-bedroom can push up to six hundred thousand."

"Two sweet for a cop's wallet."

"Hell, I got over an hour commute from Virginia just to find a place I could afford," McDonald shook his head. "Anyway, Adams Morgan attracts a lot of younger professionals from the NIH. The metro stop is a straight shoot to the NIH campus, and you can see the neighborhood is known for its nightlife. Once the professionals get hitched and have kids, they flee the city for better schools."

"What's the rental history on this place?" DeRosa asked as we ascended the stairs to the third floor.

"I did a little checking about that with a local real estate agent," McDonald said. "The place was bought two years ago by YWS Corporation for an even mil. According to district records, some safety modifications were made at that time and permits were filed to renovate two of the apartments. From what I can tell, one of the apartments belongs to Dr. Naomi Gupta and the other belongs to YWS."

McDonald jiggled Naomi's key, swung the door open, and then stepped back. DeRosa whistled through his teeth as if a beautiful girl had just walked by.

"Holy cow," I exclaimed. "Now *this* is the Naomi I knew."

Referring to Naomi's digs as an apartment would be misleading. Naomi owned the entire top floor of the brownstone, like a penthouse. The pristine open kitchen, a showstopper with pounds of granite countertops, probably never saw more than a Chinese takeout carton. The visual disconnect from the lobby to the apartment was so glaring that I dashed from room to room like a kid in a candy store. I flung open a door expecting a second bedroom only to find an enormous walk-in closet. I found shoes in every color, style, and heel height displayed like a wall of fine china.

I yelled to DeRosa from Naomi's closet. "Someone's got a fetish." I dragged my arm across a shelf, pulling at least twenty pairs to the floor. "How much money could she possibly be making?"

"I wondered the same thing," McDonald answered as he and DeRosa made their way into Naomi's shoe emporium.

"Let's hope she left a money trail, because that is something we can follow," DeRosa said. "You got anything for us, McDonald?"

"I might have somethin'. I got the call to check on the apartment approximately forty-eight hours after the time of death. Standard scenario: the victim doesn't show up for work and the cop on duty does a drive-by. The building and apartment didn't match up and although the coroner couldn't find anything suspicious, the environment didn't sit good with me."

"Is there a suicide note?" I asked.

"Yes, ma'am. It's just one line." Mc-Donald didn't need to refer to his notes to remember Naomi's last correspondence. *"I preferred the lie."*

I looked at DeRosa. "I think the note is a link. It's like the second part of the card she sent to Teddy."

"How so, CeCe?"

"Her note to Teddy implied that she tried to do something for him, but the outcome wasn't what she wanted. *I did what you said but it's not what you promised,"* I recited Naomi's original quote to DeRosa, and then I added, *"I preferred the lie."*

"Say it again, but this time include references to authorship and scientific papers," DeRosa challenged.

I was about to start when my words bottlenecked somewhere between my brain and my mouth. I tried again but found it difficult to re-create a believable conversation between Naomi and Teddy. DeRosa and McDonald nodded smugly at my ineptitude, but I refused to be beaten.

"All right. Just give me a second. I'm not an investigative expert." I paced Naomi's over-decorated bedroom. I grabbed a silky bathrobe off her four-poster mahogany bed and held it up in front of me. "Let's say Naomi tried to get a paper published. Maybe something she worked on with Teddy. Teddy knew her research had problems. Maybe she tried to make some changes, but the study still wasn't up to Teddy's standard. Then, she tried to smooth over Teddy's objections by signing off on the grant. A payoff of sorts. The bad research combined with an attempt to buy him would be tough for Teddy. He refused to play and threatened to report her careless research."

"Not bad," DeRosa complimented. "The lingerie is more than I expected."

"Thank you." I bowed deeply tossing the robe aside. "Maybe I haven't got it exactly right, but I think the note confirms that whatever Teddy asked her to do and the result of that action was more than she could handle. In fact, I think she meant the note for Teddy. She must have thought he'd be alive to see it."

"Interesting," DeRosa said.

I turned to McDonald. "He likes that word. It means he's thinking."

"You sure y'all ain't partners?" McDonald asked again.

"I'm certain." I turned to DeRosa, "What are you thinking, Frank?"

DeRosa nodded robotically, ignoring my question. "You mentioned that Naomi seemed to appear suddenly in your brother's life. Do you think she sought him out?"

I looked around the room, wondering how Naomi had supplemented her income. I hated to think that my brother had been had, but it was possible. "It could be," I answered regretfully.

"I'm going to file that away," DeRosa said, and then he turned his attention to Mc-Donald. "What else did you find?"

"Well, I questioned the apartment. However, there was no suspicion of foul play and until the call from New York, the victim didn't appear to be involved in anything requiring follow-up. I interviewed her direct supervisor at the NIH, and his comments were innocuous. The family wasn't asking questions, so the body was shipped to Michigan as requested by her parents. The chief told me to drop it."

"But?" DeRosa encouraged.

"But . . . I'm curious and I couldn't

explain the huge investment in this apartment. According to her employer, she made a hundred and thirty-five grand a year and even as a single woman, she lived well outside her means. Thing is, I'm up for a promotion this year, detective rank. I really want it, so I pushed a little further." McDonald reached into his pants pocket and pulled out a wad of papers. "I got as far as pulling up tax returns for the YWS Corporation. It stands for Young Women Scientists. According to their public filings, the purpose is to provide scholarships for young girls pursuing higher-level education in the sciences."

"Seems like a noble cause," I said after McDonald left us on our own with the papers. "Maybe Naomi had a second job working for this nonprofit?"

"Possibly." I could see DeRosa's wheels turning.

"Maybe a sugar daddy paid for the apartment?"

"Doubt it."

"Can you form a complete sentence?"

DeRosa shook his head and wandered off to inspect the rooms. I headed straight for the kitchen and filled up the remaining space in my bag with dry goods. As I rummaged through the drawers, I found a framed photo facedown under a pile of old mail. It was Teddy posing in front of the labs.

The frame felt like glass shards in my hands, and I realized it was the first time I'd seen an image of Teddy since he died. I took in Teddy's eyes; for a second I felt him with me. At that exact moment, DeRosa poked his head back into the kitchen.

"Let's wrap it up. I'm just checking the bathroom for prescription drugs. Could be a sign of instability."

I gaped at DeRosa as he turned and walked away. The mere suggestion of a man Teddy's age and build immediately upon seeing his photo sent a shudder to my core. God, I missed my brother.

I tore the back off the tacky rhinestone frame, tossed the frame in the garbage, and shoved Teddy's photo into my bag. I yelled back to DeRosa, "I'm out of here. Meet me downstairs."

TWENTY

DeRosa consulted the Metro map. "We need to head out to the NIH."

I fished around in my bag, unwrapped a roll, and handed it over. DeRosa made a polite attempt to throw away the napkin, but I nabbed it out of his hands before it became refuse.

"No sir. We save the napkin. Public bathrooms are notoriously devoid of tissue."

DeRosa swallowed the roll in two quick bites, finishing before we took our seats on the red line. The relatively new D.C. Metro system was a far cry from the crumbling underground maze of Manhattan's subways. The platform and car were clean and well lit and although it was lunch hour, the station was empty. The air conditioning seemed evenly distributed, and I didn't feel the need to avoid looking at the tracks for fear of seeing a rat.

"You ever think of moving out of New

York?" I asked DeRosa.

"Italy," he responded.

"Get out," I jeered.

"I was born in Italy. My parents came over when I was about three months old."

"Did your father work for an international company?"

Uncharacteristically, DeRosa laughed loud enough that the few fellow passengers snuck a look. "Sorry to disappoint, but my father is a mason. He builds stone walls and patios."

"Disappoint? I'm a big fan of working with your hands. Let's not forget I live on a working farm. So what brought the DeRosa family to the US?"

"I'm assuming my parents wanted to experience the American dream."

"And did it fulfill their expectations?"

"I have higher hopes for the next generation of DeRosas," he said. "Maybe we'd have more luck if I changed the family name to Prentice."

"Don't tell my dad. He barely wants *me* to carry the Prentice name. Anyway, since you're an only child, it looks like the onus is on you to pass down the DeRosa genes."

"I guess I am the last one in the line. I never thought of it that way."

"That makes two things we have in common," I answered, as I pointed to the map mounted above our seats. "Two more stops."

"How about you?" DeRosa asked. "Ever think of living more than five miles from your parents?" It was the first personal question DeRosa had posed that had nothing to do with the case. It was also rather insensitive.

"Ouch," I retorted.

"I'm only asking because the proximity and your relationship seem inversely correlated."

"I guess the West Coast would have been a more likely choice," I agreed. "Seattle crossed my mind a few years back. San Francisco was also on my radar."

"Too far to hitchhike?"

"Try not to wallow in my failure, but at one point I actually had a plan to bicycle across country." Even I chuckled at the memory. "I purchased a used cycling book at a garage sale, but I didn't get very far in that venture."

"I think I know what stopped you," DeRosa proposed.

"Do tell," I said. "I've been beating myself up for years with regret."

"You're independent, CeCe, but I get the sense that you don't like to be alone."

"Twin psychosis?"

"Not at all," DeRosa said. "You're a people person. Despite making the average citizen feel as if their every action is accelerating global warming, you have a way of pulling people into your circle. Hence, your communal living arrangement. You're the glue of the house."

"Thank you for your insight, detective." I grabbed DeRosa's arm as the subway doors opened and rushed him onto the platform.

"Hey, we got off one stop too early," DeRosa noticed too late to reenter the train.

"Your comment reminded me that we should be walking to our destination instead of consuming limited resources."

Our constant back-and-forth was evolving into an interminable tennis match, one in which the crowd inevitably loses interest while the players gain energy with every volley. I sensed DeRosa got a kick out of our repartee because he was still grinning about my planned detour when we reached the escalator. We made our way to street level and oriented ourselves in unfamiliar territory. "I'm going to make this detour work for us," DeRosa said, as he pointed to an H&R Block.

"We need a tax expert," DeRosa told the man at the counter.

"Let's see what date we have available."

"We need one now." DeRosa flashed his badge, landing us in the only office space with a door. A very nervous middle-aged woman took a seat behind the desk.

"If there's an issue with your return, we can offer you an audit package."

"Just routine investigative work, if you wouldn't mind helping out the police on short notice." DeRosa slid the YWS tax return across the desk. "The return was prepared by another firm, but I need help going through the basics. Does anything look wrong here?"

The woman took her time reviewing the YWS return. She added a few Post-its and wrote neatly on the yellow squares. Then she turned the forms towards us, pointing with the tip of her pen.

"The organization is taking in about two hundred thousand in revenue each year with five hundred fifty thousand invested in securities," she said. "That's an unusual ratio for a nonprofit."

I grabbed a pencil off the desk and did some of my own quick calculations. "The line here for scholarship expense. That's supposed to be their primary goal, but the expense is only five percent of annual revenue," I said.

"You're quick with numbers," the accountant said. "I'd also be concerned that eighty percent of the expenses are listed as *miscellaneous.*"

"There's a consultant listed at fifteen thousand a year," I said to DeRosa.

"Might be our woman," DeRosa said.

"Yeah, but it's too small a sum, given her lifestyle," I added, considering the size of Naomi's apartment. "I'm assuming only an audit would unravel the miscellaneous expenditures?"

"That's right," the accountant answered. "If you think this organization is not legitimate, then I'd track the money to its source. You need to find the entity supplying the organization with its resources."

"How do we do that?" I asked. "There aren't any officers listed and the only employee we know of is dead."

"The next person to draw on the account will probably be the largest benefactor. Someone will want to get their money back," the account suggested, "if they haven't already done so."

"How does the IRS overlook a scam like this?" I asked.

"Whoever did the accounting knows that the IRS hot button is four hundred thousand or more in contributions per year for a nonprofit. These contributions are under the ceiling."

Someone knew what was going on, and it upset me. I stood up abruptly and left the building, allowing DeRosa to wrap up the conversation. The lunch crowd was in full swing now and before long I got lost in a sea of suits and sensible shoes. DeRosa caught up and found me muttering to myself like a lunatic.

At this point, it seemed the forces of evil were fully prepared to take an axe to my idyllic existence, an existence I literally built with my own two hands. I lived in a self-contained world I had created that asked nothing of others. Living off the grid wasn't hard. Stepping back into a world where injustice reins and rotten, mean individuals succeed through deception, however, was crushing. I felt helpless and useless and embarrassingly underprepared to take on the sociopaths multiplying faster than Jonathan's peppers. And to think we had actually doubted Jonathan, one of the good guys.

Who was Naomi Gupta and what did my brother get himself into? Teddy never struck me as the type of guy angling to get into a girl's pants, but in retrospect I hoped that's all he wanted from Naomi. Getting into her *head* seemed downright scary.

"CeCe," DeRosa caught up with me and placed his firm hand on my shoulder. "I know you're losing it, but we're getting closer."

"How do you do this for a living, DeRosa?"

"Because this is what I believe in, and I'm committed enough to go down in a spray of bullets to prove it. You said you couldn't figure me out. This is my conviction."

I took DeRosa in, all of him, and I allowed my subconscious to accept a fact I had been repressing. We had only just met, but it irked me from the first night. I felt like I had met DeRosa before, even though I knew I hadn't. I had swept that niggling data point to the back of my brain, but like water through a sieve, it filtered out my fingertips and onto my canvas. I'd been drawing DeRosa for the last two weeks, not Teddy. The sketches in my attic, numbering more than ten at this point, always stopped at the same point: the eyes. The exact feature where the two men differed. Although both Teddy and Frank wore expressions of curiosity, Frank's gaze was skeptical while Teddy's was filled with hope. Not to overanalyze their traits, but it seemed fairly easy to extrapolate their chosen professions from their eyes.

"I'm sorry," I confessed as I reached out for his hand. "You remind me of Teddy, and I'm hating you for it. I'm mad because you resemble Teddy but you get to live."

"If it makes you feel better, I apologize," he said squeezing my hand lightly.

"Unnecessary." I searched for the right words to explain myself. "It's just that what you said about conviction struck a chord, a familiar one. Teddy and I were dissimilar in so many ways, but we both shared a strong belief in the potential to change the world for the better. Our paths were different — science and Freeganism — but the goal was the same."

"And is there only room for you and your brother in this world?"

"No. In fact, he would have liked you."

DeRosa let my comment lie, but I could see he itched to ask me something. He gathered up the YWS statements that had fallen to the ground, then he pulled me to a clearing near the corner of a high-rise building.

"CeCe, how did you know how to read the YWS financial statements? I thought you were an art major."

Revealing my mathematical savvy was a red flag for DeRosa, but I couldn't contain myself after viewing the YWS tax returns;

the documents were so obviously false. The fraudulent setup was recognizable by anyone involved in charity work and my knowledge of nonprofits, unbeknownst to DeRosa, made my hair stand on end. I prepared to explain my accounting acumen when I saw a familiar profile in the crowd. The telltale low brow, flat nose, and thick nape surfaced no more than fifty yards from where we stood.

"Shit," I said with unusual composure. "I just saw Igor."

"Quick, which direction?"

I pointed south on K Street toward an entrance to the subway station. With my arm extended outward, my legs kicked into high gear, and I started jogging forward to the last place Igor's head had appeared. As I moved rapidly through the crowds, people recognized a sense of urgency in my movements. Pedestrians parted and in a fleeting moment, I caught another glimpse of Igor looking over his shoulder. He glared at me, just a little too long for comfort and although my body was moving forward, I had not planned step two.

"Move it," I shouted as I tore through the crowd. I heard but ignored DeRosa, who could not run as quickly holding the stack of accounting papers. I'm sure he yelled for me to stop, but I was on a tear. My arms began to pump and my knees swung higher, practically grazing my elbows in rhythmic motion. The back of my neck flooded with pressure, preventing DeRosa's pleading strains from reaching my eardrums.

I spotted Igor once again as he made a dash for the Metro entrance. He moved shockingly fast for a stocky man with short legs. Having just exited the same station, I knew a very steep escalator lay ahead and ended in a cement floor. Regardless of the danger, I sprinted like a gazelle toward Igor.

With his squat frame in my sights, my hamstrings began to tighten as gallons of oxygen filled my lungs faster than I could exhale. A pair of elderly, lawyerly looking men passed slowly by the first step of the escalator. I knew it was the only chance I had to connect with Igor. I hoped that somewhere deep in the recesses of his twisted criminal brain, he had an ounce of good manners. And there it was. He hesitated ever so slightly to avoid plowing over the two gentlemen, providing me with the extra strides to close the gap between us.

As Igor's foot hit the first rung of the stairs, I threw myself onto the moving rubber hand rail. I stretched my arm, imagining it to be as flexible as Silly Putty, and formed a claw with my fingers. As the railing carried my body forward, I lengthened my core until my shoulder practically dislocated from its socket. With a last ditch effort, I dragged my nails into the back of Igor's neck before plummeting sideways off the escalator.

DeRosa discovered me, tangled in a ball of my own body parts, my hand raised proudly like the Statue of Liberty. He knelt down next to me, resting the back of my head in the palm of his hand, my outstretched arm resting on his shoulder.

"I did it," I croaked. "I did it."

"Did what?"

"I got Igor's DNA."

TWENTY-ONE

Officer McDonald picked us up shortly after the hordes of onlookers began to lose interest and started drifting away. With rivulets of blood dripping toward my wrist, at least a few bystanders seemed relieved that I appeared to be safe and coherent. DeRosa and I piled into McDonald's black and white, with me stuck in the back seat like a common criminal.

"I knew y'all were trouble," McDonald joked.

"Can you do us a favor?" DeRosa asked.

"I think you mean another favor," I noted from the back seat.

"As long as you don't use my name at the stationhouse. Remember, I'm gunning for promotion, not demotion."

"Can you get us access to security footage from the station? I'd like to see if Igor made contact with anyone before or after the incident."

"I can do that. What else?"

"Hello?" I said holding my hand like an Olympic torch. "I've got Igor's DNA dripping down my arm."

"That's the problem with television crime shows," DeRosa grumbled. "Everyone thinks there's some master database of instantly accessible DNA."

"Humor me," I replied.

"Officer McDonald, can you set CeCe up with an evidence swab while I head over to the NIH?" DeRosa asked and then he turned to me, speaking through the police-grade chicken wire. "CeCe, I'll pick you up at the station on the way back, but you have to promise to stay put. Do not move until I return. Igor was sizing up his opportunity today, but it wasn't the right scene for him. He'll make another attempt because this is his job and he doesn't get paid until you're dead."

"Why can't I come with you?"

"Because I'm no match for your impulsivity."

"I'll be bored," I whined.

"And alone," DeRosa answered. "You can kill time on the phone with Charlie. You owe him a call. I'll be back later, and we'll catch an evening flight."

"You're too tough on her," McDonald

remarked. "You never know with a DNA sample. It could turn something up."

"See?" I said.

DeRosa adjusted the rearview mirror to catch my reflection. "I do see, but I'd like to return you to Long Island in one piece."

"So I guess my death would be bad for your reputation?"

"Actually, I'm referring to your brains. Your insight is becoming invaluable." He smiled into the mirror before turning to McDonald. "Keep her safe. You don't want to deal with her father. Something goes wrong, he'll have you transferred so far south you'll be directing traffic in Puerto Rico."

"I'm on it," McDonald said, tipping his head once more.

TWENTY-TWO

Defying all odds of air travel statistics, DeRosa and I ended up with the same seating arrangements on the flight back to New York as we had the way down. Once again, I piled between the two children from the annoying family of five, now cranky and exhausted from touring the capital's monuments. DeRosa fared no better seated in front of me. I could see his broad shoulders shifting uncomfortably so as not to agitate the kids on either side of him.

As the flight taxied down the runway, he attempted to twist his girth over the seat to ask me a question. "What did Charlie want?"

"Plenty of drama at home." I inched forward and spoke through the crack between the airplane seats. "Jonathan and Trina are heavy into their own version of couples counseling sans counselor, and Charlie feels stuck in the middle."

"Would he rather be chased by the Russian mob?"

"Hands down," I replied, knowing full well Charlie was not a source for relationship advice — unless you wanted tips on breaking up or cheating. "Then there's Becky. Charlie thinks she's planning on moving out. Too much upheaval."

As I'd told Charlie, Becky was never a perfect fit for the house, and I couldn't blame her if she wanted out. Not that she paid rent, but free room and board wouldn't seem all that attractive in the midst of a murder investigation. Even if she could handle the constant police presence, I thought the real reason she wanted out was that she had caught on to Charlie's sudden interest in his old flame.

"What evidence does he have?"

"She borrowed the Gremlin a few times and she's been on Craigslist. Good signs she's shopping around for a new apartment."

"Did she say anything to you?" DeRosa replied.

I didn't feel comfortable explaining that Becky had probably figured out I'd slept with Charlie recently. If I were her, I'd want to leave too. "No, she never mentioned it to me."

"That's because she's avoiding you."

"Why would Becky avoid me?" I said.

"Because you slept with her boyfriend," he answered.

"What are you," I asked, "a cop?"

"I'll speak with her tomorrow. She'll need to leave a forwarding address in case we have to contact her."

"I'll see if I can talk to her when we get back," I said, wondering how I could make amends with Becky. I tried to switch the subject. "So what happened with Naomi's boss at NIH?"

"Not much, and I grilled the guy pretty hard." He sounded frustrated at hitting a wall. "It was like interviewing a cop about another cop."

"I'll bet the NIH works just as hard as the Sound View labs at quashing negative press. Naomi's boss probably prepped ahead of time and stuck to the script. Frank, try to remember that for all the amazing advancements these scientific organizations produce, getting there requires them to push the boundaries. Think about the controversy over stem-cell research. These guys are experts at managing perception. If Naomi was involved in something scandalous, it's being managed internally at a very high level."

"Then I need to find one disgruntled employee to blow it up." DeRosa turned his back to me. I suspected he could devise a way to infiltrate the NIH — no simple challenge, but one his strategic brain would welcome.

I sat back and glanced at the child next to me. I should have known better than to make eye contact. Engaging fussy children on an airplane is like catching the eye of a deranged person in Central Park; both actions have negative endings.

She was a tiny spot of a girl with old-fashioned pigtails that had worked their way into enormous knots. I had rather un-fond memories of my own bristled hair being torn at by one nanny or another. I imagined the little girl crying in frustration as her mother tugged at her hair bands. Without asking, she handed me her coloring book and a few crayons. I quickly sketched an exact replica of the youngest brother, whom I had identified earlier as the bastard child. I handed the page to her, and she giggled loudly. Stretching her arm around the chair, she handed my drawing to the brother seated next to DeRosa. The drawing came back with a big red X through it. We played this game for a while, with me drawing all her family members from memory and the brother crossing them out.

Finally, one drawing came back of an adult with chin-length hair and blue eyes, a cartoon-like character executed by someone with absolutely no aptitude for art. There was an arrow pointed at the face with the word *YOU*. DeRosa had tried his hand at a portrait of me.

I always traveled with my sketching pencils in the same worn case I've used since junior high school. If he wanted the real thing, he would get it and it would be professional. I claimed a clean sheet of paper from the little girl and the blank tableau generated the same excitement as it had since I was the same age as my airplane companion. For an artist, absence represents the beginning of something wonderful, the opportunity to literally fill in the blanks with a personal interpretation of visual stimulation. In this case, the object was me. I worked through my facial features with ease. Of course it was hard to resist covering up my own physical flaws, yet I tried to be fair without being overly generous in my self-portrait. I showed it to my drawing partner, and she smiled her encouragement. I added an arrow with the word *me* and let the little girl pass it back to DeRosa. It was returned instantly.

IS THIS WHAT YOU THINK YOU LOOK LIKE? he scribbled in all masculine capitals.

IT IS WHAT I LOOK LIKE, I wrote back.

I saw his arm moving as he wrote his reply. He passed the sketch to the boy, who then passed it on to his sister. Eventually it landed on my food tray.

GIVE CHARLIE SOME CREDIT, the note said.

My cheeks grew red with embarrassment. Did DeRosa just comment on my relationship with Charlie, my physical appearance, or both? Either way, I felt exposed by my own art. Sensing my discomfort, the little girl tugged at my sleeve, and I bent down to hear her secret.

"You're much prettier," she said pointing to my sketch. Apparently DeRosa thought so too. Suddenly I felt enormous seated between two preschool children, like a seven-foot woman in a crowd of midgets. Driven by a self-conscious urge, I fled for the bathroom like a wallflower at the school dance, but the tight confines of the water closet provided no relief. I splashed water on my cheeks, delaying the inevitable march back to my seat.

I returned to my row to find DeRosa seated in my chair. The little girl had been placed, in protest, next to her brother. I took her spot under duress, my portrait balanced

187

on the detective's knees.

"How did you read the YWS financial statements so quickly?" he asked.

"I started a charity in my late teens," I admitted without hesitation. I lifted the picture from DeRosa's lap and folded it several times before putting it in my pocketbook.

"The plane lands in twenty minutes. A confession takes less time than an interrogation."

"There's nothing to confess because I have nothing to hide. And my charity has nothing to do with the case."

"Then the floor is all yours." DeRosa swept his arm welcoming my story. He settled into his beer as I recounted the events of my early life.

At the age of eighteen, Teddy and I gained access to two separate trust funds: one established by my maternal grandmother and the other by the Prentice family. As the days ticked down to my eighteenth birthday, the tension in our house was explosive, and even a minor action like my purchasing a recycling bin was met with an argument. So fearful was my father that I would donate the entirety of my portion of the trust to an obscure environmental foundation, that he engaged a top law firm to extract my name from the Prentice trust fund. On the eve of my eighteenth birthday, my place in the Prentice line was legally removed, as well as that of any offspring I might bring into the world. My mother was helpless to fight the disinheritance and sunk deeper into her bottle.

It was a conversation I had with Teddy shortly after my disinheritance that inspired me to start a charity. He reminded me that I still had access to the other trust fund. Teddy and I discussed a future for the money at length with our grandmother, an open-minded woman who blessed us with unconditional love. With her guidance, Teddy and I decided to tackle two goals at once.

First, I would take the money from our mother's family and create a charity that funded art programs in the inner city. Art had been my savior all through my school years, and I wanted to give the same gift to underprivileged children. My grandmother's social reach was impressive, and she became instrumental in recruiting a board with members composed of former art teachers, museum presidents, and school principals. At the age of nineteen, I made myself the executor of the newly formed charity, giving me final signoff on all expenses. It was an exhilarating and heady time for me. It was also a planned fiscal nightmare. Earmarking the trust for art programs rendered me penniless, but that was the crux of the second goal. If I truly believed in Freeganism, what better way to practice it than without the cushion of money? Dumpster diving takes on a whole new meaning when your pocket is empty. My grandmother gave me Harbor House as seed money, and we held back a chunk of cash to renovate the house, with a piece put aside for major repairs. It was almost insane for my grandmother to indulge my passion, but I tried to keep in mind that this was the same woman who had happily allowed my mother to traipse unescorted through Europe a few decades previously. She balanced her whimsy with a piece of solid advice: real estate is always a good investment and ignoring upkeep is the equivalent of throwing money away.

As the plane made its descent, I wrapped up my discourse by listing the city schools that had benefited from my converted trust. "Any questions?" I asked, satisfied that I had answered DeRosa's initial inquiry concerning my ability to read YWS's tax statements.

"Yes," he said. "A decade has passed.

Can't your father see what good you've done?"

"He doesn't know all that much about my charity work."

"CeCe, that's short-sighted. You're purposely driving the wedge between you and your father deeper."

With my mouth turned down in frustration to hold back years of pent-up resentment, I presented DeRosa with the rationale I had played over and over in my head.

"How can a father not see the good in his own child? Why does my father need unbiased proof? Granted, I was a challenging teen, but I wasn't a bad person. I'm curious, I questioned, and I debated. That's how I learn and strangely enough that is how scientists bring new theories to light. He of all people should recognize these qualities in his daughter. How could my own father not see the real me?"

"I don't know," DeRosa answered, as if he took the blame for all the wrongdoing purported by males over the centuries.

"Then, I'll tell you. My father favored Teddy and he wouldn't allow me the qualities that DNA usually reserves for boys. Despite all of my father's efforts to manipulate the genetic code for the benefit of humankind, he attempted to thwart my ability to live up to my DNA, the same DNA I inherited from him."

"That doesn't make sense."

"Well that's the best I can come up with, and God knows I've been ruminating over this for years. Parents play favorites, and I'm not my father's favorite," I added. "I will take some of the blame, though. When I realized my position in the family, I antagonized my dad, and I do regret that." This last fact was a recent revelation for me. My father's kiss on my forehead days earlier had moved me, and I had to accept that although I made life difficult for my parents, my father still had room in his heart for me.

"I have another theory," DeRosa offered. "You said your father is researching epigenetics, the ability to alter a human's DNA?"

"Yes, that's his primary research."

"And solving this scientific mystery could result in epic medical discoveries?"

"Yes. If it happens, the world will change dramatically."

"Well then, is it possible that despite all his research, he can't prove it? Maybe he's come to the conclusion that DNA can't be changed and that's why he can only see you in one dimension."

I didn't have a quick comeback for that

accusation. And a hefty accusation it was. The idea that my father had failed in his scientific efforts was mindboggling. Before I could answer, DeRosa continued.

"And on top of that, you're broke."

"Completely. It's the only way to really live free."

He swigged his beer slowly, giving himself time to digest my brain dump. It was easy now to see when DeRosa thought hard. He had a tendency to clench his jaw with his bottom lip jutting out as if he were chewing on the facts. His jaw muscles ground away. For a few moments I experienced a sense of relief that I had absolutely nothing more to reveal.

"CeCe, I need to ask you a sensitive question." His voice lowered a notch, although I couldn't imagine how much heavier this conversation could get. "Did Teddy have a will, and is there any chance that you are the beneficiary of his will?"

"So now I killed my brother to get access to the same money my father kept from me?"

"Not exactly. I'm wondering if being the benefactor of Teddy's will is making you a target."

"Interesting," I replied, and for the second time in twenty-four hours, DeRosa laughed.

TWENTY-THREE

Short as it was, the trip to D.C. left us with a long to-do list, which kept me occupied Saturday. Trina, Jonathan, and Charlie were intrigued and each offered plausible explanations for the events of the past day. Our Sunday breakfast table burst alive with conversation and the support of my friends encouraged me. Trina had made a full recovery from the egg poisoning, resuming her baking duties as her appetite increased. The menu that morning included homemade blueberry pie, scones, and hand-churned butter — all my brother's favorites. I hoped Teddy had known he had an extended family in Harbor House inhabitants.

"So Becky's gone?" I asked.

Trina cut generous slices of pie for each of us. "It was strange. We barely said goodbye." She licked the knife as she talked. "All of her stuff fit in the back of a cab. It was sad."

"Charlie, do you think she was mad at me?"

"I don't know what women think," he said.

"Did she give DeRosa a forwarding address?"

Trina pulled a slip of paper out of her apron pocket and passed it to me. "She moved to the East Village."

"Maybe we can visit her after she gets settled," I offered.

"She mentioned that," Trina said.

"Don't worry about Becky," Jonathan said through a mouthful of blueberry. "You've got enough on your plate. Focus on Teddy and fill us in on the rest of the trip."

Everyone chimed in in agreement. It wasn't all that difficult since Becky and I had never formed a solid bond, although a friendship would have seemed likely given our artistic leanings. Interestingly, I wasn't the one who had found the new tenant. Teddy, of all people, met Becky through a small publishing company engaged to print a short run of his scientific articles. She was the graphic designer on the project and responsible for translating Teddy's charts and graphs into supporting visual art. She visited the labs regularly to review material, and she and Teddy struck up a friendship.

Charlie, Teddy's social director, suggested a night out and before long Becky earned a place in our circle. Trina was enamored of Becky's use of recycled fabrics and helped her develop organic dyes to recolor the materials. Charlie was smitten with her doll-like looks. She had a round face and high, broad cheekbones with sleepy lids that gave her expressions a dreamy quality. As a group, we were encouraged by her interest in building her own green fashion line, and her move into Harbor House seemed an obvious next stop. However, as my friends had noted, I had no time to babysit a whimpering tenant. Becky was a big girl and did not need our help finding a new place to live.

"So like I said, DeRosa, Cheski, and Lamendola will follow up on Igor's departure point in Brooklyn, although Frank's not hopeful on that front. A better bet is the security footage from the Metro station."

"Any chance of the camera catching you carving out a hunk of Igor's flesh with your nails? I'd pay to see that." Charlie leaned into Jonathan. "You should see my back."

"Your banter leaves me speechless," Jonathan replied, and then he turned to me as if Charlie were not in the room. "CeCe, I have no idea how you found the courage to chase

Igor. You're amazing. Can you imagine if a DNA match from your sample were found at the scene of the crime?"

"Thank you, Jonathan. You're a prince next to him." I thumbed my finger in Charlie's direction. "And as for you, Charles, if I scratched your back, I'm sorry. I was aiming for your eyes."

"You complete me, CeCe," Charlie retorted.

"Anyway, I can't believe I chased Igor. It seems crazy now, especially since DeRosa says it's highly unlikely a DNA match will be found."

"You never know," Jonathan countered.

"We'll see." I filled Charlie's mug along with my own. "DeRosa is looking into the source of Naomi's funding, and that could be huge. Money is often a motive for murder."

"What about the break-in at DeRosa's apartment?" Jonathan helped himself to seconds. "This is delicious Trina," he added, leaving a blue-stained kiss on her cheek.

"Cheski and Lamendola are going to shop my sketch of Igor around his neighborhood." I reached for a scone. "DeRosa identified three missing items from his apartment. His passport, birth certificate, and annual medical reports from the force."

"What could these three things have in common?" Trina wondered as she rose to refill the coffee carafe.

"Sounds like someone wants to steal DeRosa's identity," Charlie said. "Or confirm it. Is it possible he's not who he says he is?"

"Like an undercover cop?" Trina asked.

"Guys, don't get off track. DeRosa was interviewed on television right after Teddy's death," I reminded my friends. "Hard to stay undercover when your face is broadcast across the tri-state area."

"Then tell us more about Naomi's charity."

"DeRosa is going to subpoena the YWS bank account in order to trace the money, but basically it looks like the fake charity was her personal slush fund."

"If some person or entity gave Naomi money, they must have wanted something in return," Charlie suggested.

"Probably information." Jonathan drummed his fingers on the table. "Or access to Teddy and the labs."

"Maybe that's why Naomi was so upset Teddy broke it off," Trina theorized. "Maybe Naomi's phony efforts to keep the relationship together made Teddy suspicious, and her charade led him to uncover the fraud."

"Trina," I said with newfound hope. "That's entirely possible. Maybe someone paid Naomi to get close to Teddy in order to get access to proprietary information at the labs, almost like a security leak. Maybe whoever it is couldn't pay Naomi directly, but they could pay her through a fake charity."

"That is going to freak your dad out," Charlie said. "He'll go nuts if he thinks information is being funneled to a competitor. I'm sure that's why he's attempting to control the investigation."

"You're right, but on some level I'm okay with my dad protecting the labs," I said, remembering my father's sobering comments concerning the public enormity of the labs' scientific studies. "Teddy valued his work tremendously, and I'm sure he would have done the same thing in my father's place. The problem is that my father's attempt to control or edit the investigation may limit the police. It may cause them to miss something. If there is a connection between the labs and Teddy's death, it would be a shame if my father confused his priorities."

The thought that my father's loyalties might be skewed was not unimaginable given my childhood. My father's devotion to his career was hard for my mother, leaving her idle and depressed and turning to alcohol to numb her isolation.

"More than a shame," Jonathan interjected. "It's criminal to withhold evidence. Especially, CeCe, since your life has been threatened more than once since Teddy's death. You've been poisoned, pushed down a steep hill, shot at, and stalked on the streets of D.C. If your father has access to pertinent information, now would be the time to make his resources available to the police without restriction. In light of recent events, I think it's imperative we get DeRosa to put some pressure on your dad."

Charlie rose from the kitchen table and pointed to the gardens. "Hey, there's your mom."

Sure enough my mother and Norma were wandering through our herb garden, picking specimens from the newly sprouted stems of rosemary, basil, and thyme.

"Mom," I called out, flailing my arms by the window. The last time I'd had this warm feeling was when my mother attended one of my grade-school plays. She always stood out of the crowd of dowdy mothers in her expensive but artsy attire. She had a flair for color, typically draped in muted silks that accentuated her angular frame. From the window I noticed her face glowing with contentment. She had shiny hair and her eyes were clear. The alcohol-induced puffiness had deflated from her face.

Before I had a chance, Charlie charged outside and wrapped my mother in an enormous bear hug. His combination of good looks and outsider attitude were an aphrodisiac for my mother. I'd often reflected that it was a wonder she ever ended up with my father.

"Mom, I can't believe you came." I peeled Charlie off my mother and embraced her with abandon.

My mother motioned to Norma. "We thought a Sunday pop-in was in order."

I introduced Mom to Trina and Jonathan. Although she had already met them, she'd probably forgotten in her previous inebriated state. I could see that the housemaid was highly protective of my mother, staying close to her side. But the gracious welcome they received softened Norma's guard, and we all headed into the house for a slice of leftover pie.

"Charlie, how long has it been?"

"Too long, Mrs. Prentice, too long." Charlie's commitment issues did not apply to members of my family. He loved my mother because she was never critical of his friendship with Teddy. In fact, she encouraged it. Teddy had been a serious child, and my mother considered Charlie's carefree ways the best medicine for her overachieving son.

"Remember the absent notes?" Charlie prompted my mother.

"Do I? It got to where I could sign your mother's signature better than she could." My mother tilted her head back, remembering her unusual approach to parenting.

After we finished the pie, I offered to give her and Norma a tour of the house and gardens. We spent the most time in my attic studio, where my mother seemed especially pleased to view my artwork. She did, however, make an elaborate show of turning over Naomi's portraits so her visage faced the wall. "I never liked that girl."

The half-finished portraits of my "mystery" man consumed most of her attention. The paintings entranced her. Of course, she hadn't met DeRosa yet, and I wondered if she would presume it was Teddy's face I was struggling to capture, as I had initially. With shaky legs, she bent down on her knees and leafed through the canvases, carefully scrutinizing the progression as the man's face filled out.

"You've always communicated through

your art, Constance. I think painting Teddy is your healing. You should finish the portrait. It will make you feel better." My mother rose awkwardly with Norma's assistance, and I could see her strength waning. I decided to forgo explaining the similarities between DeRosa and Teddy. My mother's constitution was fragile, and parading pictures of my brother's doppelganger — who just happened to be investigating her son's death — didn't seem to be a positive healing tool.

I suggested some fresh air, and we wound ourselves down a back staircase and headed to the gardens. As we circled the greenhouse, we came upon the detective. I guessed Mom would have to deal with the doppelganger after all. I took the lead.

"Frank, I want you to meet my mother, Elizabeth Prentice. Mom, this is Detective Frank DeRosa."

"Mrs. Prentice. This is good timing." DeRosa shook her hand, but I could tell he was all business. His jaw was stiff, and he didn't make eye contact with either my mother or me. "The results of Teddy's autopsy just came back."

The spell of the lovely afternoon broke. Conversation halted. My mother's lower lip trembled, and I noticed Norma wind her arm through my mother's elbow. DeRosa plowed forward, seemingly ignorant of my mother's adverse reaction.

"Mrs. Prentice, to your knowledge, did your son ever complain of an itchy tongue or develop red blotches around his mouth?"

"Not that I'm aware," she responded cautiously, knowing full well that this question could be better answered by the revolving door of nannies and maids that ran her household.

"CeCe, do you have any recollection of your brother experiencing discomfort after eating?"

"I don't, Frank," I said coldly. I intended to shut him down, but it was evident that this unexpected opportunity to interview my mother would not be squandered.

"Mrs. Prentice, did the pediatrician ever mention the possibility that Teddy had a food allergy?"

"That's a loaded question," my mother replied, her voice straining to stay on keel. "The children never saw a traditional pediatrician. All their medical exams were conducted at the labs by staff members."

"Is this true, CeCe?"

Just when I thought there was nothing more in my personal history that could possibly be intertwined in my brother's case,

DeRosa hit upon a sore point. Since the time I was a child, I received all medical attention through the labs. I had, in fact, never seen a doctor off the labs' campus. If only my connection to the labs had stopped as an adult. Unfortunately, Freeganism does not provide medical insurance and as a result, I still relied on Teddy's access to the labs for my medical needs. All my records were housed on the campus and at Teddy's insistence, I kept up with annual visits.

"My mother is correct. Teddy and I never saw a doctor outside of the labs. Neither has my mother."

She lowered her head as if in embarrassment at revealing the ultimate control my father had over all of our lives.

"Well then, I regret to inform you both that the esteemed Sound View staff neglected to inform you that Teddy had a severe allergy to macadamia nuts." DeRosa banged away at his iPad. "I'll forward the coroner's report to you, but according to the summary notes, Teddy had an anaphylactic reaction to a macadamia nut. There were faint marks at his neck, drawn downward to his chest. The coroner suspects they were made by Teddy's own hands."

"Mom, is that possible? A macadamia nut?"

"I don't know. You're father handled all this. Maybe he knew. I never even filled out the school medical forms. Anyway, no one worried about these things when you were children. It's only now that food allergies are a big deal."

"Can't you develop allergies later in life?" I asked DeRosa.

"Yes, and the coroner did note that here. Apparently, you can also test positive for a sensitivity but not have an anaphylactic reaction until multiple exposures occur."

"So he might not have known. Or maybe Teddy realized this sensitivity as an adult. I'm sure it's easy to avoid macadamia nuts — they're not as common as a peanut or almond."

"It's possible," DeRosa said. "Are you absolutely sure, Mrs. Prentice, that you had no idea Teddy had an allergy?"

My mother shook her head.

I relegated the visual image of my brother's last gasps of air to the far recesses of my subconscious — an act my mother appeared incapable of performing. With shoulders sagging and the skin around her mouth growing slack with remorse, it was evident that my mother could not bear the weight of the news. She cupped her hand to her mouth and for a second I thought she might regurgitate. Heaving sobs welled up from her chest and she reached forward for DeRosa while Norma struggled to pull her back in the opposite direction. Strangely, my mother's eyes had been locked on the detective throughout the entire episode. It may have been an inopportune moment for my mother to recognize the flickering resemblance between DeRosa and Teddy, but I suspected this had just transpired.

"Mom, you need to sit." Norma and I led my mother, her steps growing increasingly smaller, back toward the kitchen. Her movements became so constricted that I suspected she was having a full-blown anxiety attack, yet her eyes remained glued on Frank DeRosa.

Trina, God bless her soul, spotted the crisis immediately and slid a cushy chair across the room to receive my mother. Exhibiting expert skill, Trina forced my mother's head between her legs and placed a brown paper bag over her mouth to regulate the balance of oxygen and carbon dioxide. With the color from my mother's face drained to gray and her throat dry from overexhaling, she spoke for DeRosa's ears only.

"Maybe it isn't an oversight."

"What are you saying, Mom?" I knelt next

to her, my arm wrapped around her bony back and my hand clasped to her shoulder.

"I think what your mother means is that it's possible someone connected to the labs had access to Teddy's medical records and used the knowledge of his allergy to create the perfect murder. It's possible he received a very high dose of the nuts' condensed natural oils." DeRosa turned to me. "Are you getting this, CeCe?

"I think so," I said, as I made room for more mind-bending information.

He rubbed his jaw, thinking out loud. He spoke as if every assumption he proposed were a puzzle piece being strategically moved into place. "It is nearly impossible to commit a murder without leaving a clue. If someone wanted to murder Teddy leaving little to no trace, using nut oil in a baked good would be ideal. People allergic to nuts typically look for the nut in the food. If it were just oils, Teddy wouldn't see a nut and therefore, wouldn't bother to ask. We also know that he ate something in his office, which means this person would have had to enter the facility."

"Or already be there," I added.

"That's what I'm thinking. Almost five hundred people come and go from the labs each day, but full-time employees are there regularly without question. And a select group of full-time employees would have authorization to pull personal files."

"This makes almost every scientist at the labs a suspect."

"Yes. And your father isn't going to like that." DeRosa pulled out his iPad and sent off an email, supposedly to my father. "I'll meet with him tomorrow."

TWENTY-FOUR

The Monday-morning train to the city was packed so thick with commuters that I had the uncomfortable sensation of swimming at a public pool on a scorching summer day. I had nothing against the masses of honest working people trudging through the routine of a forty-hour week, but I knew I'd never be one of them. It had nothing to do with my near-royal lineage, which at this point was merely a pencil line connecting me to previous generations of insanely rich people. In my adult state of poverty, I should have revered the carload of earnest business people crammed neatly in rows of two or three. Instead, I reacted like a caged animal at a petting zoo hoping to grab some kid's candy bar and then scurry back to my lair. My analogy was not far off, since I could probably pick up about a dozen half-eaten Danishes wrapped in butter-soaked paper had I waited around the train station long enough. My stomach grumbled with discontent at the mere suggestion of pre-eaten pastries. Craving partially eaten food is the litmus test for a true Freegan.

Hoping to achieve a Zen moment that would last long enough for the train to creep its way from the Jamaica stop all the way to Penn Station, I located my sketch pad and made room on my lap. By looking at the reflection in the window, I could stare directly at a man located two seats ahead and to my left without being obvious. I attempted a wistful, vague expression as I let my eyes loll softly at the passing landscapes morphing from suburban green to brick and mortar. For all the unsuspecting man knew, I was caught in a meandering daydream. In reality, I was studying his face and capturing his features on my pad. As always, I worked top down, focusing on his hair. Just like shoes, hair can tell an awful lot about a man. My subject was a particularly neat man with his short, almost military-style cut, parted and swept slightly to the side. I imagined him skimming the sun-tipped ends with a comb and then checking to make sure his quarter-inch sideburns were symmetrical. The rest of the commuters appeared rumpled and drowsy, but this man's posture was alert, almost anticipatory, and his suit and shirt remained crisply starched.

The man had caught my eye from the platform when he got out of a car chauffeured by his wife. Seated at the wheel, his wife stood out in contrast, still wrapped in her bathrobe, hair tousled, and gripping a travel mug loaded with caffeine. The scene seemed benign — harried wife drops husband at the station and then rushes home to hustle the kids to the school bus. What really grabbed my attention was the couple's goodbye kiss. The man had leaned tentatively toward his wife and air kissed her as if he were a woman protecting his make-up. It's these obscure, meaningless moments that always seemed to crowd my head as if I had anti–attention deficit disorder. I had a tendency to linger too long. This was probably why I'd never be able to manage a regular, nine-to-five job.

Since I had nothing better to do than sketch a complete stranger, I gave the man's eyes a suspicious slant and turned his lips in such a way that it appeared he was withholding a pertinent fact. I pulled his shoulders back and lifted his chin to create an exaggerated sense of self. And then, just because I could, I made his right sideburn a tad longer than the left, a fact I'm sure would drive the man crazy. I imagined him gripping my picture, frantically looking for a pencil with an intact eraser to even out my artistic license.

As I finished the intricate pattern on the man's tie, the train rolled into Penn Station so slowly I could have walked alongside. The majority of morning riders seemed pleased with the train's feather pillow landing, as if horns and whistles might insult their morning coma. My guy, on the other hand, had places to go. He rose quickly and positioned himself against the door, ready to spring in action. Since I didn't have a briefcase or work paraphernalia to slow me down, I fell easily into pace behind the man. We led the rush, but the foot traffic bottlenecked at the base of the escalator, leaving me so close to the man that I spied the faint markings of a single closed earring hole. Sure enough when the escalator unloaded, the man bee-lined straight into the arms of an equally neat man awaiting his arrival, and this time there was no hesitation in their kiss.

I chuckled out loud to no one in particular and watched with pleasure as the man's face lit upon seeing his companion. If I had taken my trip in reverse, my sketch would have revealed a completely different scenario, a happy pairing of two people counting the hours until their next meeting.

I left the couple in peace and headed toward the subway. Tremont Avenue Elementary School was a hike from Penn Station. I joined the mobs of straphangers on a subway north to the Bronx until I reached 174th Street, a shaky neighborhood in the shadows of the Cross Bronx Expressway. The art program at Tremont had been all but obliterated when the last art teacher retired with no replacement in the budget. My monies allowed for two new teachers and enough supplies to last a decade. I relinquished all supervisory control because I fell madly in love with the teachers hired to revive the program. Both are experienced professionals yet somehow immune to teacher burnout, and I trusted them implicitly. My only condition was the ability to see the money at work.

On this particular day, I had to escape Harbor House. I should have tried to follow up with Becky via phone or her new address, but I had wimped out. I figured we'd catch up in the city in the next few weeks.

I also didn't want to hang around the house and obsess over the news of Teddy's autopsy results. I had absolutely no memory of a nut allergy, and I grew weary trying to re-create every morsel I had ever seen my brother ingest. Teddy was not an adventurous eater by nature, and I had to assume he knew to avoid sensitive foods. Most importantly, I did not want to be in shouting range when DeRosa met with my father to request full access to the labs. As it stood, my father had received wind of my dramatic pursuit of Igor, and it did not thrill him. DeRosa's inability to control me was a disappointment. In fact, my ill-planned vigilante act so unnerved my father that he'd appeared once more on my front porch. He'd arrived at the crack of dawn that morning, obviously squeezing me into his busy day. He was frustrated, and it showed with a thin row of perspiration forming along his thinning hairline.

"Constance, this is unacceptable," he had said. "Isn't it enough that you are already in danger without creating it yourself? I am working very hard to keep you safe, and your actions are making it difficult."

"Dad, you can't control everything and you know you can't manage me of all people."

"This family is not having another funeral," my father had said, actually stamping his foot for emphasis. "For once, Constance, do as I say."

The meeting between DeRosa and my

father was scheduled for early today and in a fit of self-preservation, I decided to make myself scarce. I took advantage of my exile and booked myself as a guest artist at Tremont Elementary in the South Bronx. This meant I got to enjoy an afternoon in an art studio equipped with tiny chairs and desks and enough glitter, glue, and string to challenge Santa's workshop. It was a safe haven for both me and the children of Tremont Elementary.

Along the walk from the subway to the school, I nodded pleasantly at the heroin-addicted prostitutes who either started early or were finishing up a long night. It was unimaginable to me how parents could walk their children to school along this parade route of destitution. Although my art program was a drop in the bucket compared with the sums of money required to overhaul the area, it was all I could do short of loading these kids in a van and transporting them back to Harbor House in search of asylum. On the upside, I could probably pick up some Dumpster diving tips from my young charges.

Before every school visitation, I planned an art lesson that was both educational and fun. Today I was assigned to work with five- and six-year-olds. The objective was to have the children learn the letters in their name by designing each symbol into an animal. I illustrated my name on the board, carving my two Cs into giant crabs. Although many of us enter school already counting to ten and spelling simple words, the task seemed well beyond the kindergarteners and most of the first-grade classes. And it wasn't just the letters that were daunting. Apparently, inner city children have little to no exposure to animals besides rodents, pit bulls, and bugs. I stumbled my way through the lesson, revealing my unfamiliarity with urban names such as Taneisha and Ka'sheena. On my third attempt to spell Du'vaine (having grossly misplaced the apostrophe), I changed the project to freestyle watercolors.

By the end of the school day, my back hurt. I thanked the teachers profusely for indulging my whims and dragged my beaten body back through the overcrowded hallways, sincerely regretting that I had not driven into the city. Standing on the building's stoop, I scanned the neighborhood now filled with children running aimlessly among the crack addicts and streetwalkers. Even an experienced Freegan would have trouble rustling up a meal here. Like a prince on a horse, Charlie's blond head stuck out of the crowd like the white man he was. He leaned against the car with his hands shoved deep in his pockets and long legs crossed casually, as if posing for an ad. The only thing that fit properly into the scene was the rundown Gremlin.

"Someone is getting detention," Charlie reprimanded.

"A girl can't get a day off to contribute to society?"

"Not if her disappearance freaks out her housemates and sends her bodyguard cop into full metal jacket mode."

"Oops, I never thought about that."

"S'alright sweetheart," Charlie said as pecked me on the cheek. "I figured you had a bit of wanderlust in you, so I called the school to see if you scheduled anything in the 'hood today."

"You know me well."

"I know you well enough to know that you don't feel like going home just yet, so I thought we'd take a side trip to Brighton Beach." Charlie shrugged his shoulders impishly. "Who knows? Maybe we'll get a lead on Igor. You're already in trouble with Frank; how much worse could it get?"

"Fantastic."

"Your chariot awaits, Miss Prentice."

Charlie was correct in his assumption. Like characters in a play, I wanted to erase myself from a storyline where I was a central figure: Teddy's autopsy revealed that he'd eaten something with macadamia nut oils, triggering an anaphylactic episode. The incident alone could have appeared to be a tragic mistake. It was entirely possible that Teddy himself purchased a sweet in the lab's cafeteria ultimately causing his demise. However, his death wasn't isolated. When combined with the threats on my life and Naomi's suicide, a pattern was emerging. People associated with Sound View Laboratories had a difficult time staying alive.

Fatal allergic reactions happen within minutes. The fact that Teddy died in his office meant he ingested something while there, which led DeRosa to believe that the murderer had unfettered access to the building. To further that theory, Teddy's medical records were housed at the labs, making every authorized employee a suspect. The investigation was now at an important juncture. DeRosa needed to wrestle control from my father because, whether my father liked it or not, odds were good that someone associated with the labs was causing deaths.

Before distracting myself with the neat-looking man on the train into the city, I'd tried to predict the conversation between my father and the detective. Should I assume DeRosa could even make a dent in my father's hubris? I expected this meeting would be a shadowboxing event where both maneuvered for the most advantageous position. They each wanted Teddy's death solved, but on their own terms. Although DeRosa was a team player, he also seemed like he was used to being the captain of that team. I sensed my father's back-seat driving got on his nerves. Still, it was imperative DeRosa understand that if he couldn't bring the investigation to a swift end, then my father — with his endless resources — would make it happen.

My mother's meltdown and her admission that our father controlled a lifetime of our medical assessments allowed DeRosa a window into my father's overriding authority. After my mother's hurried departure the previous day, I'd reminded DeRosa that my father defended many a controversial scientific hypotheses in front of highly educated panels of PhDs. Dr. William Prentice was used to being on the defensive and was therefore a formidable match.

"What's your strategy?" I'd asked DeRosa Sunday afternoon.

"To avoid having you tell me my strategy," he'd replied.

"I promise to just listen."

"I'm going to let your father talk about Teddy from a father's perspective. It will give me room to compliment Teddy and develop a rapport."

My father loved to talk about Teddy and his achievements because it was a direct reflection on him. DeRosa, it seemed, had already figured this out.

"Don't corner him," I'd directed.

"I'll try to remember that, Nancy Drew."

"And don't mention my name. He'll clam up."

"I already checked that box."

Charlie drove toward Brooklyn with the windows down, the radio blasting, and his arm draped over the car door. He sang along to the top hits of the seventies, slapping his free hand on the car in time with the beat. This was a guy who hadn't a care in the world, and I loved him for it. I was also aware that if I conjured up an image of Teddy right now, Charlie would burst into tears. I mentally arranged the men in life and ranked them on a fictitious scale of emotional expression. If Charlie was an eight, my father ranked in the decimals, with DeRosa, Jonathan, and Teddy inching up the scale. Teddy'd had a zest for life, but he lived within the serious constraints of his professional career. It was almost as if wasting time would have an impact on all humanity. Jonathan, I felt, had "found" himself in his twenties and was confidently content in his choices, leaving him firmly anchored at a 5 on my emotional-expression scale. The enigma DeRosa exposed very little of his light side. However, given his penchant for puzzle-solving, I expected to see his joy emanate if and when Teddy's murder was solved.

I pointed to an iPod-sized gadget adhered to the Gremlin's dashboard. "What's this thing, Charlie?"

"*What's this thing,* she says with ignorance," Charlie emoted with Shakespearean flair.

I attempted to pry the device off the dashboard, but Charlie swatted my hand away. "Charlie, just tell me what this freaking thing is."

"A Dollameter, my dear. This 'freaking thing' is a Dollameter," Charlie sang out as he leaned on the horn, willing a double-parked tow truck away with a screeching honk.

"Should I know what a Dollameter is?"

"The next greatest invention, targeted for the Green market. A high-tech must-have that will make me rich beyond my wildest dreams. And in contrast to you, my unpretentious and charitable friend, I plan on blowing it all on booze and women."

"*Blowing* being the operative word," I commented wryly. "Charlie, since you've only sold a quantity of one and that sale is to yourself, why not give me your best product pitch?"

"Certainly." He turned to face me despite driving forward, a bad habit he'd adopted as a teenager. I called it driving with his ear. I grabbed the steering wheel and aimed for the white line.

"Charlie, eyes on the road."

"Good point. Anyway, the Dollameter links your automobile's real-time mileage to the amount you paid per gallon of gas. The device calculates the cost of each trip the driver makes. It's almost like counting the calories as you eat. This way, an environmentally concerned driver can decide if the trip is worth the money, hence putting themselves on a gas-to-dollar diet."

"But don't you have to take the route at least once for the mileage —"

"A GPS can estimate the mileage for different routes."

"That's actually pretty cool," I said.

"Then you could divide the Dollameter's

output by the number of passengers and get the cost per rider. You could even program it for that. It would promote carpooling."

"Yes, but the additional riders would add weight to the car and lower the gas mileage per dollar driven."

"We'd be encouraged to pick only slim friends."

"Mean and funny all at once. A reality show in the making. What should we call the show?" I asked.

"Too Fat to Fit?" Charlie suggested.

"Thin Gets You In?" I said, riffing off Charlie's title.

"I like that, and I bet I could retrofit the car seats with built-in scales so when the passenger sits, the seat would register their weight."

"Maybe the Dollameter could also track single drivers of SUVs and add environmental points to their license?"

"I like how you think. We'll call it the Dollameter Tax." Charlie stretched his arm out the window to slow traffic and maneuvered the car into a tight parking spot behind an oversized eighties Oldsmobile. "And now that we've solved the world's problems, let's give the Gremlin a rest and explore Igor's hometown."

Neither Charlie nor I had ever been to

Brighton Beach. At first glance, it looked as though time froze thirty years ago: the Berlin wall had just fallen and the first transmissions of MTV were indoctrinating the Soviet countries with American pop culture. Women wore more make-up than Tammy Faye Bakker and sported big, overly processed hair, all of it bleached blond. If only I had known shoulder pads were going to make a comeback, I could have been a millionaire again. The stretch of beach, unexpectedly beautiful, was inundated with Speedo-sporting men over sixty. Despite the cool June temperatures, the ocean was afloat in dissidents accustomed to the icy Black Sea.

"This is some crazy shit."

"I'm getting naked," Charlie answered, pretending to remove his shirt.

"The clothes stay on in public or I'm driving home."

Charlie wrapped an affectionate arm around my shoulder. "That implies the clothes come off in private."

We strolled the beach arm in arm and I relaxed into our friendship, thankful for Charlie's constant presence in my life. Eventually Charlie would meet the woman of his dreams and I'd become Aunt CeCe to his children, but for the time being it was easy enough to play the part of sometime girlfriend. Our affair had always been casual, and I accepted Teddy's death as the cause of our current needy affection.

"So can I tell you a little more about the Dollameter?"

"Of course," I encouraged. Charlie had been tinkering with something for as long as I could remember. His intense creative energy mixed with a casual attitude made him so enticing to me. He didn't take himself too seriously, which allowed him to explore boundaries without worrying about consequences.

Charlie lengthened his stride, taking on a confident swagger. "An automotive company that produces very small, very intelligent, some might say *smart* cars" — he winked with exaggeration — "has expressed interest in the Dollameter."

"How much interest?"

His jaunty walk came to a stop as he scanned the storefronts. He pointed to an ornately adorned restaurant made to look like a Russian orthodox church. "Let's just say I'd like you to be my guest at the Volna restaurant situated across from the beach in the heart of Little Odessa."

"A flush Freegan? Tempting."

"Come on, CeCe. For one night, let's not

eat garbage."

"I'll make that decision after I taste the food."

Charlie steered me toward the restaurant, ignoring my weak protests about waste and overconsumption, and before I knew it, I was sitting comfortably in a booth dripping in red velvet with Russian icons mounted on the wall. The music was dark and moody, putting me in a food coma before we even ordered. Charlie ordered plates full of pierogis and kielbasa with beets and pickles on the side. A gross and excessive smorgasbord of items arrived that would hopefully transport well in the doggie bags I imagined filling. Although the pounds of food overwhelmed me, what bothered me most were the shots of vodka Charlie was consuming like water.

"Your liver is crying for a rest. I swear the whites of your eyes are turning yellow with every *cheers.*"

"Don't worry, CeCe. I'm a good drunk."

"You are a good drunk, Charlie," I said, and I meant it. When Charlie got his groove on, he could motivate a barroom of nuns to dance on the tables. "But I'm concerned about your motivation to get sloppy. Since Teddy's death, you haven't exactly been Mr. Happy Hour."

Charlie wiped his mouth with the cloth napkin, his expression turning grave. "CeCe, remember when I missed the sixth-grade field trip to the Hayden Planetarium because I overslept?"

"I do. And you missed a good one. I remember thinking how cool it was because at the end the teachers let us stay to see the Pink Floyd light show."

"Thanks for reminding me," Charlie threw back another shot and continued his remorseful walk down memory lane. "How about the time I cut school for a week and convinced my mother I was participating in an Eagle Scout convention? I wasn't an Eagle Scout. Hell, I was never even a Cub Scout."

"Teddy was the Eagle Scout. You just pretended to go to meetings with him."

"That's what I'm talking about. Or, one of my worst memories, the day I took the bus back from MIT mid-semester because my parents wouldn't pick up a drop out."

"Stop the 'woe is me' attitude. You know I don't do the therapy thing, so just tell me what's bothering you."

Charlie fiddled with the empty shot glass, waiting for me to coax a confession out of him. Fat chance.

"Look, Charlie, I'm not doing drama

tonight, but I'll go as far as saying that your best attribute is not running with the pack. You would have never thought up the Dollameter or the handful of other ideas you've patented if you were tied behind a desk redesigning widgets for a major corporation."

Charlie's eyes misted, and I watched as the youthful energy seeped from his body like a balloon with a pinhole leak. "CeCe, you and Teddy were the only people in my life that kept me on track."

"I think Teddy kept us both in check." I nabbed a choice piece of sausage with my fork. "Did you really take the bus home from MIT?"

"I was waiting for the bus when Teddy came and got me," Charlie said.

I reached across the table, extricated Charlie's fingers from the shot glass, and wrapped his hand around mine. "I admit I'm not Teddy, but I'm still here for you."

"Not for long."

"Am I going somewhere?"

"DeRosa is into you."

There it was again, except this time it came with a third-party endorsement. Up until this point, I thought I imagined DeRosa's backhanded compliments. I recognized the standard *what's a nice girl like you doing in a place like this* flirting, but De-Rosa's advances seemed harder to decipher than a five-star Sudoku puzzle. I felt flattered and deceived all at once. For Charlie's sake, I maintained a poker face. I anticipated that one of us would leave our intermittent relationship soon, but I didn't expect it would be me.

"So just because a guy expresses interest, I get the vapors and lose the ability to think for myself?"

Charlie's inebriated lips were working slowly, his words loosening at the ends of sentences like he just received a shot of Novocain. "Frank is good for you. He's solid, but he's got enough going on upstairs to keep you on your toes and versa visa." He mangled *vice versa,* making it sound like a Russian delicacy on the Volna restaurant's specials board. For all I knew we'd actually ordered it.

"I'm not looking for a bridge partner," I said as I calculated the tip for Charlie and counted out money from his wallet.

"I'll make you a bet, Ms. Prentice." Charlie stuck out his pinky finger, and I automatically hooked mine around his. "I'm not putting out for you anymore, no matter how much you beg. I'll bet my lack of attention will drive you straight to DeRosa by the end of the summer."

"What do I get if I win?"

"If you lose, you get DeRosa; if you win, I'll have to lower my standards and ravage your body against all protestations." Charlie fumbled his way across the table and slapped a wet kiss on my mouth. "Either way, you win, CeCe."

As we were leaving the restaurant, Charlie yanked a flyer off a community board in the lobby. "Ce, check out this ad for a roommate. *My bags are packed. Friendly, single female, looking for roommate. Just need enough room for my Springer.* I think we've just found the perfect match for Becky. Do we know if she likes dogs?"

"Please, let's not count Becky out just yet. Maybe she'll change her mind." I dug my hand deep into Charlie's front pant pocket and fished for the Gremlin's keys. "I'm driving tonight."

TWENTY-FIVE

Charlie and I returned home just as the sun set. The view from Harbor House was spectacular at any time of the day but this, a summer sunset, was by far my favorite. There was something about the consistency of the solar drop that amazed me, that absolute moment when the sun dips below the horizon and you know, without disappointment, that it's over. Sunsets are denied to those who move too quickly through life. But for a Freegan who savors all things free, a summer sunset is the perfect gift. As the last of the rays disappeared, the setting sun highlighted an unwelcome sight. In an unpleasant repeat of the night Teddy passed, Harbor House's lights were ablaze.

"Oh shit, not again," I moaned. I poked Charlie in the chest as he slept off his vodka-induced stupor. "Charlie, wake up. Something's going down." Charlie's head tipped like a rag doll. I sighed.

Maybe he was right. Maybe I needed someone like DeRosa. At the least, I needed a guy who wasn't drooling, I reasoned as I pushed Charlie's head into an upright position before abandoning him in the car. I headed up to the house to face the music, knowing full well my disappearance had infuriated DeRosa.

"Hey everyone," I greeted my friends cheerfully, hoping to defuse the police crackdown on my whereabouts.

DeRosa, Cheski, Lamendola, Jonathan, and Trina sat stone-faced at the kitchen table. Excluding Jonathan, the other three had their arms folded across their chests in a protective gesture. Jonathan's fingers were laced gently together, forearms extended on the table as if he were arbitrating a heated divorce.

"Look, I'm sorry about today," I apologized to a room of deaf ears. "I just needed a little down time."

Again everyone ignored my chatter, and I took the opportunity to slip into a kitchen chair and join the table.

Trina had positioned herself so close to Jonathan that she was practically on his lap. "I don't like this idea one bit," she said with tangible fear in her voice. "There has got to be a better way. Jonathan is not a cop."

"He just needs to sit for an interview," DeRosa stated matter-of-factly.

"An interview?" I interceded. "Is anyone going to fill me in?"

"A job interview. With a company called Relativity.com." Trina included me in the conversation now. "The police uncovered Naomi's charity backer while you were out. Now DeRosa wants Jonathan to go on a phony interview to find out more about the company."

"Why you, Jonathan?" I asked.

"Because Relativity.com is a genetics-based company, and Frank believes that my background may help me probe deeper than someone without my knowledge base. The company happens to have an opening for a geneticist, and they're headquartered in Stamford, Connecticut. It's only about a forty-five-minute drive from here, making it a plausible fit given my background and location."

"So why not just accompany the team on a police interview and feed them questions, Cyrano de Bergerac style?" I countered.

Trina's eyes swelled with relief at my idea.

"Because if the company knows they are being interrogated, we won't get squat," Cheski said with impatience. "CeCe, having access to Jonathan is a trump card that might lead to a break in the case. Let him do this. There's a chance we can get him in for an interview before the week is over."

Cheski had a point. Naomi's source of funding was the best lead we had, and I understood that this strategy was probably in our best interest. I decided that now was not the right moment to play devil's advocate.

"So tell me about Relativity.com."

Jonathan turned his palms up and spoke with an even tone. "From what I can gather, Relativity.com is using traditional DNA research for nonmedical commercial uses. Their products are gimmicky and somewhat misleading. Basically, for three hundred bucks, the purchaser obtains a DNA ancestry kit. With a quick swab of the mouth, mailed back to Relativity.com in a sealed receptacle, the user's DNA is decoded and fed into a database that links it to possible ancestral migration patterns. The final purchased product is a map that matches the user's DNA to world populations as well as a percent distribution ranked by close matches in a specific area."

"In English, Jonathan. What does their ad copy say?" I asked.

"The idea is that an individual can track where their ancestors originated from through DNA analysis."

"I kind of love that stuff," I admitted.

"You and millions of other saps around the world," Cheski added heavy on the skepticism. "These rackets are gold mines. You send 'em some spit and find out that gramps is from Poland. No kidding, have you seen my last name?"

"Or mine for that matter," quipped Lamendola. "Like I might be Irish?"

"Frank, did you ask my dad about this company?" I asked. "My father knows everyone in the industry."

"He is not aware of this company, but he had nothing good to say about that branch of the industry in general. Your father has a particular distaste for companies like Relativity.com that attempt to commoditize DNA analysis into a hot-ticket item for Christmas," DeRosa said. "He is extremely pleased we uncovered this connection, but if I can't put the pieces together soon, your father is going to be banging down the front door at Relativity.com himself."

The table flooded with supposition and theory, all of us tossing around what little we understood of Relativity.com. As we chattered away, I watched DeRosa physically push himself to the periphery, lost in mental overdrive. As per his earlier bouts of intense focus, I could see his brain slicing and dicing the facts and clues in a furious attempt to detect a legitimate pattern. His jaw ground away as if he had a stick of beef jerky stuck between his molars. He was ten steps ahead while the rest of us were still trying to connect the dots. I shot forward in the timeline, attempting to meet the detective on his trajectory. "Frank, how does Naomi fit in?"

DeRosa now rose and started to pace. This was a new side to him, and I could almost touch the nervous energy emanating from his every step. His usual reserve had been swallowed by frustration. So determined was his gait, I feared he thought that the faster he walked, the closer we'd get to solving the case. In a move that signaled his growing exasperation, he ran his fingers through his thick, dark waves before summarizing his thoughts.

"Turns out Naomi was a bit of an empty suit. Lamendola did an exhaustive background check on Dr. Gupta and discovered that her MCAT scores were too low for an American medical school. Jonathan, what did you say the cut off is for Yale?"

"No lower than thirty-five."

"And Naomi scored a fifteen. As a result, her only option was an off-shore school.

Yugoslavia, of all places," DeRosa said with surprise as he continued to circle the table like a hyena on the hunt.

"Technically, Slovenia," Lamendola corrected. "Right on the border of Italy, about a two-hour drive northeast from Venice. Nearest town is Bonetti."

DeRosa halted and drew his finger to his chin. He raised his eyebrows looking quizzically at Lamendola. "Did you say Bonetti?" he pronounced the town like a true Italian with a hard accent on the *n*.

"You know the place?" Lamendola asked.

"Neither here nor there, but you're sure the town is Bonetti?"

Lamendola nodded in the affirmative. DeRosa's lower lip dropped a quarter of an inch — imperceptible to the rest of the room, but it was the type of facial change I registered. Then he resumed his pacing.

"Right, so back to Naomi." DeRosa's thoughts were now tumbling out faster than dice on a craps table. "My guess is that Naomi spent most of her time cruising the canals of Venice. Anyway, enough speculation, let's assume her training is less than stellar, given her low entrance test scores. What we do know is that she supplemented her medical school training, or lack thereof, under a pile of awards and honors she actively compiled. Based on Lamendola's research — impressive, by the way — Naomi conjured up a falsified bio highlighting her early years as an orphan in India. Of course, she grew up in Lansing, Michigan, which we confirmed by speaking with her parents this morning."

"Were her parents helpful?" I asked.

"They were," DeRosa said. "Her parents are from India, but Naomi was born here. As it turns out, she's the youngest. Her siblings are doctors, and I could tell by the tone of the conversation that the parents pushed the children very hard. I wouldn't be surprised if Naomi went to great lengths to keep up with her sister and brother. But she may not have been smart enough for a medical career."

"How far did she go to keep up?" I asked.

"Apparently she manipulated every affirmative action policy on the books, even claiming on one application —" He stopped abruptly to draw a well-deserved breath. "What did she claim, Lamendola?"

"That she was half black and half Native American."

"Yes, and this bothers me. Naomi has now exhibited a pathological pattern of lying from an early age, possibly caused by her family dynamic. Teddy must have picked up on this. But what's interesting to me, very interesting in fact, is that her so-called training occurred in Eastern Europe, which is not so far from Russia. If we could make some connection between Naomi and Igor or Igor and Relativity.com, we might have something. And that's where you come in, Jonathan. I don't need much for a warrant."

"I'm in." Jonathan stood and shook DeRosa's hand. "Whatever you need."

The detective reached for his wallet and counted out two hundred dollars. "First thing tomorrow, I need you to get a haircut and shave the beard. I want you to buy a white, collared golf shirt and a pair of pressed khakis. Good shoes and a belt and absolutely no thrift shop finds. Cheski and Lamendola will beef up your resume to cover the gap since you've been farming. Be back here by ten thirty sharp and we'll do some practice runs on your background. Got it?"

"I got it."

"One more thing, and please don't argue: you need a professional manicure to soak the farmer out of your hands."

Jonathan's face dropped at the mention of a manicure.

"I'll handle that," Trina interrupted.

DeRosa nodded. "And Jonathan, try to

remember that before the farmer was the scientist. You need to play the role." DeRosa turned to Trina and, with the poise and assurance of Clark Kent, said, "Trina, you have my word. He'll be fine."

Then it was my turn to receive his Superman strength. "CeCe, I have a feeling we scared off Igor."

"How so?"

"Because chasing him through the streets of D.C. like a madwoman sends a message that you're not afraid."

"But I am afraid. I'm terrified."

"Trust me on this one," DeRosa said. "If Igor tracked us in D.C., then whoever he's working for knows we saw Naomi's apartment. We're gaining on them, and that puts them on the defensive."

"Won't that just make them angrier?" I shot back.

He glanced at his watch, ignoring my irritation. "Look, I can't stay here tonight."

"Frank, you can't just ditch me like this," I yelled as he grabbed his coat and headed to the door.

"I have something personal I need to attend to. But I feel confident leaving you here with Lamendola," DeRosa stated. He turned to Lamendola. "You good with that?"

"I guess I can do that, Frank. I've got a change of clothes in the car."

"So that's it?" I said incredulously. "You haven't even told me what happened with my father."

"Tomorrow, CeCe." And with that, Frank DeRosa departed.

I had to admit his excuse hurt. Something personal? Like a girlfriend, or a wife? Did DeRosa owe me anything? I guess not. Maybe I exaggerated Charlie's observation that the detective was "into me." Just because he liked me didn't preclude him from liking someone else. Again I was struck by the complete transparency of my life compared to DeRosa's Fort Knox exterior. I couldn't just get up and go home, the way he could, because this was my home, and my entire background and family history was on display for people I'd met only two weeks ago.

The heaviness in the air gave way to nervous laughter with DeRosa's absence. Lamendola also assured me I'd be fine, and the room moved its focus to Jonathan's upcoming adventure. Cheski and Lamendola began pumping Jonathan up for his first undercover exploit. Trina lovingly stroked his soon-to-be-shaved Unabomber beard and then hugged him like he was stepping onto the space shuttle.

When the kitchen phone trilled, I walked out to answer it, taking the opportunity to disappear. There were a lot of moving parts in this case, and I needed a few moments to organize my thoughts. Before I could make a hasty exit, Trina grabbed my arm and led me to a far corner of the kitchen.

"Here," she said, handing me a phone number scribbled on a napkin. "A woman with a Spanish accent called earlier and said it was urgent. I think maybe it was the woman who came to the house with your mother the other day."

"Norma?"

"Yes, I think so. She called at the same time this Relatively.com stuff exploded. Maybe that's her calling back."

"Thanks, Trina." I held her close and whispered in her ear. "I'm sorry Jonathan has to do this for Teddy and me."

I hurried to the one and only phone in the house: a wall-mounted, rotary-dial throwback with a five-foot spiral cord. Charlie had his own cell phone, but I had refused to give in to the inane cellular chats that dominated our public spaces. On the issue of communication devices, my stubbornness was admittedly ridiculous, since I was too young to have grown up with the antiquated clunker in our kitchen. I had, however, come to love the weighty feel of the handset, snug between my ear and shoulder. Cell phones have a way of making conversations disposable and if this was in fact Norma, I assumed it was a message worth keeping.

I answered and received a tentative hello in response.

"Is this Norma?"

"Yes, Miss Prentice."

"You called earlier."

"Mrs. Prentice, she very drunk. She is drinking all day."

"I'll come right over."

"No, no. You come tomorrow. She sleeping now. I just think, I should call."

"Okay, Norma. I'll be there first thing in the morning."

"One more, Miss Prentice. Your father. He very sad today. No work. Home all day."

The news of my father's unexpected hiatus astonished me. He had never missed a day of work in my entire memory. His life was his work and even if he were at home, he would hole up in his library to read scientific papers. I placed the phone in its cradle and sank down the wall. Just as my rear end swept the floor, Charlie stumbled in the front door, wagging a floppy finger at me. Disheveled and cotton-mouthed, he picked up midsentence, as if we had been deep in debate.

"So that's it. It's over between us. Don't even think of knocking on my door tonight." And then he crawled up the stairs like a toddler refusing the hand of his mother.

Twenty-Six

I sat on the kitchen floor until well past lights out. The house was quiet, but I was anxious. I had to admit that a few hours of moronic television would have provided an escape from my own circling thoughts. Unfortunately, Harbor House was television-free — a hasty decision, it now seemed. I felt too jumpy to sketch, and food was out of the question given my earlier Russian gorge. I wandered through our library of used books and found an old atlas. I cracked the spine, letting the odor of mildew fill the room, and then turned the pages until a map of southeast Europe appeared. Bonetti, Italy. There it was, right near the border of Yugoslavia, now Slovenia.

Without questioning ethics, I decided it was time for a firsthand look at the police evidence stored on the second floor of my house. I tiptoed upstairs, heading for the room Frank had commandeered for police use, only to be sidetracked by the closed door to Becky's room. I laid my hand on her door and listened for signs of life although I knew she had already moved out. I counted to ten and then turned the knob. The door swung slowly on its hinges as it drew my body past the threshold.

As strange as it seems, a creaking floor board or rattling chains would have made me feel safer, if only to break the eerie silence of an empty room. I tried to remind myself that this room was technically mine, merely a few square feet of space in the house I owned. I flicked the switch, but the glare only highlighted the barren remains of a hasty departure. Scraps of material littered the floor and a random pile of unmatched socks, undergarments, and hangers lay in a corner. Becky's sewing equipment, her lifeline, had been removed. The only thing left on her cutting table besides straight pins and loose threads was a picture of Becky, Teddy, and Charlie, arm in arm, taken shortly after she moved in. By all accounts, the trio seemed happy, gleeful even. Given Charlie's grip on Becky's slim waist, I guessed they had begun their affair by the time of the photo. Teddy, ever the diplomat, showed no offense at being the third wheel. Instead he seemed pleased for the social outlet. I guessed Becky left the photo on purpose; her way of saying thanks and goodbye. I inched my way backward out of the room, fearful to turn my shoulder on the unknown. Closing the door, I moved swiftly down the hall to the room DeRosa and his partners had been occupying for the last two weeks.

Between the excursion to Washington, D.C. and my field trip to the Bronx, it appeared that a serious amount of investigative work had gone on. One wall of the room was papered with a map of the East Coast indicating Naomi's movements over the last two years. The facing wall included photos and bios of everyone involved in the case.

What caught my interest was the file cabinet in the corner of the room. I walked over and gave each drawer a solid pull, but the cabinet was locked. In a childish move, I shoved my shoulder into it, but no amount of roughhousing would jar it open. I searched around the room for a key, running my hands under the edge of the conference table and behind the cabinet, then grabbed a chair and felt around the molding above the door. Still nothing. Perched on top of the chair, I noticed a light on in the bathroom across from the room where

Lamendola was sleeping. I let myself down from the chair and made my way in silence across the hall. No key in the bathroom, but Lamendola's door was slightly ajar and his pants hung on the back of a chair. I tiptoed across the room and slid my hand into the pants pocket, pulling out a set of keys. I felt a twinge of guilt that was quickly overshadowed by my annoyance at DeRosa. I did not feel ready to be released from his protective custody, but apparently my safety had been reprioritized.

I tiptoed back to the conference room and worked the keys quickly until one slid easily into the lock.

The top two drawers were stuffed thick with files. I opened one to find a thorough history of my mother, although it appeared that nothing of note took place after I was born. Another file contained years of press releases from the labs, and yet another included awards and grants bestowed to the labs. There were also recent aerial shots of the labs, my family's home, and Harbor House, all taken with a telephoto lens. The overheads were so crisp, I was able to detect Jonathan and Trina on the grounds of Harbor House. This got my back up. Freegans were used to living on the low-down. Worse, the evidence of our surveillance was stored in my own home. An acid taste filled my mouth, and I crumpled the photos and tossed them in the wastebasket. I wondered how DeRosa would like it if I had hired a private investigator to sniff around Freeport.

I persisted in my snooping for a good hour, and it quickly became evident that nothing in our lives was beyond scrutiny. Charlie's file read like a chapter of *The Catcher in the Rye,* and my own file was riddled with words like *dissociative.* Before long, I located a file on my father, the largest of the bunch, which began with his many achievements in high school. Unlike Naomi, my father's accomplishments were genuine, and I didn't begrudge him the honors he had accumulated. To his credit, he was a producer, and not for the purpose of filling a resume. He didn't just develop theories, he tested and proved them with enough evidence to receive FDA approval.

I flipped through the sheaves, stopping at a report with a raised seal issued by US Immigration and Customs Enforcement, dated three days earlier. The memo was addressed to DeRosa and gave an exhaustive list of international travel as recorded on my father's passport. The travel log was dense with entries, since my father had traveled regularly on behalf of the labs for over forty years. I scanned his jet-setting itinerary, overwhelmed by the volume, until one destination stuck out like a flashing neon sign. Twenty-nine years ago almost to the day, one year before the birth of his children, my father traveled to Italy, landing at the Trieste airport.

I scrambled for the atlas downstairs, tearing pages in my hurry to locate the correct map. Trieste was an Italian city on the far eastern peninsula of the country. At the top right of the boot and a stone's throw from Bonetti, Trieste was mostly likely the nearest airport to the town. Something about the timing of my father's trip troubled me.

Back upstairs, I fumbled for my mother's file, searching madly for a similar notation. I felt the familiar seal through the papers and spotted the evidence immediately. Entry to Italy through Trieste. At that moment, I realized I had no idea how my parents had met. I'd always assumed they'd known each other through a network of wealthy North Shore families. Now it seemed entirely credible that my parents met on my mother's European travels. Maybe they had fallen in love in Italy. Maybe Teddy and I were conceived in Italy. How could it be that I had never heard the stories a normal family repeats with religious devotion — the day Mom and Dad met, that one magical moment that secures your entry into the world? I pushed my brain a little harder without a single memory surfacing.

I carefully put everything back in place and locked the cabinet before slithering back to Lamendola's room, wondering if I could pull off the key swap twice in one night. I didn't like my odds, especially when I heard a faint ring from the kitchen.

When I'd cleared the door, I walked quickly down the hallway and then made a mad dash down the stairs to catch the phone before losing the caller. It was too late for a purely innocent call.

Please, let my mother be okay, I thought.

I fumbled for the phone in the pitch-black kitchen. "CeCe?" I heard my name through the receiver. No Spanish accent.

"Frank?" I said softly.

"Bad timing earlier," he said. "I realize I left you hanging."

"Yeah, by a rope." I caught myself avoiding the windows for fear of spotting an intruder. "I know it's late, but can we see each other now? I'm a little shaky."

"Can't do it. I'm at JFK."

"Let me guess, you're booked on the red-eye to Trieste, Italy."

"Wha— how did you figure that out?"

"I haven't figured anything out. I happened upon the US Customs report in my dad's file," I admitted. "And then I checked my mom's file."

"Really?"

"Are you surprised I went through the files or surprised by what I found?"

"I expected you to look, but I hadn't thought to check your mother's file. What's the timing?"

"One month before my father."

"I'll make note of that," he said. "I'm actually calling because I need a favor."

"You can ask, but I'm not making any promises."

"I need you to sketch a head shot of me from memory. Then, I want you to age it at two points in time: me in my mid-fifties and then in my seventies. I'll give you a fax number for my hotel. Have Cheski fax it to me the minute you're done."

His request caught me off-guard. Outside of Igor's quickie head shot, I wasn't in the business of criminal art. "Come on, that's stretching the limit of my talents. You need a practiced police sketch artist familiar with aging techniques."

"I've seen experts who don't hold a candle

to you. You've got something special, and all I'm asking is that you put it to good use."

The compliment flowed over me like warm water, and I could feel my hesitance slipping away. I didn't consider DeRosa an especially persuasive individual, yet here he was working his magic. I started to think there was more to his meteoric rise in the police department than simply hard work. In fact, he had easily worked his way into my home, established a network of contacts in Washington, D.C., convinced Jonathan to shave his beard and go undercover, and won over Charlie while flirting with me. And now it seemed that after ditching me without explanation, DeRosa planned to change my career path and hire me as a police sketch artist.

"I have no idea where you're going with this, and I'm not even sure why you're traveling to Italy. Really, it was just a stab in the dark on my part. I happened to notice your reaction earlier at the mention of Italy and it stuck in my head, but I guess you won't tell me the purpose of your trip."

"Not yet."

"Can I get a photo of your parents at least? That would give me a starting point."

"It won't help," DeRosa replied. "Trust me."

"Let me think," I said as I re-created his face in my mind.

"What are thinking about?"

"Your earlobes," I said. "You and Teddy have the same earlobes."

"Is that unusual?" Frank asked.

"Eighty percent of the population's earlobes are detached. Like mine." I pulled my blond strands back and tugged on my ear, remembering my mother's lobes.

"One facial feature down and only a few more to go," DeRosa noted.

I started to explain why I couldn't do the drawings, digging deeper into a list of excuses. He said nothing; he planned on winning this one. My options were disintegrating, and I realized that one of DeRosa's gifts was his ability to pull back. The less he said, the more you prattled on, ultimately giving in to his will. I tried another tactic: tit for tat.

"How about this? I'll do the drawings, but you'll need to tell me what happened when you met with my father. Your meeting must have hit a nerve. I got a tip that my mother is drinking again, and my father took his first day off in a half a century." I pressed my ear into the hollow cup of the receiver and placed my hand over my own mouth, trying to stop myself from rambling. If my theory was right, I'd need DeRosa to break the silence first. Not talking was harder than it looks and much quieter than one might expect.

Apparently, I was not up for the challenge. I folded within seconds.

"Frank, you still there?"

"Still here."

"So about my dad?"

"You're familiar with the phrase 'blood is thicker than water'?"

"Of course."

"I'm reluctant to share certain information with you on the outside chance you'll pass it on to your father."

"What are you saying?" I was filled with uncertainty. "Are you suggesting my father is a suspect in Teddy's murder?"

"Not necessarily," DeRosa replied in a way that almost made it a question.

I shifted the phone to my other ear. "That's not very convincing. I'm not a big fan of my dad, but you realize there's no way in hell my father laid so much as a finger on Teddy."

"I agree with you completely."

"But you think my father is somehow involved?"

"At this point, I don't want to say that your father is part of this." DeRosa sighed and started again. "Your father is involved to the extent that the labs are involved."

"I think we've established the fact that my father wants to solve Teddy's death, but you're concerned that he also wants the labs to come out clean in this tragedy."

"Yes."

"And you can't guarantee that."

"That's right."

"Okay, so what did you ask him?"

"It's better if we didn't discuss it."

"Look, if you can't tell me what you said to him, then can you tell me what he said to you?"

DeRosa grunted something that sounded like a curse. "Clever. You're getting better at this."

"Well?" I pushed.

"Okay, we'll do it your way. Your father said that as a man of science, it was important to put aside subjective interpretations and bring forth objective, indisputable evidence. He asked that I use the same criteria in my effort to find Teddy's murderer."

I listened intently, my ear so tight to the phone that it started to perspire. "What else did he say?"

"He mentioned something at the end of our discussion that I latched onto. He said sometimes a scientist invests a lifetime of study only to discover the results don't match their hypothesis, and although it can be devastating, it must be accepted as another type of truth."

"I hate when he talks like Confucius," I grumbled. "What kind of truth does he mean?"

"He means being wrong is information in and of itself," DeRosa said, sounding as if he were enjoying the challenge. "The police academy teaches you to make direct and obvious links in a case. But on some level, your father is right. Sometimes the wrong answer is really an open door. Pushing your brain to think external or tangential to the facts can often reap a larger reward."

"And that's why you're getting on a plane to Italy?"

"Maybe."

"I won't push you, but you said earlier that you thought Igor was not an immediate threat to me. How so?"

"At first I thought your life was being threatened because you knew something. The murderer may have known that you and Teddy were close and suspected your brother alerted you to something right before his death. Carrying around that information would have made you a target.

Same goes for Naomi, another individual close to Teddy." It was almost as if DeRosa were thinking out loud. "But then I took your father's advice and pretended that was an incorrect assumption. Which led me to another conclusion."

"Okay, I'm listening," I said.

"If Igor wanted to kill you," DeRosa said, "he would have. In D.C., he ran from you as opposed to fighting back. He's had enough chances at this point. The eggs could have contained a lethal dose of poison, but they didn't. On the day of the funeral, Igor could have shot you point-blank in the limo and then pushed the car down the hill and into the water to hide your body. Instead, he pushed the limo down the hill and engaged in a shoot-out with the police. I'm starting to believe both events were for show."

"I could have done without the visuals."

"Yes, but the visuals were meant for someone. I think Igor was sending a message."

"What if you're wrong?" I asked. "What if Igor's just warming up? What if he wants to scare the hell out of me before he kills me?"

"Or he's dragging it out to scare someone else."

I made one last attempt to hold my tongue

to see if DeRosa would keep talking.

"There's one more thing," he said.

Finally, my advantage! "Go ahead."

"My assignment to the case came with a recommendation."

"From whom?" I asked.

"Your father. Apparently, he did some research and specifically asked for me."

"He's a stickler for quality. He wants this crime solved."

"Well, let's hope I can deliver. But I'll tell you something: there's a good chance I can't solve Teddy's death and remain within your father's constraints."

I hung up the phone less than a minute later with a sense of empowerment. It was past midnight, but I still had enough energy to work on the sketches. I had no idea why DeRosa wanted them, but at least I was involved. I turned on the kitchen light and made myself a pot of coffee, creating the illusion of safety. I spread out my art supplies on the kitchen table and focused on capturing DeRosa's face as it looked now. It was hard to believe that he and I were close in age. As I drew, I realized there was nothing old about his face, rather it was his expressions and movements that gave him an air of maturity. I kept that in mind as I took on the aging process, a real challenge.

First, I worked with gravity, figuring anything hanging low by thirty years of age would move in the same direction over time. DeRosa had a heavy lid, which would most likely pull down the corners of his eyes over time. This initial change had impact, and I got a sense of where I was going. When I hit a roadblock, I accessed our library, grabbing any book with photos to study common facial lines and their changes over time. As ridiculous as it seems, I found it quite helpful to analyze an old *LIFE* magazine with a photo spread of the Kennedy family over decades. I knew that President Kennedy had suffered from back pain, and I could almost see the discomfort etched into his face. Similarly, I had noticed that DeRosa, when deep in thought, would crinkle his forehead. I expected this would worsen with age, so I increased his brow lines. Because he did not smile much, I was softer around the mouth, assuming these muscles were not getting much of a workout. I anticipated his hair remaining thick, drawing only a slight widow's peak, one of his better qualities. The one feature I couldn't save was his nose. All noses enlarge with age, and since DeRosa was starting out with a slightly larger proboscis, I added some heft and spread.

People age differently, a genetic fact I'm sure my father could speak volumes about. Some gain weight in the face for a fuller, puffy image. Some lose muscle tissue and bone density, causing a hollow-cheeked effect. I decided to try both a thin and heavier version, ending up with four final executions. It was much harder to predict De-Rosa's aging process since I did not have access to family photos. I did, however, make one assumption based on his Italian olive skin: his Mediterranean glow ensured he would never look washed out or pale, so I kept his face light on the wrinkles, almost smoothing with age.

I assessed my completed work and arrived at a pleasant conclusion: Frank DeRosa's physical attributes, it appeared, would stand the test of time.

TWENTY-SEVEN

Jonathan's makeover was astonishing. I actually had difficulty trying to find the person I knew. Sans the thick beard and unruly hair, here stood a mild-mannered man who appeared to be no more than an eager job candidate. There was, however, an unanticipated skin issue that Trina was able to obscure with make-up. Jonathan had worn a beard for so long that the skin underneath was baby pink compared to his sun-beaten forehead. A quick application of blush on his lower cheeks and chin and some gel to force his hair over his brow, and the discrepancy was barely noticeable. With his shirt tucked in and belted and his rough hands smoothed with pounds of hand cream, the ruse seemed believable.

"You could sell me insurance in that get-up," I remarked.

Jonathan caught his reflection in the mirror, fiddling with his hair like a young boy at the prom. His transformation was probably more of a shock to him than to the rest of us.

"Really? Then my expectations were too low. I was hoping to sell you a set of kitchen knives."

"Or a vacuum with lots of useless accessories."

"I think I could pull that off," he said, with amusement.

"But can you pull this off?" I hinted at the potential danger, feeling terribly guilty that my good friend had volunteered for this charade. "Seriously, I'm worried."

He held out a small device, almost imperceptible in his palm. "I've been instructed to hit the panic button in case of emergency."

"For real?"

"No. This is actually an empty razor case from my first shave in ten years," Jonathan said, tossing the object on the counter. "Lamendola will drive me up and stay on site, and I have his number preprogrammed in a cell phone the police provided. Cheski is going to stay here with you. It's just an interview, CeCe. Please don't worry."

"I get the sense you're actually looking forward to this."

"Is it that obvious?" He scratched his

newly shorn hair. "I'm starting to wonder if it's not too late for medical school. I sort of enjoyed the prep work for the interview. It's been a while, but the basics came back pretty quickly." Jonathan grabbed a medical genetics book and flipped through the tome as if it were a Dr. Seuss book. "I studied DNA links and got sidetracked by multiples. Look here, CeCe. I tabbed this page to show you the various combinations of twins."

"I had no idea there were types, other than identical and not." Despite growing up in a medical household, my father had been mum on things related to our personal bodies. When it came to issues of hygiene, puberty, and sex, we were entirely on our own. It was almost like growing up in Victorian times, when modesty had been a sign of a good upbringing. My father was adamant in his repression, never entertaining a frank conversation of twin births — or any birth, for that matter. Given that Teddy was the miracle child, delivered straight from heaven on the wings of an angel, it may have seemed unnecessary to educate his children on the finer details of reproduction. For a brief period in time, I had feared that merely kissing on the lips would result in twins. As for Teddy, I had no idea how he came to understand the changes of a young boy's body, but I suspect that Charlie was probably his source of remarkable yet erroneous information. I know that I personally had fallen victim to Charlie's sideshow fabrications. It's hard to admit, but in high school Charlie actually seduced me into thinking that sex would increase my hormones, resulting in a larger cup size. That fact has yet to be proven.

Jonathan opened the book to reveal a series of medical drawings showing fetuses floating contentedly in sacs filled with what looked like warm, squishy fluid. Whoever the artist, they had made sure to etch a mild, almost Mona Lisa smile on the amoebic faces. It was sweet and endearing, and it reminded me of the subtle power of the pencil. All it took was a centimeter turn of a line to completely change an expression. Not to read too far into this artist's agenda, but these particular babies had their palms placed gently together in a praying position. I doubted a layman would pick up on this detail, but I suspected a subliminal attempt by a clever artist to sway the reader's thoughts on Darwinian theory.

"So which figure is me and Teddy?"

Pointing to two cherubic fetuses floating aimlessly next to each other, Jonathan said,

"Most likely, you and Teddy are the standard dizygotic version of twins. Dizygotic is medical code for two separate eggs and two separate sperm."

"How ordinary. I hoped for something with a little more genetic buzz."

"Actually, with dizygotic twins, there's always a slim chance of the sperm originating from two separate men."

"As in a threesome?"

Jonathan blushed in response to my question. I almost felt bad putting him on the spot when he was about to risk his life on behalf of my brother.

"I'm sorry, you don't have to answer that."

"No, it's good practice for my interview," Jonathan said, regaining his exposure. "Here's a valid example. A husband and wife have sexual relations in the morning and on that day the wife is ovulating. That 'meeting,' shall we say, results in a fertilized egg. Later that day, the wife entertains her lover while her husband is busy at work. Unbeknownst to her, she has dropped multiple eggs in one cycle. Her afternoon 'meeting' begets another fertilized egg. Two babies, one mother, two fathers."

"Half-siblings born on the same day. How would anyone discover the twist of the tryst?"

"Well posed, CeCe," Jonathan complimented my linguistic gymnastics. "Here's the answer. There may be obvious physical differences and genetic traits that would otherwise be impossible to replicate given the pairing of only two people. Eye color is a typical give away. But a definitive answer would be found in a genetic test of paternity."

"Very cool," I said.

Jonathan had captivated the room. Cheski leaned over my shoulder to scan the pages of the medical text, and Trina was rapt with newfound admiration for her almost-doctor boyfriend.

"Paternity testing is another genetic product offered by Relativity.com," he said. "That's why I wanted to brush up on it."

Lamendola honked the horn then, and we sent Jonathan off in a flurry of good wishes. I had asked the policeman to call the house phone as soon as the interview was concluded. Jonathan seemed so gung-ho about his fake interview that I was afraid he'd actually accept the job and leave us to till the soil ourselves.

"I need to see my mother," I announced.

"Is she slipping?" Trina asked.

"I'm not sure what to expect, but I don't think it will be good."

■ ■ ■ ■

Against my wishes, Cheski trailed behind me to my parents' house in an unmarked car. He apparently wasn't convinced of DeRosa's new theory concerning my safety. Being followed by a cop, even one who was looking out for your best interests, was unnerving. As a result, I drove like a sixteen-year-old with a new learner's permit. I waffled between driving too slowly or too quickly, with inordinately long pauses at street signs. I felt frazzled by the time we arrived, but I was fully prepared to scrape my mother off the floor. A chance meeting with my father, however, would be an entirely different matter. I wasn't sure I could handle two parents in one day.

I leaned my head into Cheski's car to give him the lay of the land. "My dad gets driven to the labs by a town car every day around midmorning. I see the light on in his library, so it appears he's running pretty late. Just so there aren't any surprises, I'm alerting you that there may be an incident if my father and I cross paths. If you haven't heard, we're not exactly best friends."

"Then let's move the Gremlin out of sight. Gimme the keys, and I'll re-park it," Cheski said, sporting a faint smirk. "Don't worry about your dad. I'm pretty sure I could take him down if push came to shove."

"Good to know." I gave the hood of his car a hard slap.

"Hey, CeCe," Cheski said. "You've got good intuition. Listen to it."

"You think I'd make a good cop?"

"I actually think you'd make a great sketch artist," he answered. "Frank's sketches were damn good. I faxed them this morning. You got some talent."

Too bad my father can't see that, I thought as I opened the oversized front door, heading straight for the solarium only to find my mother's lounge chair empty.

"Miss Prentice," Norma whispered from behind. "She is in the den. Come."

It had been nearly ten years since I walked the intricate web of the hallways of my childhood home. The house, or rather mansion, was so enormous it was easy to get lost, a never-ending game Teddy and I played as children. Wandering toward the den, I experienced an overwhelming sensation of Teddy — a sense of déjà vu, as if at any moment he'd reappear. That bubble popped when I discovered my mother curled up on the couch, shades drawn and an empty bottle of scotch on the floor, her gray pallor lit only by the glow of the television.

"Jesus, Mom. You were doing so well," I sighed with disappointment. I spoke quietly to Norma, requesting a pitcher of cold water and some aspirin. Then I closed the door. "Mom, you look dehydrated. Your lips are chapped."

She nodded out of habit, barely registering my arrival. I knelt on the floor in front of her and pushed her fair hair from her eyes. "Will you let me put some lip balm on you?" Again, the weak nod. I found a small pot of Trina's homemade, organic lip moisturizer in my bag and gently swabbed my mother's mouth, which appeared puckered from an over-abundance of alcohol. Her breath smelled harsh, and I grew concerned that she may not have eaten in a few days. Since this was the worst I could remember her being, I wondered if her horrific condition had been enhanced by pharmaceuticals.

"Mom? Did Detective DeRosa upset you?"

This time I got a faint croak, and I could see her dry eyes attempt to cry.

"I know he looks kind of like Teddy. It's subtle, but it's there. Almost like seeing a ghost. It freaked me too, Mom. Maybe it caused you a little setback, am I right?" I held her hand and she squeezed it with so little passion that I could have mistaken the gesture for a muscle spasm. I realized that the best I could offer her at that moment was company, so I settled on the couch and watched television next to her. Today's programming was a matinee of the Prentice family home movies.

"Oh my god. This must be one of our first vacations at the beach." I let out a controlled squeal. "Look at how cute Teddy was. So chubby." The footage was classic. Typical summer family day, complete with shining sun and gentle waves. Teddy's diaper poked out of an ill-fitting bathing suit as he sucked down a bottle. The only thing missing was me, as if my parents had planned to document our family life at the exact time I took a nap. I let the tape roll for about ten minutes, while Norma and I tried to ply my mother with analgesics and water.

"Norma, this may not work. I think she's going to need professional help this time."

"No, no," Norma protested. "I can do this. It has happened before. Tomorrow is a new day."

"Well then, let's start." I ejected the DVD from the recorder and popped it into my satchel so it was unavailable for repeated showings. "Clean slate, no dwelling on the past." I kissed my mother gently and without thinking twice, hugged Norma, replaying my childhood years when I'd relied on the help to navigate my day in my mother's self-imposed oblivion. "Norma, I trust you, but if there's no improvement by tomorrow, I'm going to call a doctor."

On my way out of the house, I chose a hallway that placed me outside of my father's office. I could hear him talking on the phone and though I couldn't hear his words, he was speaking, as always, with authority and purpose. I pushed my toes directly up to the door hoping to eavesdrop. Instead of more words, I caught the shuffle of feet approaching from behind me — a heavy step, definitely a male. I started to panic until I remembered a neglected closet located a few feet to my left. Moving swiftly, I opened the door and stepped inside.

Blackness engulfed me and I felt a whole new fear: being trapped in the closet. I tried to control my breathing, convincing myself I was exaggerating the circumstances. Realistically, I was in my childhood home, mere yards from my mother, Norma, and my father. I tried to focus on that fact, breathing deeply through my nose and slowly out of my mouth. My controlled respiration quickly gave way to something I can only describe as the frantic gasps of a pregnant woman in the throes of the Lamaze technique. The trigger was a voice.

"Are you ready, doctor?" The voice had a distinct accent, not unlike the waiter from the Volna restaurant.

"Not today," my father responded with a dismissive tone.

I listened as the footsteps moved back down the hall and then with every ounce of strength I could muster, I willed my paralyzed body to walk out of the closet. Without a second to spare, I caught a glimpse of a man as he turned the corner heading away from my father's office. The bulky frame and thick neck were unmistakable. Igor. I wanted nothing more than to step back to the quiet confines of my closet, but I had been spotted as easily as a red wine stain on a white shirt.

"Constance?"

"Daddy."

Daddy? I was suddenly seven years old again, standing sheepishly at my father's feet. Only this time, his shoulders were stooped with age and I almost had to bend and look up to see his face. For the first time, I felt a physical advantage over my father. Time had worn his frame down, and Teddy's death had beaten him. Even his earlobes sagged, although they were covered by the coarse ear hair that only older men can produce in such volume. His other hair had thinned terribly, so unlike Teddy's thick mane, and his bare scalp revealed red patches of eczema. His eyes were watery and red-rimmed, and I wondered if he had been crying. His voice had been stern on the phone, but his face displayed worry.

Over his shoulder, I could peer into his darkly paneled library. I detested this room; it was where all family punishments were doled out, although *family* punishments might be a bit of an exaggeration since most penalties had been directed toward me. I cringed. The room had been like having the judge's chambers in your own home, with no jury of peers to hear your case.

Many a curfew was assigned in this room, privileges were revoked, and life sentences were issued that stretched until your eighteenth birthday. I think even Charlie got caught up in the crossfire a few times, earning punishments by association. If it hadn't been for the confusing Igor sighting, my demeanor toward my father might have been more forceful.

"Dad, you caught me off-guard. I stopped by to see Mom."

True, but it was a sidebar to the question

I really wanted to ask: *Hey Dad, did you know your limo driver tried to kill me two weeks ago?* I had no choice but to continue the inane conversation because I had no clue as to my father's involvement. Did Igor work for my father as more than a driver? If so, I couldn't get out of the house fast enough to scrub the bull's-eye off my forehead. On the other hand, was my father even aware of Igor's chosen profession as a fairly inept hit man? Maybe he'd be better off driving himself to work today. I wasn't sure whose safety was worth protecting, but I selfishly voted for mine.

"Your mother isn't here. You'll need to ask the maid."

"Dad, the housekeeper's name is Norma, and I already saw Mom. If you haven't noticed, she's not well. I think she needs medical attention." I did my best to sound annoyed and impatient. Letting my fear surface would only raise suspicion. He was accustomed to my terse attitude and that's what I needed to deliver.

"I'll check on her later," he said with indifference, turning his back to me. "Is there anything else before you leave?"

Before I leave? Gee, Dad, it almost sounds like you're telling me to get going. If you give me a sec, I can catch up to Igor and borrow his gun, and then we'll discuss who's leaving.

I controlled my internal musings and addressed my father. "What happened to Tony? He drove you for years. Did he retire?"

"Indeed. Now the car service sends a new and more incompetent driver every day, as if I had requested nothing more than a taxi. I don't even remember calling for the car today."

I wasn't sure if my father was lying. Did he know Igor or not? I didn't have an answer. If my father didn't know Igor, then Igor was up to no good, using the same cover as the first time: the scheduled driver.

"I think I'll go back and check on Mom," I said.

"Fine," my father replied, stepping back into his office.

I ran down the hall, turning corners like a bobsledder. I burst through the front door, expecting to see Cheski waiting patiently to save my life, but the driveway was empty. Exposed and vulnerable, I stepped quickly back inside for cover. I darted from window to window, hoping to spot the policeman parked on the grounds. But he was gone, and so were Igor and the town car. Not encouraging.

I headed back to the kitchen and picked

up the house phone. I don't know what possessed me, but I pressed the last call button, jotting down the previous five calls made from the house on the ever-present pad of paper next to the telephone. I'd check later to see if my father had in fact called for a car. I stuffed the note paper in my bag and dialed Harbor House. Charlie picked up on the first ring.

"Charlie," I wheezed, my chest constricting with each breath. "Thank god you're there."

"Fucking Becky," Charlie spit into the phone.

"Sorry to interrupt. I'll call back later." I would have laughed at my own punchy joke had I not feared for my life. Unfortunately, Charlie was not in the right mindset for my quick wit.

"What are you talking about?"

"Forget it, Charlie. Just listen. I saw Igor."

"Where?"

"He came to pick up my dad at the house," I whispered. "He's posing as a limo driver again. I mean, I couldn't tell if my father knew him or not."

"Did he see you?"

"No. Maybe. How would I know? I do know that Cheski is gone."

"Get in the Gremlin and drive home immediately. Take a back route."

"I can't do that."

"CeCe. You can. You need to get out of there."

"No, I really can't. Cheski has the keys. I'm not even sure where he parked the Gremlin."

"Your mom has a car now. Get in it and get home. I'll call Lamendola in Connecticut and have him track down Cheski. Wait, what am I saying? I'll call the precinct and they'll send a car over. Just stay put until I can send help. In fact, don't move away from the phone."

I contemplated my options. Staying in the house made me feel as safe as a well-fed turkey on Thanksgiving, but Charlie's advice had merit. Parents always tell children to stay put if they're lost. *Someone will come find you.* The problem was I didn't want to be found. I wanted to get lost. Very lost.

Charlie must have been reading my mind. "CeCe, I know what you're thinking. Stay in the house."

"Okay. I'll stay, but just talk to me a few more minutes to calm me down. What's up with Becky? Did you just find out that her room is empty?"

"Sort of, but now is not the time to talk

about that. Let me get off the phone and try to reach Cheski."

Charlie ended the call, leaving me terribly alone. I gave it about thirty seconds before making a management decision. Staying in the house was not an option.

A doctor's home is generally organized, so if memory served me correctly, there would be spare car keys in a jar in the pantry. My movements were deliberate and tight, as if I were trying to conserve energy in case I had to react to something disastrous. I located a set of BMW keys and slipped silently into the garage. I knew nothing about cars, but the vehicle directly in front of me looked like it cost a mint. I never understood the numbering strategy behind car models; I had to assume the 750 above the BMW's bumper meant that, idling in neutral, it could outrun the Gremlin. I hesitated, not because I was afraid to get a scratch on an $80,000 luxury vehicle, but because I was petrified. If Igor suspected I was in the house, he could be waiting for me to leave. Maybe he was, at this very minute, surveilling my every move. For all I knew, the Gremlin had a tracking device. Maybe that's how Igor knew that DeRosa and I had flown to Washington. Maybe that's how Igor ended up at my father's house within an hour of my arrival. If I left by the main drive, there was nothing to stop him from running me down in his oversized death limo. Call me crazy, but three trips to the hospital in as many weeks seemed excessive.

Plan B was insane but doable. My old five-speed Schwinn was leaning against the back wall of the garage. It was dusty, and rust dotted the chain, but it came to life when I cranked the pedal with my hand. Of course, I loved the idea of going green, but an ancient bicycle that maxed out at ten miles an hour didn't seem like the best getaway vehicle. I weighed my options. I could stand in the garage, go back in the house, or flee.

I decided to pedal for my life.

I found a nylon drawstring bag and shoved my satchel inside, then I bungeed the pack to the back of the bike. Instead of opening the garage door, I rolled the bicycle out a side door to avoid drawing attention. Across the semicircular patio, there was an open clearing that spanned a hundred yards. If I could make it as far as the pool house unnoticed, then I could safely enter the wooded path. Even if Igor saw me from his car, a vehicle would never make it through that path. If someone were on foot, the bike gave me the advantage of speed.

Every minute of internal debate seemed wasteful now. I took the plunge with the same gusto I invested in a Dumpster dive.

My legs swelled with adrenalin, and my knuckles turned white on the handlebars as I pedaled like a maniac. I kept my head low, as if by some miracle I could actually dodge a bullet. Mostly I prayed my legs would hold up. I was fit, but I wasn't an athlete. As I neared the path, an uncomfortable thought entered my mind, a loose thread I had yet to consider. If my father was connected to Igor and if my father was in fact a player in Teddy's death, then his movements also needed to be evaluated. He knew I was in the house and that Igor was on the premises. If my father had spotted me leaving by the back exit, he could easily have called Igor and have me intercepted when I hit the main road.

I was already in forward motion, unfortunately, so there was no turning back. *Please,* I thought, *let my father be innocent in this mess.* If Igor were at the other end of the path, I didn't stand a chance.

The entrance to the path was almost entirely overgrown with vines and weeds. I plowed the bicycle through the bramble, ignoring the thorns biting at my legs. About halfway down the slope, I stopped and looked over my shoulder. The path was thick with growth and I wouldn't have been able to see anyone until they were within ten feet of me. Not much of a buffer when I realized that Igor could be approaching. That would be an unpleasant meeting. *Hey, remember me? I'm your contract hit.*

I pedaled for what seemed an eternity, but was probably no more than ten minutes. With the main road breaking through the bush line, I felt an enormous sense of relief — until Mother Nature decided to screw with my already less than perfect day. The skies opened as I cleared the tree cover, pouring buckets of cool spring rain on my head, and a vicious wind picked up to toss debris in my way. I forged forward, the bike wheels slipping out from under me each time I turned the handlebars. With each fall I seemed to revive my injuries from the cascading limo drop I'd suffered the prior week. I did my best to ignore the torrential downpour, the gaping hole in the knee of my jeans, my skinned elbow, and my bloody chin. Like a fisherman on the open seas, I wiped streams of rain from my face, giving myself just enough vision to locate a neighboring estate where I knew I could cut at least two miles off the trip by sticking to a well-used horse path. If I could make it through that estate, I'd only have to pedal on the main road for a few hundred yards until it intersected with Snake Hill Road, a famous North Shore rollercoaster of a road that spun in spirals like a cotton candy machine.

By the time I made it to the top of Snake Hill Road, my heart was pumping like a champion cyclist in the Tour de France. The hill peaked in a ridiculous tumble of twists and turns, and I accepted there was no way in hell I'd make it down the hill in one piece on the bike. I untied my bag from the back fender and ditched my beloved five-speed in the bushes, sloshing my way down the slick hill. With about a mile to go before I hit level ground, I could just make out the top of Harbor House through the sheets of rain. Feeling quite desperate — not to mention cold and bruised — I decided to cut through the neighboring lots built precariously into the side of Snake Hill Road.

About twenty feet off the paved road, I accepted the foolishness of my plan. My feet gave way to the muck with each step as the rain tore through the earth, creating crevices a team of beavers couldn't mend. I'd had it. I was exhausted, drenched, and terrified. I needed refuge.

I walked to the nearest house, a charming

and welcoming Dutch Colonial, for cover. The driveway felt solid under my feet and I picked up my pace, nearly running for the front door.

The roof over the portico provided welcome relief. I ran my sleeve across my face and pulled my hair back just in case the owner thought a crazed lunatic had stopped by. God knew I certainly looked like one. I considered saying just a few words out loud so that my first sentence to a complete stranger didn't tumble out like a desperate rant. Then I peeked in the narrow window next to the front door, ready to smile and wave to my unsuspecting neighbor just to reassure them.

As soon as I leaned toward the window, though, my neck snapped backward like a whiplash victim, and I withdrew my finger from the doorbell. My heart, which had been headed back for a normal beat, cranked up to stroke level, and I actually wondered how many times in one day a person could experience unbridled fear before causing irreparable damage.

Inside the house, Igor sat with his elbows resting on the oak dining table, sipping a cup of coffee and reading a newspaper. From the front porch, which was raised a good five feet from the driveway, I could see past a smattering of other homes straight down to Harbor House. I guessed the view was even better from the second floor of the Colonial. Forget high-tech surveillance and tracking devices; Igor was a good old-fashioned villain with a pair of binoculars. There was nothing magical about his powers and nothing spectacular about his evil ways. He was simply an awful person who had camped out behind my house for the sole purpose of tracking my movements.

I darted my head to the sidelight on the other side of the door and again I pulled back within a millisecond. I couldn't believe my eyes. Sitting directly across from Igor was Becky. And, unfortunately for our friendship, she was neither gagged nor bound and seemed to be there entirely of her own free will.

I couldn't put the pieces together fast enough, but the strands of information swirling in my head were trying to connect themselves in a fluid story. A story where a young, attractive girl *just happens* to make friends with a young, successful doctor, ultimately befriending the doctor's friends at the exact time she *just happens* to need a place to live and the friends *just happen* to have an open room. Out of nowhere, the young doctor is murdered and the young girl packs her belongings and virtually disappears within days of the death.

I started to cry, and it was no small whimper. These were the tears of a defeated person, an outpouring of emotion born of cumulative crushing blows. The kind of tears you shed as a child when you realize the world is just too big for a three-foot human being. I slid off the porch, letting the rain wash me down the driveway like a twig being carried by a gushing river. My movements were off kilter, almost jerky, and I wondered if I weren't going into some kind of shock. My body temperature was most likely dropping, and the effort to ride the bike through the woods and rain and up the hill had probably drained me of necessary electrolytes.

There was a small shed to the right of the driveway. I knelt by its side, hoping to find the strength to move my sorry self out of a very dangerous spot. From my vantage point, I could see around the back of the house where Igor had parked his town car — the same car I had seen earlier in my father's driveway perhaps an hour ago. Snake Hill Road was no more than fifty yards away and I realized that, given the weather, Igor and Becky were probably staying put. Besides, they wouldn't think to look for me out the front windows of the house.

I stood up like I was balancing on wobbly stilts and walked defiantly down the middle of the driveway as if I had lived in the charming Dutch Colonial my whole life. My gait was no better than a DWI driver walking the white line, but I didn't care. *Fuck them. Let them put a bullet in my back,* I thought. *I've got nothing to lose at this point.*

Then I realized something. I had seen them, Becky and Igor, but they hadn't seen me. They might see me when I returned to Harbor House, but they would have no idea that I knew I was being watched.

I picked up my pace.

This could be the major break we'd been waiting for.

TWENTY-EIGHT

"Holy shit!" Charlie screamed as he charged toward me.

I was on all fours, crawling through the front door of Harbor House and across the foyer. My slow inching seeming ridiculous, but it was all I could manage. If Charlie hadn't spotted me, I would have kept moving like a wind-up toy across a nursery floor. I was on auto-pilot, a mechanical mess. I just wanted to get somewhere that wasn't where I had been.

"Becky," I managed to say. "And Igor."

"I know," Charlie said. "I know. It's my fault. If I hadn't been drunk the other night, I would have picked up on it. I read the flyer wrong."

Trina came running in then with a pile of blankets and a piece of torn paper. "Oh my god, CeCe, where have you been? Cheski drove all over town looking for you!"

Charlie stripped the waterlogged clothes

from my body and wrapped me in the blankets while Trina ran upstairs to run the bath, but not before handing Charlie the ripped flyer.

"Look CeCe. The flyer says *Singer* not *Springer*," he said as he shoved the ROOM-MATE WANTED ad from Volna restaurant in my face. "I thought the person looking for a roommate had a springer spaniel. I read it wrong because I was shit-faced. The person who placed the ad has a Singer, as in a sewing machine. I think Becky posted an ad for a roommate in Brighton Beach. That puts her in the same neighborhood as Igor. I checked the Dollameter because it registers the mileage for each trip. There were at least a dozen trips matching the mileage from here to Brighton Beach. Igor and Becky were meeting all this time."

"I can beat that." I spat a mouthful of rainwater on the floor. "Becky and Igor are drinking coffee at 132 Snake Hill Road right now."

The police conference room on the second floor of Harbor House was jam-packed with men wearing matching navy blue jackets with the block letters FBI emblazoned across the back. The number of people in the room coupled with the exploding energy made me feel like I had been dropped in a box of Mexican jumping beans. The initial disarray, however, was misleading. There was an organized efficiency controlling the room, and people were moving strategically, like chess pieces on a checkered board. Within two hours of my announcement, a SWAT team of highly trained law enforcement agents descended upon Igor and Becky's hideout, closing the surrounding roadways on our idyllic peninsula. There was only one main road leading in and out of town, but it was apparent that the dynamic duo had either gotten a tip or had stepped out for dinner; by the time the FBI arrived, the house was stripped clean. With no one to cuff or shoot, the FBI agents had descended upon Harbor House, making themselves comfortable in whichever rooms they could fit.

I leaned over to Cheski, who was crammed next to me at the conference table, and whispered in his ear, "So did you run out for a cup of coffee this morning instead of covering my ass?"

"No, I spotted Igor leaving the house after I parked the Gremlin. I ran back to get my vehicle, but I lost him." He said this with a tremendous amount of guilt.

I gave his arm a comforting pat and

relaxed my face. "I'm kidding. Charlie already told me you spotted Igor. What do you think he was up to?"

"I think he wanted to take your father on a joy ride," Cheski grumbled under his breath.

"What stopped him?"

"The housemaid and your mother were in the house. Your father would have had to go willingly, otherwise the commotion would have tipped someone off. That's why he posed as a driver again."

"Apparently it works. My father never questioned him and clearly, I jumped right into Igor's limo on the day of the funeral. So is that our only theory?"

Cheski shrugged. Obviously the only other option was that my father knew exactly who Igor was.

"What does DeRosa think?"

"Hard to say," Cheski answered with a hint of annoyance. "Kind of tough to phone in police work from Italy."

"Do you have any idea why he's there?"

"He's got an appointment with the director of Naomi's medical school today, and I guess he'll shop Igor's picture around."

"How about the pictures I drew for him. What do you think he needs those for?"

"Beats me, but Frank has figured out

some crazy shit before, so I'm gonna have to trust him here."

"Crazy shit? Like what?" I was intrigued by the lore of the famous Detective Frank DeRosa.

Cheski turned to me. "Well, about a year ago, the Freeport police found a dead body in the back of a Mercedes. The guy that got whacked was the owner of the car. Someone killed him and stuffed him in the trunk. The car was untouched, in pristine condition, about five years old. Everyone from the mayor on down figured it for a drug deal gone bad." Cheski started to chuckle retelling the story.

"But not Frank?"

"No sir. And see, that's the good part. A lesser cop would have taken the opportunity to pin the crime on a street thug dealing that corner. Even if the dealer didn't do it, you have a chance to put him away for life. But that's not Frank's style. He's all about the truth."

"So who dunnit?"

Cheski shifted in his chair and started to gesture, pointing here and there to map out the story. "Turns out, this guy, the dead one, is having an affair with the wife of a local merchant. The merchant pegs the guy because he's seen the Mercedes in his neighborhood a few too many times. By chance, the guy has the Mercedes up for sale, posted on Craigslist. The merchant makes arrangements to see the car. He shows up at the guy's house, slits his throat, and stuffs him in the back of his own swanky car."

"How did Frank figure it out?"

"I have no idea, but the mayor almost blew a gasket because he had already done a press conference accusing the drug scum of the job."

"That sounds like Frank." I smiled. "So when does our fearless leader return?"

"We called him about an hour ago. He needs one more day."

I planned on continuing to grill Cheski, but he received an urgent text from Lamendola.

"Hey, hey. We got a name." Cheski rose and sought out the only FBI guy in a suit and tie. "Jonathan's interview went so well they're taking him out to dinner with the lead investor of Relativity.com, a guy named Peter Dacks. Jonathan says this Dacks has a faint accent. He thinks he may be Eastern European. How fast can we get a line on this guy?"

"Jonathan needs to leave there immediately," I said.

The room fell silent while a roomful of strangers all came to the same conclusion. I voiced their thoughts in few succinct sentences.

"Igor and Becky were watching us. They might know it's a phony interview, and that Jonathan is a setup. If this Dacks guy really is crooked, then Jonathan is in danger."

As I spoke, Cheski punched the pad of his phone and waited for a reply. "They're not at a restaurant," he relayed. "The dinner is scheduled for a yacht owned by Peter Dacks. It's docked off a pier in Stamford."

The well-dressed FBI man held his hand up to quiet the room and in a very grave voice said, "If the boat leaves the dock, we may have a hostage situation on our hands."

With swift efficiency, I was removed and deposited downstairs. I broke the news to Trina, who alternated between dry heaves and bouts of bawling. After several minutes, Charlie and I took her out to the greenhouse, where he forced her to smoke a stash of herbal plants he had dried and pounded into a moist clump.

"Charlie, I'm thinking this may be a bad idea. You realize the Federal Bureau of Investigation is within spitting distance."

"Yeah, and what have they done for us so far?" Charlie inhaled the pungent smoke.

"They were too late to catch Igor and Becky, and they should have connected the dots back to Jonathan faster than they did."

I ignored the familiar smell and watched as Trina's eyes mellowed and her tense shoulders released. The air inside the greenhouse was warm and moist, creating a sauna-like experience. We formed a powwow circle on the cool stone floor of the greenhouse and began to toss around facts that just days before seemed utterly random.

Trina tilted her head up to glass roof of the greenhouse and let the smoke drain from her lips. Rain still pounded on the panels with relentless power. "Who the fuck gets on a boat in the middle of a downpour? This is not a business dinner."

Charlie and I nodded in agreement.

"Trina, did you offer Becky the eggs at breakfast?" I asked my head tilting lazily in her direction.

Trina thought back to the morning of the poisoning. "You know, I did, but she said she'd already eaten." Trina took another deep drag on the cigarette and let the smoke roll out before she spoke again. "Bitch."

Charlie turned to me. "What was the name of the publishing company Becky worked for initially? I remember the company approached Teddy first about publishing his papers. He was really psyched about it. It's not like he was shopping the stuff around."

"It was something like University Presses." I tried to recall the name. Strangely enough, Charlie's herbal smoke sticks had a mind-opening effect. "Wait, I've got it. It was called University Medical Press. I remember the acronym UMP stamped on the cover of something in Teddy's office."

Charlie took out his phone and Googled the name. "Dead end," he said showing us the page for the URL, which simply read *Page Under Construction.*

"A front." I watched droplets of water feed a gutter leading to a water basin. "How could Teddy miss that?"

"He had no reason to question it," Charlie answered. "Let's face it, Becky was hot. She shows up, offers him a little cash to publish his papers. She always comes to his office, so there's no effort on his part."

"Why? Why was Becky here?"

"Someone wanted to keep an eye on Teddy," Charlie said as he lit another stick and passed it to Trina.

"I think there's more to it. Becky did more than watch. She ingratiated herself into the group. She had to have an agenda."

We all sat for a few minutes wondering

297

what her role had been in Teddy's death. Trina was the first to offer an explanation.

"Befriending us gave her information on Teddy twenty-four/seven. Even if she wasn't with Teddy, she could still find out about him through his closest friends."

"It also gave her a reason to be on the labs' campus. It gave her access," Charlie added. "If you hang around long enough, the security guards start to recognize you and after a while you just stop signing in."

"That's an excellent point," I agreed. "Becky probably could come and go without raising suspicion. I bet she made sure to be seen there regularly with Teddy inside and outside."

"I have a question," Trina said. "She was with us almost a year. That's a long time. Why would she be watching Teddy for so long?"

"And you know what I think is weird?" Charlie said. "Becky showed up almost to the day Naomi left. Think about it. Naomi shows up on the campus and starts dating Teddy. Then, she takes a new job at the National Institute of Health and Becky appears."

I picked up on Charlie's train of thought. "Is it possible Naomi and Becky have the same boss? Maybe they were tag teaming each other." I rose to crack the window. "Oh shit, Cheski is on his way over."

Charlie threw a plastic baggie across the room and shoved his lighter into a potted plant just as the policeman opened the greenhouse door.

"Officer Cheski," Charlie stammered.

"Smells like my kids' room," Cheski said, pulling a wooden stool up to our circle. He sat down, and I realized he was more interested in the investigation than causing us problems.

"Come join us," I said. "We were playing cop and might need some help."

"Let me hear what you've got," he said.

"Keep going," I instructed Charlie. "You were on a roll."

"Okay. How about this? Someone, let's say it's whoever Naomi and Becky work for, wants the labs to study something that they will ultimately benefit from."

Cheski raised a finger. "So you think Naomi and Becky are connected?"

"Are they?" Charlie asked.

"We think so," Cheski answered.

"I knew it," Charlie said. "So whoever they work for places Naomi on the campus to whisper in Teddy's ear. Scientists work together all the time, so it doesn't seem out of place."

"Did Naomi seem out of place to you guys?" Cheski asked.

I fielded that question. "She fit in the labs and at least in the beginning she seemed to be girlfriend material. After a few months, you could sense the tension. She must have been pushing him."

"Pushing him how?" Cheski asked, testing our ability to work through the case.

"To forward research that Naomi's boss would profit from," Charlie added speculatively, "until Teddy backed out."

"So they murdered him? That's a little extreme." Cheski's insight revealed the leaps we were making.

"What do you and DeRosa think?" I asked Cheski.

"Murder needs a motive with teeth. Teddy had to be a realistic threat to be expendable."

Cheski's phrasing bothered me. "Teddy was too smart to be expendable."

"You're right, CeCe," he conceded. "Teddy was the opposite of expendable. In fact, DeRosa thinks Teddy was about to reveal that the labs were being manipulated to do something highly questionable. He didn't back out. He stepped up and threatened to publicize what he thought may have been criminal activity motivated by profit."

"When you say profit, how much are we talking about?" Trina asked. "How much money needs to be at stake to murder someone?" She was transferring her fear to Jonathan's situation.

"These mega medical companies live and die by their patents and their products," Cheski replied. "As soon as one patent expires, they need to have another in the pipeline. The research takes millions of dollars, so yes, pushing expensive research on the labs would make sense. If the pipeline dries up, these medical groups are screwed because they've already made the upfront investment."

"I'm thinking of something very ugly." It was hard to say, even to my friends. "If Teddy thought the labs were being scammed, the first person he would have approached was my father."

"So he knows something," Charlie said.

"I'm starting to realize that," I said, remembering now that DeRosa was hesitant to pass information on to me for fear it would get back to my father. "But let's get back to the connection between Becky and Naomi before we bring my dad into it. Let's say that Teddy realized Naomi was a phony. He gives her a chance to come clean. Maybe he sees something good in her, but he can't get her to crack. That seems to have been the tone of the card she sent him. Anyway, he calls her and tells her that he's about to reveal the truth. With her reputation and high-end lifestyle on the line, she kills herself."

Cheski nodded in agreement and then added, "We also think it's possible she killed herself before someone else could. Based on the cash in the YWS account, someone was paying her a lot of money. Her failure made her a liability."

"Seriously?" Charlie said. "That's twisted."

"It's not pretty," Cheski agreed. "But before she died, Naomi probably accessed Teddy's medical history, which was stored at the labs, hence the macadamia nuts."

"Most probably delivered in a cookie or cake," Trina finished.

"That leaves Igor. Why would he hang around?" I asked. Then I answered my own question. "Because there was still one person who knew the truth: my father. For sure, Teddy would have told my father that the labs were being manipulated into something unethical. The more I think about it, the more I'm convinced that my father knew exactly what Teddy had figured out."

"I'm going to fill in a blank," Cheski said.

"Relativity.com."

"Charlie, give me your cell phone," I said while I dug up the phone numbers I had transcribed from my parents' house phone. The paper was a bit worse for the soggy bike journey, but the numbers were still legible. I dialed each of the numbers, getting a hit on the third. "Yesterday morning at nine a.m. sharp, my father called Relativity.com's corporate offices."

Cheski took my phone and listened to the end of the Relativity. com message. "You got this number off your parents' phone history?"

"I did."

He jotted the number down and headed for the door. "This is good, CeCe. It's going to be hard for your father to deny knowing anything about this company now."

"I'm scared." Trina was riddled with alarm.

"Me too," Charlie confided as he Googled Relativity.com. He spent a few minutes reading before summarizing his findings. "According to their site, Peter Dacks, CEO, has 'a unique blend of industry experience in the medical field'."

"Which means he's not a doctor and he's not a scientist," I said. "So, basically he has no medical credentials. That's why he needs

Sound View! He has no medical background."

"Correct," Charlie replied. "There is, however, a touched-up picture of a guy in his mid-fifties trying to look forty."

Trina scooted over to get a better look at the man who was likely holding her boyfriend hostage. "Bastard," she spit.

I leaned over Charlie's shoulder and took a hard look at the photo. Peter Dacks had a polished appeal, well put together, an obvious choice for a company front man. His pearly whites alone must have cost thousands. Although it was just a headshot from the shoulders up, you could tell Dacks was fit in the way men strive for when they want to defy the aging process. To complement his youthful physique, his blond hair had been highlighted and his "healthy glow" was most likely refurbished every two weeks at a tanning salon. As with every face I encountered, I stored it in my head, thinking that at some point I'd see it again.

"Relativity.com must be working your father as we speak. I'll bet Peter Dacks is forcing him to continue whatever Teddy was working on," Charlie said. "That's why Igor came after you. It was a sign to your father."

"Charlie, that's exactly what DeRosa said last night — that Igor's actions were meant as a message to someone. As in, *if you don't do this then I'll kill your other child.*"

"But why can't your dad just say what's happening?" Trina pleaded, as if my father could somehow turn off a running faucet and save Jonathan at the same time.

"Because he must be involved at a much higher level. Let's face it, I was almost murdered, twice, and the insanity still hasn't stopped."

"Peter Dacks must have something on your father," Charlie said. "Something big. Otherwise he would have allowed Teddy to stop whatever it was he was working on."

"So that begs the question, what was my brother working on that got him killed?"

"And what does Peter Dacks have on the labs that your father doesn't want made public?" Charlie finished.

"I bet that's why DeRosa is abroad," Trina added. "Jonathan thought Dacks had a Slavic accent, you think Igor is Eastern European, and Naomi was educated in an Eastern European medical university. That's the link."

"And DeRosa knows it," I said. "He's always one step ahead."

TWENTY-NINE

By 8 p.m., the rain had stopped and Jonathan remained on-board the yacht, bobbing in the same spot it had been three hours before. Trina, Charlie, and I were invited back into the conference room for an update. As it stood, the boat hadn't left the dock, which put the FBI in a quandary. So far, no foul play had occurred. Jonathan visited the bathroom twice to send text messages, indicating his ability to communicate freely. Although Cheski and Lamendola had strongly encouraged Jonathan to walk off the boat in return texts, I suspected Jonathan had been sucked into the world of science he now longed for. Cheski, Lamendola, and the FBI were under intense pressure, and that was only exacerbated by Jonathan's stubbornness about vacating the boat. His texts were transcribed by hand on a mounted white board while various interpretations were voiced.

COMP. VALID. PRODUCTS REAL.

DACKS ???, BUT NO CUSTOMER FRAUD.

BIZ MODEL = LOTS OF DNA. NEED TO BUILD DATABASE.

"So where are we?" I asked, hoping someone with a badge would step up to the plate.

The man in the suit was an FBI agent by the name of David Swell. The name worked nicely for him because he was, in fact, a decent guy. Dapper without a bit of pretense. His hair was combed, his suit was tidy, and I'm sure he had a pleasant wife and three nice kids stashed away in the suburbs. Adding a feather to his cap, he didn't seem the slightest bit turned off by our Freegan ways, even offering us the leftovers from the bureau's take-out Chinese dinner.

"We have three maritime police boats strategically anchored in the exit points of Long Island Sound," Agent Swell said. "We've also got a helicopter that's circling sparingly so as not to raise suspicion. And the area around the dock is blanketed with undercover cops." Swell described the situation without raising unnecessary alarm. "I'm impressed with your friend Jonathan's eagerness to help, but at this point he needs to get off the boat. Peter Dacks is not who he says he is."

"So who is he?" Trina had no patience left.

"According to Interpol, his name is Piotr Dackow and he was born in Belarus. He was a small-time scam artist in his hometown and his specialty is falsified papers. When Communism crumbled in the Eastern Bloc, he filled the gap across the Slavic countries by providing phony passports, licenses, and certification in any area required by the payer." Swell passed around a file with photos of Piotr Dackow, alias Peter Dacks.

"What do you make of Jonathan's text messages?" Charlie asked.

Swell looked at the messages on the board and then addressed the group. "I think Jonathan is telling us that the bones of the Relativity.com business are legitimate as far as the product sold. With his background in genetics, he seems to be confirming their primary product, which tracks the customer's familial relatives.

"I think he's also reporting that Dacks is a bit slippery. My guess is that he comes off as a slick salesman and that's not Jonathan's speed. The last text is the most important and it has taken some research to understand what he's uncovered, but we've confirmed that companies like these — companies that compile DNA samples — are dependent on growing their information base. They're in the business of making conclusions based on volumes and volumes of DNA and then packaging and selling that information. To feed their database, they need DNA samples. The richer their database, the better the product and the more products they can offer."

"Why?" Trina asked.

Swell spoke slowly and clearly, and I sensed that this one point was a crucial factor in the case. "Because one single case of anything is an anomaly. But two, three, four, or four hundred cases make it real. If you have an unexplainable symptom, it's an isolated case, until it's not. The larger the DNA database, the greater chance your inexplicable symptom can be explained. Relativity.com's current product of tracking relatives over generations is rather benign, but it's based on the same premise. The more DNA samples in the database, the more connections that can be made across family lines."

I had no medical or genetic training, but I had grown up in the family business and had come to understand a few basics by sheer osmosis. My exposure helped me to an important conclusion.

"And the labs, through years of research,

are probably one of the largest private holders of DNA samples," I said.

"Yes," Swell replied.

"And Teddy was working on decoding the human genome, which is essentially the Rosetta Stone of all of that DNA."

"Right again."

"So the combination of Teddy's work and gaining access to the labs' DNA database has the potential to make Relativity.com a genetic giant," said Charlie, my brilliant-yet-underrated sometime bedmate. "By tracking relatives and then linking their medical histories, Relativity.com has the potential to own the key to life. More than that, they'd own your personal key." He let his eyes travel across the room to ensure that everyone understood the impact of his next statement. "And that's what Teddy figured out. And knowing my best friend, he was disgusted by Relativity.com's attempt to sell information, the most intense personal information; namely, your own DNA code."

"The end game," I said to myself, wondering if DeRosa had gotten this far. The room fell silent. Even the soft shuffling of papers and keyboard tapping came to a halt.

Trina broke the silence. "Cheski, give me that cell phone." She redialed the last number called and waited with arms crossed until Jonathan picked up and then in a very loud voice she barked, "Jonathan, you were supposed to be home hours ago. The children are asking for you. You promised to read them a bedtime story tonight." And then she hung up.

Swell was flabbergasted, as were the other FBI officers, whose fingers erupted in a mad flurry of activity flying across keyboards and phone pads. Within minutes Cheski's phone rang back.

"It's Lamendola," Cheski reported. "Jonathan is getting off the boat."

Trina's face beamed with intense satisfaction, and I watched as her chest swelled with pride. "There, it's done. Unfortunately, that's the extent of my powers. The rest of you have to figure out what this Peter Dacks is holding over Dr. Prentice's head."

THIRTY

The futon in my studio was a mess of rumpled sheets and battered pillows when I woke the next morning. I stripped the bed and gathered up the piles of clothing that had formed in small heaps around the room, then headed to the basement laundry. Because I was nice, I included a few pairs of Charlie's boxers that had gotten tangled in my bed sheets. Our laundry setup was cumbersome and complicated, and I'd be the first to admit that Freegan clothes washing was difficult at best. In an attempt to conserve water, we collected and captured rain through a serious of drains and tubing that led to a cistern in the basement. A foot-activated pump lifted the water from the container into a washing machine only Laura Ingalls Wilder would have envied. The washer looked like an oversized mixer designed to whip up ten gallons of frosting. The base of the machine sat on a flat wood-burning stove with just enough air flow to allow the fire to catch.

Once the water heated up, we put a sparing amount of nontoxic detergent in it and then turned the crank to spin the clothes. Not surprisingly, used or discarded detergent was impossible to come by unless you can find a way to scoop up buckets of bubbles before they pop and dissipate. I detested this chore because every load made me pine for a spanking-new white t-shirt from the Gap. My Freegan weakness. Once you go Freegan, you have to accept that you will never wear a perfectly white piece of clothing again. The washing exercise was antiquated enough that I had lobbied hard for a low-energy, low-emission Scandinavian machine that cost as much as flying to Sweden to have your clothing dry cleaned by the royal family. I'd been outvoted.

As if the washing wasn't bad enough, you still had to pray for a sunny or breezy day to hang the clothes on the line. The only upside was that process gave me ample time to think.

As I turned the handle on the machine, my shoulder braced against the contraption to intensify the speed, my thoughts kept going back to what Teddy learned in the days before his death. If he wanted to make an accusation, then he must have had proof. Scientists live for proof, and I was sure my brother had documented his findings. He would never have pointed a finger randomly without having his test tubes in a row. At the least, he must have presented something concrete to my father, his mentor and professional confidant. Based on my father's actions (or rather, his inaction), it appeared he had dismissed it all initially. This would have upset Teddy tremendously, hence his noncommunicative behavior in the days preceding his death. We knew that Teddy was on to Naomi and that he had probably figured out her connection to Relativity .com. Through Naomi, he had probably learned that Dacks was squeezing the labs for DNA samples. Teddy must have been horrified when my father refused to stop the transfer of personal information to Relativity.com. Teddy probably threatened to go public.

The most likely places to search for his findings were his apartment and his office at the labs. Unfortunately both had already been thoroughly picked over by the police without uncovering anything of substance. I considered another angle. Was it possible that Teddy tried to leave information with a neutral party? Had he told Charlie, his best friend, something in passing? Had he engaged in conversation with a peer at the labs? Had he unknowingly left the information with my father without realizing my father's potential involvement?

Or had Teddy attempted to make contact with *me* in the days preceding his death? If Teddy suspected my father of something sinister then a likely sympathetic ear would have been his twin sister, for the sole reason that I would have believed him without question. A slam dunk. If Teddy had come to me and said, "CeCe, Dad did something wrong," my reply would have been an emphatic, "No shit, Sherlock." But given the gravity of the situation, the information might have put me in danger, so Teddy would have taken my safety under serious consideration before telling me anything. Of course, I was now in danger anyhow, but I still had no idea what Teddy had known. Somehow, the threats against my life would have been more understandable if I knew what the hell was going on.

It was a long shot, but there was one place my brother could transfer information to me without anyone knowing. And he wouldn't even have needed to leave his office building to complete the task. I stopped my churning mid-cycle and ran upstairs to the house phone.

"Dr. Grovit, it's CeCe Prentice."

"Yes, dear. How are you? I've been thinking about you since Teddy passed," the man replied with genuine compassion. "A horrible affair. We're all devastated here at the labs. A loss for the entire scientific community."

"Thank you. Your condolences mean a lot to me."

"What can I help you with? I wondered if you might call for a sleeping pill or such. Nothing to be embarrassed about in times of stress, you know."

"No, that's not it. I'm holding it together." Then, choosing my words carefully, I revealed the purpose of my call. "Dr. Grovit, this may sound odd, but since Teddy's death, I realize that I need to act like an adult. A good place to start would be finding my own doctors instead of relying on the labs' medical staff."

"Actually, I think that's a wonderful idea." As soon as he said it, I sighed with relief. "I'd be happy to recommend a number of doctors in the area."

"Wonderful. Can I come by today and get my medical files?"

"I see no reason why not. The files are your personal property and what with all the new privacy laws, I'd almost prefer patient files to be in the hands of the patient rather than a messenger service."

"Great. Just leave them at the front desk and I'll swing by this morning. Thanks again." I hung up the phone and paced the kitchen. I wasn't thrilled to be going to the campus because there was always the possibility of meeting up with my father. For all I knew, Dr. Grovit's amenable response was staged and he was dialing my father right this instant. By the time I got to the labs, my file could be reduced to the height and weight chart from my childhood. I decided to try another tactic to avoid a possible interception of my files. I called the main number of the labs and waited until I reached a live operator.

I modulated my voice trying to recapture the tone of a balanced person following up on mundane paperwork. "Good morning, can you transfer me to Records, please?" The operator pressed some buttons and within seconds my call was propelled through the labs' phone network.

"Records," the wonk on the other end of the line grunted. I imagined a troll toiling away in a sun-deprived corner of the campus's basement. I hoped he was so happy to hear another human voice that he'd start work on my files immediately.

"Hey there. I'm a patient of Dr. Grovit's."

"Check."

"Check, what?" I asked.

"Got a request for paperwork for a patient of Dr. Grovit's about two minutes ago."

"Yes, that would be me. Constance Prentice." There was no reaction to my name. I was thrilled that the guy in Records had no idea who signed his paycheck each week. "I'm in the building now and I thought I'd come directly to Records to pick up my file."

"Save me a trip upstairs. I don't like going upstairs."

"Well then, I'm happy to do it. Just tell me where you are."

"Wait," he said as my heart sunk to my knees.

"Is there a problem?"

"I got two files for Prentice," he answered. "Actually, I got a bunch, five in all. Big family, huh?"

"Yes, there's quite a few of us. I'm Constance."

"Let me put the phone down," he said, and I listened as he shuffled across the cement floor. I counted to twenty in my head, continuing to thirty until I finally heard the troll shuffle back to the phone. "Okay, walk to the back of the main building and then take the elevator to the basement. Go through the double doors and turn right. I'll be waiting."

I bet you will, I thought. I grabbed the keys to the Gremlin and shouted upstairs for Cheski.

"What do you want, CeCe?"

"I need a chaperone."

The labs were in full scientific swing when Cheski and I arrived at nearly 10 a.m. The administration and staff were on their second cups of coffee, hammering away at theorems and experiments with gleeful enthusiasm. Cheski was the first to comment.

"Everyone is smiling," he huffed. "They must be pumping in extra oxygen."

"Despite what I think about my father personally, it's actually a nice place to work." I waved politely to a few familiar faces. A few doctors came up to me to express their condolences, but as always with death, the interactions were slightly awkward. The employees knew something was wrong. I presumed everyone knew about Naomi's suicide and the threats on my life. So although I received broad smiles, some of the doctors tilted their shoulders away from me, as though murder was contagious and I was Typhoid Mary. I understood completely. Post-death interactions, especially those involving murder, never come with directions. It didn't help matters that Cheski's entire presence screamed *cop*. We followed the directions to the Records department and exited the elevator on the basement level.

"In all my years of police work, I've never been to the morgue," Cheski said.

"I'd only take you to the morgue if I knew Igor was resting comfortably on a slab."

"I'd pay to see that."

"Just wait, I think this visit will be just as interesting." I pushed my way through the swinging doors leading to the Records department. I rang the old-fashioned bell and then waited to hear the familiar shuffle from the stacks. To my great surprise, a jaw-dropping specimen of human perfection stepped from behind a file cabinet. As it turned out, the Records troll was one camera shot away from a Calvin Klein underwear advertisement. He was amazingly tall with a perfect physique and eyes that swirled like warm chocolate milk in a mug.

"Hi, we spoke earlier. I'm Constance Prentice," I said as I stuck my hand out over the counter. The man standing behind the counter made no attempt to return my shake. Despite his rebuff, I couldn't stop smiling. My pearly whites, unfortunately, went largely unnoticed because the Records guy refused to catch my eye. My head bobbed up and down trying to find a way into his line of vision, but I quickly realized why he'd chosen to work in the basement. Despite his extremely pleasing physical attributes, this man probably suffered from a severe social disorder. I restrained myself when I realized he wanted nothing more than to be left alone.

"What have you got for me?" I asked, pulling my hand back to reduce his anxiety.

"More than I expected," he said and pointed to four full cardboard boxes marked C. PRENTICE. "You must be a sick one."

"I'm much better now," I replied and winked for good measure.

"I got a lot of boxes myself," he answered, and I nodded in the solidarity of the sick.

"Thanks so much for your help."

"Just doing my job," he responded and then stepped back to expand his personal space. "Sign here."

As I signed my name, I asked what I hoped would be an ordinary question. "So each time a patient's files are pulled from Records, someone has to sign?"

"Yup," he said and then scanned down a list of signatures. "You got pulled two months ago." He pushed the paper toward me and indicated a signature. T. Prentice signed in mid-April.

"Good to know," I said, hoping that whatever Teddy had found in my file would help us. "Have a great day."

The Records guy gave Cheski and me a rolling cart for the boxes and told us to leave the trolley at the main reception desk by the front door.

"What next?" Cheski asked as we boarded the elevator. "A visit to the psych ward?"

"Nice. And you're supposed to be a protector of the people." I smirked. "You get the car, and I'll wait here with the boxes." I rolled the cart back to reception. As I parked the cart, I heard my name from across the lobby. The voice was low, steady, and very familiar.

"Constance."

I could have bolted through the front doors, but I hesitated one second too long. Just enough time to hear my name again.

"Constance," my father repeated. "I'd like to see you in my office."

My boxes remained in a pile by the front door and I didn't want to leave them unattended. When Teddy had pulled my files two months ago, he must have stashed something in the folders, I was sure of it. I caught Cheski parking the Gremlin near the front doors and gave him the *two minutes* signal with my fingers. As long as he transferred the boxes safely to the trunk, I'd be okay. I turned and followed my father.

Dr. William Prentice's office bordered on spectacular with wide open views of the Long Island Sound. On a clear day, the Connecticut shore was in full view and I wondered if he hadn't sat here with a pair of binoculars watching Jonathan squirm his way through an interview on Peter Dacks's yacht. For some reason, I felt renewed confidence, as if the connections between the players were being laid as thick as cable wire so strong I could get across them like a tightrope walker. With that in mind I refused to be interrogated by my father, instead putting myself on the offensive.

"Have you addressed mom's illness since we spoke? Your negligence is upsetting to me."

"Negligence? That's an accusatory word to use with a doctor."

"If the stethoscope fits," I let the implication linger.

"Your mother is entering a facility tomorrow."

Unbelievable. He couldn't even say the word *rehab,* instead watering it down to a generic facility. Even if the love between my parents had diminished, I hoped that an ounce of respect remained. Yet my father, in his capacity as a doctor and a husband, could not bring himself to admit my mother's obvious struggle with alcohol. I wanted to lash out at him with an exhaustive list of charges that climaxed with the death of my brother. But up to this point I had nothing definitive to back up such claims. I somehow knew that Teddy had placed something in my medical files for me to find, and I was too close to the answer to let anything get in my way. So I held my tongue between my teeth and squashed my urge to point a finger at my father.

"You asked me here," I said with my arms folded tightly across my chest. "Did you want something?"

"I fear you think I had something to do with Teddy's death."

"And since when does my opinion matter?"

"Frankly, Constance, your opinion doesn't matter, but you seem to have gotten the ear of Detective DeRosa and your opinions couldn't be farther from the truth. I have been working closely with the police department and have done nothing but encourage the detective to find the truth."

"That sounds like you know the truth."

"I know I did not kill your brother." My father answered plainly, but his face was a mangled mass of contradiction.

"Do you know who killed Teddy?"

He parsed his words with extreme precision. "My knowledge is not that specific."

"Who the fuck are you? Bill Clinton?" I shouted with explosive anger. "It's a yes or no question."

"Life is complicated, Constance." He rose to a standing position, indicating my dismissal. No problem there. I was happy to depart, but I yearned for one last dig. My father had consistently underestimated me and I expected he thought I knew very little about the case. He had no idea I'd spotted Igor at his home and he was unaware that I saw Igor and Becky together. I also knew that he had been to Bonetti, Italy, in close proximity to Naomi's medical school. It was a fact I could not contain. So I dropped a heavy hint.

"DeRosa is in Italy," I said.

My father lifted his head and stared directly at me. I held his gaze steadily while he processed the information.

"I have work to do," he replied.

"Ciao," I replied.

I left my father's office, heart pounding in my chest. I found my way to Cheski on legs too thin to support my fragile body. He noticed the change immediately.

"You okay?"

"Do you think it's possible my father had something to do with Teddy's death?"

It was apparent the officer could not maintain a poker face. He opened his eyes a bit too wide in an attempt to convey surprise at my question, but I knew where his head was. We climbed into the Gremlin.

"Come on, Cheski. Has DeRosa said anything to you?"

"You want the statistics first?"

"If they'll help," I answered.

"Okay. There are thousands of cases where a son kills a father, but the reverse is almost an unheard-of crime," Cheski said as he pulled out of the lab parking lot.

"Go on."

"Fathers rarely harm adult children, but," he said, tilting his head back and forth as he presented both sides of the argument, "parents have been known to make bad decisions."

"Decisions that could harm their children?"

"That's what we're trying to find out

now." He drove in the direction of the police station as opposed to Harbor House. "Lamendola picked up Becky. She's being held at the station."

"Was she in the East Village?"

"No, that address was bogus."

"No surprise there. How did you find her?"

"I got a call when you were speaking to your father. You know the ad for the roommate that Charlie picked up in Brighton Beach? The FBI dismissed it because Charlie was too high to explain the connection. So this morning Trina thought to reply to the email listed on the ad."

"But why would Becky talk to Trina?"

"She didn't know it was Trina. The girl played to Becky's ego and pretended she was a retailer in SoHo interested in carrying Becky's clothing line. She gave Trina an address to meet at and Lamendola scooped her right up."

THIRTY-ONE

The interrogation room at the police station was barren except for a worn metal table and two hard-backed chairs. By the look of the chairs and the lack of decoration, I suspected the strategy was to make the guilty party so physically uncomfortable that they confessed quickly. It seemed as though it worked. Becky shifted anxiously in her seat, with nowhere to look but directly at Lamendola seated across from her. Lamendola forced his shoulders and chest across the table, maintaining an aggressive and dominant position. He started by running through what seemed to be a list of standard identification questions. Becky refused to answer a single one. Her arms were folded snugly across her body and her bare legs were entwined tightly around each other like twisted pipe cleaners.

I was sitting with Cheski in an adjacent room watching the drama unfold on a mounted closed-circuit television. I had a hard time believing the person in front of me was my former housemate. Last time I saw her, she was taking afternoon tea on a bleak day with her pal Igor. I studied her countenance, her soft, full cheeks replaced by strains of sheer panic. She clearly had no idea she was going to ever be holed up in an interrogation room.

Lamendola was getting nowhere with her when a stray piece of paper inspired me. I bummed a pen from Cheski and started sketching, my eyes glued to Becky's face. It came easily since I had already worked out similar features a week ago. It was the shape of her nose that caught me, the flat bridge leading to eyes covered by a slight Asian lid. I interpreted her features quickly and then handed the sketch to Cheski.

"Give Lamendola my sketch," I directed. "Have him tell Becky you're holding her father in a room across the hall."

Cheski's eyebrow rose quizzically until he took one look at the sketch. He patted me on the back. "Damn good work," he said, taking the paper and leaving the room. I watched through the camera as he handed my sketch to Lamendola and grumbled in his ear. Lamendola smiled smugly as if he'd just came into possession of an opposing team's playbook, which wasn't far off. My sketch showed two faces, a man and a young woman. The triangular area punctuated by the eyes and leading down to the nose was practically identical in both faces. Juxtaposed next to each other, it became immediately obvious that Becky was Igor's daughter, a fact none of us had detected until my drawing was completed. The sketch worked like a charm, bringing Becky to tears at the thought that both she and father had been caught and were being interrogated simultaneously.

As she studied my sketch, her hand rose to her mouth. I figured she had just realized I was nearby. She stood up and approached the camera, staring directly into the lens. "I'm sorry, CeCe," she cried, tears tumbling down her round face. Lamendola led her back to the chair and asked her if she wanted a lawyer.

"I didn't do anything." She covered her face with her hands.

"First tell me your name," Lamendola said firmly.

"Rebekkah Volwitz."

"Your father's name?"

"Stash Volwitz."

I was taken aback hearing Igor's real name; it transformed the crime from a fantasy world of guessing and supposing into reality. Matching a name to my initial drawing was frightening as it gave Igor, now Stash, a form and identity. I wasn't being chased by an apparition. Stash Volwitz was a real person with intent to harm. And if I wasn't mistaken, his intent was to harm me.

"Who do you work for?"

Becky looked down at my drawing and ran her hand across the sketch. "I was helping my father," she said, her blue eyes wet and moist.

"Whom does your father work for?"

"My uncle," Becky said without hesitation. "My uncle Peter."

Lamendola sat back, clearly caught off-guard by Becky's reference to Uncle Peter. Her comment must have set Lamendola's head spinning. In an amateur move, he looked into the camera as if he needed coaching.

I grabbed Cheski's arm. "He better not screw this up. This is a huge break."

Cheski spoke into a small microphone that was wired to Lamendola's ear. "Get a last name for the uncle," he demanded.

Lamendola's eyes lit up as if he just remembered where he had left a set of lost car keys. "Your uncle's full name?" he asked after a slight pause.

"At home he went by Dackow, but here he goes by Dacks."

"Where is home?" Lamendola asked as he jotted down notes.

"Slovenia."

"When did you immigrate to the United States?"

"When I was five. My uncle helped us come to the country after my mother died. Uncle Peter is my mother's brother."

"How did your mother die?" We watched Becky's face fill with grief. I almost felt sorry for her, but I knew in my heart that she and her father had done something unforgiveable.

"We were very poor. Everyone in our village was poor except my uncle. He always had money." She wiped her eyes with her hands.

Lamendola retrieved a box of tissues and gave her a second to collect herself.

"My uncle recruited villagers to participate in drug trials. It was easy money. You just had to be healthy. People would take the pills and every few months, American doctors would give you a checkup to determine if the pills had an effect on you. But one time, my mother and about ten other villagers got sick right away." Her sobs seemed endless as she replayed her mother's final days.

"My mother was in terrible pain and throwing up blood. I stayed home from school and sat by her bed until she passed. My uncle paid the villagers to keep quiet, but my father wouldn't accept the money. He pressured my uncle to bring us back to the United States with him instead, and he did. Now my father works for my uncle in security at his company."

"And you are also employed by your uncle?"

"Sort of."

"Explain."

"The girls from home work for a living" — Becky paused — "if you know what I mean."

"But you've grown up here." Lamendola's voice was laced with sympathy. He was losing perspective, forgetting she was a suspect in Teddy's death. "Why would you need to do that type of work, Becky?" He made a critical mistake by using her first name.

Cheski groaned through the microphone and admonished Lamendola's overly familiar line of questioning. The message got through, and his face went from kind to cold in a matter of seconds.

"I'm not legal," Becky offered. "My uncle kept promising he'd process my paperwork.

333

He knew how these things worked, but he wanted me to help with a job. He told me all I had to do was get close to Teddy, but just as a friend. No . . . intimate stuff. There was another girl before me, but she wasn't good at it, my uncle said."

"Was that Dr. Naomi Gupta?" Lamendola asked.

Becky nodded affirmatively.

"What was the purpose of staying close to Dr. Prentice?"

"I had to tell my uncle anything Teddy said about his work. I tried taking notes after we talked, but the medical terms were confusing. It was hard and I kept disappointing my uncle, especially if we had plans with Teddy's work friends. I didn't understand what they were talking about."

Just as Charlie and I had suspected, Becky and Naomi worked for the same person, Peter Dacks, both assigned to watch Teddy at different points in time.

"Were you trying to be Dr. Prentice's girlfriend?"

"No, Teddy wasn't interested in me that way," Becky said, as if she were apologizing for not successfully selling her body to a disinterested client. "I promised my uncle I could still stay in Teddy's life by connecting with his friends. That's how I met his sister and the people at Harbor House. I was actually happy for once." She looked away, lost in thought now.

It wasn't that she had fooled us into thinking we were all friends; we were all friends because when Becky was with us, she wasn't acting.

"Tell me what happened the day Teddy died."

"I was trying to break away from my uncle. I thought I could actually make it as a clothing designer, and then he came to see me. He asked me to visit Teddy's office. He knew it was easy for me to enter the building because the receptionist had stopped asking me to sign in."

Cheski whispered to me, "Now we know why her name didn't appear on the visitor's list." I nodded and then turned my attention back to the interrogation. I knew I was about to hear something that would make me terribly upset. I saw that Becky, too, could see it coming as she continued to twist and turn her body like a snake shedding its skin.

"And you brought him something?" Lamendola led her.

"I didn't know," she screamed, practically clawing at the policeman. "How could I know there was something in the cookies?"

She stood and started pacing around the room, her movements frantic as she recounted her horror at the site of Teddy choking. She had snuck a cookie in the car ride over with no reaction, so she assumed a piece had simply lodged in his throat. She attempted to give Teddy the Heimlich Maneuver, but he shoved her away. He must have known an obstruction was not the cause of his choking; the symptoms would be entirely different. Becky's story was mesmerizing and dreadful, a nightmarish account of my brother's last breaths. I caught my reflection in the monitor's screen, my hand partially over my eyes, as if I could soften the gruesome blows.

Becky rubbed her throat as she spoke. "I realized it was hopeless and I knew my uncle was behind it. I opened Teddy's office window and crawled out."

Since she had never signed in, no one remembered her presence on the day Teddy died.

Lamendola sat stone-faced, pen idle in his hand. When Becky crumbled to a halt, he stood abruptly and stormed out of the room, leaving her alone with her confession. He joined Cheski and me, and we watched the monitor as Becky cried like a baby. Her remorse was genuine, but it was

336

too late to recant.

"I can't believe this," I said, circling the room and swinging my arms as if I were addressing a packed stadium. "Becky killed Teddy. She just admitted it!" The confession was startling despite having seen her with Igor. I'd known she was guilty of something, but I couldn't comprehend that someone I lived with had killed my brother. Part of my resistance was that I bought her protestations. I actually believed she had no idea the cookies were tainted. She may have been desperate to gain citizenship, but Becky did not premeditate Teddy's murder. However, she had made one fatal error. She could easily have called for help. In a building filled with medical professionals, a swift injection could have saved Teddy's life. She could argue there was no intent to kill, but there was also no intent to save. She watched him die and, knowing she had done something wrong, purposely snuck out of the building.

"Now what?" Lamendola asked. "Where do I go from here?"

"We need to know the connection between my father and Dacks," I said.

Lamendola and Cheski stared blankly at each other, as if this were beyond their job description. On some level, I knew they felt sorry for Becky's unwitting involvement in a complicated murder case. She was adorable and sweet and had clearly been a victim of her uncle's evil manipulation.

"Come on guys. If Frank were here, he'd ask the hard question. Get in there and get it done."

Thirty-Two

Becky was emotionally spent, which gave Lamendola an advantage. Once her own secrets were out, there was no reason for her to lie. It was like the end of Halloween, when everyone takes off their costumes and returns to their regular selves. Becky's face was relaxed and she was resting her elbows on the table in a sign of defeat. At this point, it was likely she'd say anything just to get out of the interrogation room.

Without mincing words, Lamendola asked, "Why did your uncle want Teddy dead?"

"I don't know," she replied, shifting her eyes, hazy with grief, upward as if the answer were pasted on the ceiling tiles. "I really don't know."

"You never asked your uncle?"

"I didn't know he wanted Teddy dead. I thought he wanted information from Teddy, but he never said he wanted to kill him. He didn't speak to me of these things. He only spoke to my father about business," she said, using the word *business* loosely.

I leaned into the microphone to speak to Lamendola, "We need to locate Igor. Find a way to ask her without letting on that we don't have her father in custody."

Lamendola pretended to take copious notes, giving him time to phrase his next question.

"You and your father were staying at a house located on a hill above Harbor House," he said, "You vacated the residence recently. I need the exact address of your next location." Becky offered up an address in Brighton Beach, assuming that her father was also being detained. Within seconds of stating the location, Cheski was out of the room, calling for two cars and backup. I grabbed the microphone and spoke once more to Lamendola.

"Ask about my father. Now." I barked loudly enough that the policeman covered his ear reflexively.

"Did your uncle have a business relationship with Dr. William Prentice?"

"Dr. Prentice helped my uncle come to the United States," Becky replied, avoiding the camera as if she were about to be punished. "I wasn't supposed to know that, but I heard my uncle and father talking about it once."

There it was. The connection. There was now no doubt my father and Peter Dacks had a personal relationship. I was startled and yet not at the same time. I knew the truth would surface at some point. My father knew Peter Dacks, and Peter Dacks had arranged to kill my brother.

"When?"

Becky bit her bottom lip like a child and held out her fingers one by one. "I'm guessing thirty, maybe thirty-five years ago?"

Lamendola called for a uniformed cop to cuff and process Becky. In a poorly planned move on my part, I exited the room at the exact moment she was being led away. She made a vain attempt to plead her innocence mouthing the words *I didn't know* in my direction, but it was useless. Her words hung in the air like moist droplets falling precipitously to the floor. No matter what she wanted me to believe, Teddy was still dead.

Lamendola met me in the hall and escorted me to Frank's temporary office, the converted butler's pantry off the main room of the Laurel Hollow Police Station. The last time I had visited the room, I'd regurgitated into the waste-paper basket. I felt the same heave of nausea as I struggled to process Becky's confession. It had left me unsatisfied. Becky was a pawn in a bigger plan. She was weak and desperate and although her confession was helpful, it didn't uncover the root of the issue.

"DeRosa is holding on the line," Lamendola opened the door, motioning to Frank's desk. He picked up the phone. "Okay, I've got CeCe, here."

"Hey," I said, sinking onto his swivel chair. "Where are you?"

"I'm on my way home," he said, and I secretly hoped that when DeRosa said *home,* he meant Harbor House. "Lamendola filled me in already. I'm sorry you had to hear Becky's statement firsthand."

"I'm okay," I lied, feeling as if I had been pummeled by an overly aggressive masseuse. I had actually had more energy after my frenetic bike ride through the pouring rain than I did at this particular moment. The gaps in Becky's confession were the source of my energy drain. "It's not enough," I said to DeRosa, "is it?"

"It's not," he replied. "Becky's confession gives us a reason to pick up Dacks, but it's not enough for a conviction. I don't want to bring him in unless we've got something solid."

"I'm tired," I moaned into the phone.

"I know. But I need you to hold on just a little bit longer."

"So what are we up against?" I asked.

"Well, according to Becky, she had no idea she was being sent to kill Teddy. Knowing what she knows now, she can assume that was her uncle's intent. But it's her word against Dacks's, and he will portray himself as a successful businessman while Becky will come off as a prostitute. And both parties will claim they had no idea that Teddy had an allergy to macadamias. We need to know what Dacks has on your father."

I countered, grasping at straws. "Dacks was taking DNA from the labs, and Teddy wanted it stopped. That's not enough?"

"I know you're disappointed, but the fact is, your father allowed it. There's no law against transferring DNA, even if your brother didn't like it."

"Seriously? Are you saying that I don't own my DNA?"

"It's a gray area," he said, "but let me explain it this way. As long as something is attached to your physical body, it's yours. Once an organ or a tissue sample or swath of DNA is removed from your body, it's finders keepers."

"Frank," I shot back, "why are you working against me?"

"I'm not. But I know what it takes to win a court case."

"And what does it take?" I demanded.

"With no eyewitnesses and only circumstantial evidence, the district attorney will need something airtight to put Dacks behind bars for Teddy's death."

"So what's your theory?" I asked over the din of airport sounds. I assumed Frank was working his way through Customs as I heard a sea of voices in a cacophony of unrecognizable languages. As if the noise were not enough, the phone reception started cutting in and out, increasing my frustration.

"Peter Dacks was blackmailing Dr. Prentice," he started. "Instead of money, your father handed over DNA and potentially the result of Teddy's research, the decoded genome. Your father has been acting like he's trying to protect the labs, but he's really trying to protect himself because Dacks knows something very damaging about him. Teddy figured it out and confronted your father. With pressure from Teddy, your father probably tried to call Dacks's bluff. Dacks retaliated by killing Teddy, allowing him to resume his blackmail against your father. The threats against you were a message to your father that Dacks was serious."

"Where does that leave us?"

"We need to find Igor and get him to talk. We'll offer him and his daughter a plea bargain if he throws Dacks under the bus," he wrapped up.

"Don't hang up yet, Frank," I urged. "Did you find something in Italy?"

"I found what I was looking for," he replied. "And some things I didn't expect to find."

THIRTY-THREE

Cheski heaved the last of the boxes onto the kitchen table. He was skeptical but open to trying anything. "They say twins have an ESP thing."

"Well, since the police haven't picked up Igor yet, my medical files are all we've got," I said, as I lifted the lid on the first box. Jonathan was just making his way downstairs, having slept a full ten hours after his almost-hostage situation. "Jonathan, we need you."

"Again?"

"Yes, but first you need to fill us in on the interview."

He rubbed his eyes, thick with sleep, and looked around the room. "Those FBI guys kept me up half the night and then they cleared out like they were never here. Unbelievable."

I poured him a cup of coffee and motioned him to sit down. "So Teddy's work on the human genome is really linked to Relativity .com?"

Jonathan sighed with an enormous sense of loss. "It's hard, you know, to see good work, genuine work, gone bad. It's like when giant corporations co-opted the Green movement. They end up getting it all wrong but with some decent packaging, they can dupe the public."

"You wanted this job, didn't you? You wanted it to be real."

"Relativity.com is real. The problem is that it's a perversion of reality. There's no doubt the company is actually collecting and tracking DNA. And they are producing sellable products. But Dacks is a megalomaniac."

I handed Jonathan his coffee. "I'm sorry, I know you're disappointed."

"It's okay. I'm trying to take this development as a sign that I've reached a juncture in my life. I'm more than a farmer."

"You are, Jonathan," I said, wrapping an encouraging arm around his shoulder. "In fact, you're Houdini. Tell us how you got off the boat so easily."

"Well, except for Peter Dacks, everyone else was a scientist — a believer, shall we say. Most of the time, we were caught up in the beauty of work, the possibility that the

347

human genome could be uncovered, ultimately saving millions of lives through the early intervention of gene therapy. That is, until dinner was served and Dacks joined us. What a sleazeball. The way he treated the waitstaff was deplorable, barking orders like he was Henry the Eighth. I don't think the others were on to Dacks's master plan." Jonathan paused for effect. "His plan was to be the sole source of decoded DNA."

"Frightening," I said.

"Also, I'm not convinced the employees are even aware of any link between their company and Sound View Laboratories. But Dacks, he's a piece of work. He grilled me without mercy." Jonathan scratched his head as if he just realized his hair had been cut.

"Tell me what the scumbag did," Cheski said.

"Well, he seemed to know I had worked briefly at the labs. That concerned me because he kept pounding away at how much I knew about the place. He kept trying to trip me up with dates and then he'd make off-handed references to the Prentice family to see if he could catch me. But I didn't give in." He smiled. "Slinging manure around a farm for a few years builds up a certain type of endurance. I guess by the end of dinner he realized he couldn't break me, so he didn't have a reason to keep me. Trina's phone call, staged loud enough for the entire table to hear, was a wake-up call for all the guys around the table who had families. It was like the school bell went off. They all got up to leave, and I blended in with the crowd. Simple as that."

"Peter Dacks is going down," Cheski threatened, "and the faster we dig into these files, the faster we can bury him."

Trina and Charlie joined us at the kitchen table, and I willingly allowed my personal information to be shared without discretion.

"May I start?" Jonathan said.

"Go ahead," I replied.

"CeCe, you're a healthy twenty-eight-year-old female with no prior medical issues?"

"That's me."

"So I can't understand why there are four full boxes. I should be able to slide your file under a closed door."

"That does seem odd," I noted, remembering the Records guy's comment about my precarious health.

"Well, let's get started," Trina said as she popped a top off one of the boxes.

The volume of papers did confirm my earlier assumption. Apparently, Teddy and I had been tested for everything from diphtheria to lice on a quarterly schedule. Dr. Grovit's notes were copious, and I had to imagine that even he thought the level of detail requested by my father was unusual. That may have been the reason he so easily released me from the grips of the labs.

"I see you got your period at thirteen," Trina remarked with a giggle. "A late bloomer."

"Thank you for notifying the entire table," I responded. "I'd like to think of myself as a work in progress as opposed to a late bloomer."

"Call me when you're in full bloom," Charlie said.

"All right, enough jokes about me. Focus on the files."

We spent a good hour poring over my paperwork. Random remarks about my health were tossed around the table, and I allowed for some level of mirth at my expense. I had to admit that as much as I thought my father didn't know me, from a medical perspective, nothing seemed off-limits. After reading a short narrative on a series of nightmares I'd had in fifth grade, I came upon a one-pager with a diagram made up of circles, arrows, and numbers.

At the top of the page, was a notation: *T to C.*

"I think I just hit paydirt," I said waving the paper. "Look, there's a note from Teddy at the top. T to C. That's Teddy to CeCe. It's from him."

I laid the paper on the table for all of us to study. The diagram was fairly simple. There were two circles with a line connecting them, almost like a dumbbell. Inside each circle were two, single-digit numbers. Extending vertically from the line were more circles hanging like upside down lollipops. Again, the circles each contained two numbers.

"What is it?" Lamendola asked, and we all looked to Jonathan.

Jonathan crumpled his bottom lip and tossed his head back and forth like a pendulum. He held the paper up for a closer look and then traced the lines with his finger. He flipped the paper over, looking for additional information, and found another series of numeric notations on the back.

"It's the result of a paternity test," Jonathan said with controlled composure, but his chest was expanding and deflating too quickly for my comfort.

"Can you interpret it?" Trina asked.

"Well, the two larger circles at either end

351

of this line are the parents." Jonathan pointed to the slightly larger circles so everyone could get acclimated. "Here, this is an allele. It's used to determine paternity since a child must share one allele with each of his parents. We each have two alleles, one allele from each parent. The numbers in the circles are the allele indicators. This parent, for example, has a 3 and a 7. Any child related to this parent must have either a 3 or a 7 as one of their two alleles. The child's other allele must be a match from the other parent."

"So each person has two alleles," I confirmed. "One from one parent and one from the other. That's why each circle has two numbers."

"Yes," Jonathan said.

"Well, I'm no rocket scientist," Cheski admitted, "but based on these number combinations, some of the people in this diagram are not related. There are way too many different numbers."

Jonathan hesitated, and I could tell we were getting drawn into murky waters. "That would be correct."

"Can you interpret it for us?" I asked Jonathan.

"As Cheski pointed out," Jonathan said, pointing to the circles, "reading the diagram is fairly easy. If Teddy meant this as a message to you, then he ensured it could be read by a layman."

"So with one parent providing a 3 and a 7 and the other parent providing a 1 and a 2, the children would all need a mix of only these numbers."

"Yes," Teddy said.

"The two circles to the left have the numbers 4, 5, and 8," I remarked. "The circle on the right has a 1 and a 9."

"That's right. There's a story here and you can read it," Jonathan said. "The note was in your file and it's meant for your eyes. Before you begin, let me mention that just because this paper is in your file, it may have nothing to do with you."

"Bullshit," I said, "but I admire your diplomacy. I'm pretty sure that both Teddy and I are represented in this diagram." I grabbed a pencil off the kitchen counter and jotted down the numbers. I was buying time because it was easy enough to see the outcome of the diagram. My hand was shaking slightly, and I decided to dispense with the charade and state the obvious.

"Two of the children, the circles to the far left, are not related to these parents because neither child shares that cell thing with either parent," I said.

"An allele," Jonathan said. "It's called an allele."

"Okay. But, this child, to the right, is related to one of the parents because they have one allele matching one parent. If Teddy and I are the circles to the left, then this diagram would show that my parents adopted twins."

"Oh CeCe." Trina gripped my arm. "I'm so sorry."

"Are you kidding? That may be the best news I've heard in weeks," I laughed. The revelation, although astonishing and completely unexpected, was encouraging, if only because it would explain a lifetime in exile. Of course my father disliked me. We weren't even related! And as for Mom, her lack of maternal instinct now had meaning. Maybe these were just two wealthy people who adopted simply to fill up space on their annual Christmas card.

"But," Jonathan said, giving me a nudge to continue.

"Well, I guess it also shows that one of my adopted parents had another child by birth. This is just supposition, but I'm wondering if my mother may have come to the marriage pregnant, lost the child and then adopted Teddy and me with my father. Her depression may have come from this loss.

Or maybe she gave that child up for adoption, yet another possible reason for her depression."

Cheski turned the paper over and pointed to the markings on the back, "How 'bout this, Einstein. What do you make of all these Xs and Ys."

"Basic biology," Jonathan answered. "Male DNA contains an X and a Y chromosome. Females have two Xs."

"I was hoping for a triple X." Charlie smirked.

"Do you ever stop?" I reprimanded him. Then I turned to Jonathan. "So basically, this key on the back shows which circles are males and which are females. I'll be able to find out if Teddy and I had a stepsister or stepbrother. Is it step? Or half? Whatever."

Jonathan turned the paper front to back a few times, making mental notes of the chromosomal key. He grunted a few times, seemingly lost in his own thoughts. "Maybe."

"Here, let me do it." I grabbed for the pencil again. The Xs and Ys were multiplying, and it was no longer as simple to decipher the diagram. I flipped the paper over a few times, making notations of gender in each of the circles. As I penciled in the last of the circles, my hand slowed to a screeching halt.

"Oh my god, this can't be," I said as the room spun around in a blurry haze. I was stumbling and falling despite being seated and felt as destitute as I had the night I found out Teddy was gone. Even that could not match the depths of my sorrow at this particular moment. "Jonathan," I wailed, "tell me I'm wrong. Please."

"I can't." Jonathan opened up his arms and let me fall into his chest. "I'm sorry, CeCe. I wasn't expecting this."

Charlie was the first to break my grip on Jonathan. "Come on. Don't hold it in."

I read the diagram, my voice weepy and thin. I wanted my friends to be the first to know what had struck me so hard.

"The circle to the left is my father," I began. "He's not related to any of these children. Not one of his numbered alleles is shared by any of the children." The first bomb dropped without protest from my friends. "The circle to the right is my mother. She is related to one of the children. That child is a girl and that child is me." I paused for a second, allowing my friends to digest the information. "The two children to the left are boys. They're not related to these parents. One of the boys must be Teddy. Teddy has a brother, but he doesn't have a sister." I wiped my face with a dish-towel; there was no tissue with enough absorbing power to soak up my tears. "I don't have a brother. I'm not a twin. Teddy's not my brother."

The room exploded in chaos. The news was shattering. Everyone seemed agitated and at a loss for words. Trina simply cried, while Charlie stared into space, his entire childhood landscape upended. Lamendola and Cheski communicated in police terms I did not understand. Everyone seemed as disoriented as if we had been deposited in a circus funhouse. I could only speak for myself, and I felt as if I had lost my brother twice — once to death and once to genetics. Most importantly, none of us knew what to do with this new piece of information. What was Teddy trying to tell me with it? We weren't twins, but that information alone was not enough to complete the picture. So my father adopted twin boys? Since when was that a crime? What happened to the other boy?

"Stop. Everyone stop," I yelled. "Charlie, go get me your laptop." I jolted back from the table with supreme purpose and ran upstairs to my studio. I rummaged through a pile of junk at the foot of my futon and located the still-drying satchel I had carried yesterday as I bicycled home from my parents' house. At the bottom of the bag was the DVD my mother had been watching when I checked in the other day. I charged back down the stairs and instructed Charlie to insert and play the disc.

"My mother was watching these home movies when I went to check on her yesterday. I didn't see the whole thing, but I thought it was strange that I wasn't in the film. Most of what I saw included only Teddy and my parents."

The film booted up and the screen filled with happy families at the beach. My dad, under a brightly stripped umbrella, held Teddy and rocked him to sleep. As with the first viewing, Teddy looked adorable and cozy and completely content. The camera panned wide, picking up my mother as the waves pushed her ashore. Her one-piece suit was wet and clingy, revealing a slim figure with a little extra padding.

"CeCe," Trina said, "I'm embarrassed to say this, but your mom looks kinda pregnant. It's subtle, but she could be four or five months in."

"I think so too. I also think I noticed it the first time I saw the footage, but I blocked it out."

"That would mean that Teddy is older

than you."

"Yes, and based on the timing of this film in late summer, I guess my birthday is not in June."

"More like October," Trina added.

"Now I know why Teddy always hit milestones earlier," I said, remembering how awful I felt that he could ride a bike and swim a year ahead of me. "I could barely roll over when he started to walk. I'll bet he's easily six to eight months older than I am." I watched my mother drying herself with a towel, her face distant and disconnected. The camera paused and when it restarted, it appeared that someone else, maybe my mother, was filming.

"There's another thing I'm noticing now," I said. "When I first saw this at my mother's house, I thought it was our annual vacation to Cape Cod. But look." I pointed to a row of stores in the background. "Those signs are in Italian. This was taken in Italy."

"Oh man," Charlie said, "this is getting too close for comfort."

The camera swept the shore again and refocused on a man walking on the sand toward my parents. The lens zoomed in on the man, singling him out from the crowded beach patrons.

"No!" I screamed at the top of my lungs.

"No, that's insane." I didn't need to sketch this one out with a pencil and paper because I'd already done part of the work for De-Rosa. I knew how to add age to a face, and as a result I had a pretty good idea of how to reverse the lines of time. And I knew for certain that the man walking toward the camera was Peter Dacks, alias Piotr Dackow, looking thirty years younger.

"That's Peter Dacks," I screeched, jabbing my finger at the screen.

"No fucking way," Charlie said loudly.

"Believe me, it's him. His teeth are bad and his hair isn't as blond, but damn it, that's Peter Dacks. Wait until he gets closer."

The man walked to the umbrella and it was obvious from his casual demeanor that he knew my father. He knelt down in the sand and for a quick second was out of the frame. When he came back into focus, he sat next to my father and cradled a second baby boy. Every last molecule of air in the room disappeared, sucked deep into our collective lungs.

Charlie pressed pause and we sat there frozen, all of us, staring wide-eyed at the screen. It was faint, but behind me I heard something whispery, a breath and then a gulp. I turned my head slowly, moving Jonathan aside with my arm to get a better look.

DeRosa was watching the screen from behind us. I had no idea how long he had been standing there. He seemed to be equally as mesmerized by the video. He was stone-faced, but something foreign and unfamiliar was pooling in the corner of his eyes. Tears — surely a novelty for Detective Frank DeRosa — formed like rain drops and rolled down his cheeks.

"Frank," I said, and the entire room turned in unison. "Is it you? The other boy in the video?"

"I believe so," he said, his voice bereft and wan.

THIRTY-FOUR

DeRosa walked into the room, shaking hands with the men and hugging Trina.

"*You're* Teddy's twin?" I said, almost in awe of his presence, a near biological replica of Teddy.

"I am."

"How did you find out?"

"The pictures you sketched. I had heard my parents talk about Bonetti in passing as a child. Not often, but every once in a while. The town came up when we found out about Naomi. I thought the connection was too strange, so I went to see my parents right after leaving Harbor House." He pulled a chair from the kitchen table and then rubbed his face, as if he couldn't contain his own disbelief. "It was difficult for them to admit. My parents are good, loving people and they only wanted the best for me."

"Are they your parents?" I asked.

"No, they're not. They were living in Bonetti, a childless couple, struggling financially. My mother went to a clinic in Yugoslavia, an hour's drive across the border, to find out why she couldn't have children. Fertility intervention in a Roman Catholic country was unavailable at the time. There she met a man I suspect to be Peter Dacks. He offered my parents the deal of a lifetime: he would get them a baby boy and help them resettle in New York. They handed over their measly savings and agreed to take a baby without asking questions."

"So what did you do with my pictures?"

"I went to Bonetti hoping to find someone who looked like me, maybe my father. It was a long shot."

"Did you find anyone?" I asked.

"No, but I was able to get some information. I showed your photo to every storekeeper in the town and the same name kept coming up: Margiotta. Then I went to the local police and between the last name, my year of birth, and the sketches, they felt able to make some calls to the Margiotta family. I spoke to this man." DeRosa pulled out his cell phone to show me the photo of a man in his mid-fifties. The similarity between my sketch and the man was uncanny. "If my assumptions are correct," DeRosa said, "he may be an uncle. We chatted for a while, and I showed him the sketches and explained my predicament. He had a brother who disappeared at seventeen. This brother had a girlfriend at the time, and the families had been worried she was pregnant. That's all he knew, but I suspect the girlfriend gave birth in this same clinic that my mother attended, and the clinic is probably associated with Naomi's shady medical school."

"How does my father fit in?" I asked, passing the cell phone picture around the room for the others to see.

"That part is ugly, CeCe." DeRosa hung his head in dismay. "I'm not sure I'm ready to talk about it. It's too personal."

"We've come this far," I pleaded.

Jonathan motioned to the rest of group, and my roommates left the house without making a noise. DeRosa whispered to Lamendola and Cheski, and they patted each other on the backs, shaking hands the way people do at funerals.

"Can we go up to the studio?" DeRosa said.

"Sure," I said, and we made our way to the spot of our initial meeting. I remembered it clearly because that first night, I despised him and his overconfident tone. This time, however, his bravado had been

364

defused. Unfortunately, that made me nervous; I had come to rely on DeRosa's steadfast control.

I flicked on the light and he made a beeline to my portraits, setting aside the paintings I had done of him. He stood back to study my work.

"I need to tell you something and at the risk of sounding dramatic, it's the closest thing I've seen to pure evil."

"You're upsetting me." A million thoughts raced through my mind, fighting for answers I didn't have. *How did Teddy and Frank get separated? Who was my father? What did my mother know? Did I have other siblings?*

"I don't mean to scare you, so let me qualify this conversation. Although we have uncovered many facts in the case, some of what I'm about to say is supposition."

"I trust you."

"Okay, here goes." He went on to unravel a story so spellbinding I was afraid to budge for fear of missing an important detail.

"Teddy and I have a number of recessive features in common. As you pointed out, we both have attached earlobes and we both have a hint of a cleft chin. But you know from your paintings that we are not identical. I can see here," DeRosa said as he gestured to a canvas, "the way you started to sketch my eyes, it's not exactly the same as Teddy. However, the similarities are almost spooky. It bothered me initially. I'd never worked on a case where I resembled the victim. And I know it threw your mother for a loop."

"Can't fraternal twins have things in common?"

"Yes, but Teddy and I have too much in common."

"But you're not identical twins?"

"No, we're not. It would have been obvious if we were. I did some research. Actually, the director at the medical school in Slovenia, where Teddy and I were born, explained it to me after pulling our file. Our conception is called polar body twinning, a rare version of twins. A thorough DNA analysis would confirm this."

"Explain," I said.

"Identical twins share a hundred percent of their DNA."

"Okay," I said.

"And that's because identical twins form from a single fertilized egg that splits in two."

"Jonathan explained the egg-and-sperm combinations to me earlier. Fraternal twins are no different than siblings, and that's why they don't necessarily look alike. Two eggs, two sperm. So what are these polar body twins?"

"Apparently, it's unusual but there's a chance an egg can split *before* it's fertilized and subsequently meet two separate sperm. In that case, the twins are almost identical, sharing seventy-five percent of their genetic material. A close but not perfect match." DeRosa's face turned grave. "I think your father ultimately searched for identical twins, but Teddy and I were the next best thing."

"Searched? You're losing me."

"Do you remember when you explained the concept of epigentics to me? The ability to alter but not change DNA. You said Teddy explained to you that some geneticists believe extreme external factors can trigger switches on a DNA strand, essentially turning the switches on or off. A person programmed to handle stress can be deprogrammed as a result of negative stimuli."

"Okay, I remember that conversation."

"I think your father is testing this epigenetics theory with Teddy and me."

"That's insane."

"I know, but hear me out. Your father . . ."

"Stop there," I interrupted, holding both my palms forward. "Call him anything else but my father. I'm disgusted."

"The man is still your father," DeRosa said calmly.

"Oh no, you must have come in a few minutes too late," I said with pure pleasure. "William Prentice is not my father. Jonathan helped me decipher Teddy's medical notes on my family's genetic tree. I have no idea who my father is, but I can say with complete confidence that I'm not related to that bastard."

Frank practically fell backward onto the futon. The frame shifted under his weight and he caught his head in his hands and started to laugh uncontrollably.

"Did you think that maybe we were all related?" I asked, but he kept on laughing. "Frank, seriously. Don't tell me you sat on that plane for umpteen hours thinking that you, me, *and* Teddy were siblings."

I grabbed a clean painting rag and helped Frank wipe the tears from his eyes. He was emotionally spent not to mention jet-lagged. He regained his composure momentarily, bracing his hand on a ceiling beam as he stood. "I've barely slept in the last four days. I have no idea what I'm thinking. I'm relieved to learn, however, that you are not a half-sister or first cousin or whatever."

"So now my genetics aren't good enough

for you?" I feigned offense to lighten the mood.

"Your genetics are just fine," DeRosa said. "In fact, they're more than fine. This issue is my genetics and the game that man attempted to play with my life."

"Go on. Tell me."

"Dr. Prentice's life work focused on two medical fronts. Decode the human genome and then figure out how to manipulate it. To test the manipulation theory, he took two nearly identical babies and separated them shortly after birth. He gave one baby all the many privileges a wealthy family could afford, and he gave the other baby nothing. Worse, he did everything in his power to limit the second baby's opportunities."

At this point, DeRosa's anger swelled and his took on a sharper and more forceful tone. "He gave the baby to a poor, uneducated family and then deposited them in a rundown slum in Freeport, a crime-ridden area with a lousy school system. The boy's parents were immigrants in an unfamiliar country. They did not speak English, nor did they ever master the language, thereby increasing the chances the boy would fail. Then Dr. Prentice watched both boys in hopes that external factors would send them on opposing paths despite having almost identical DNA. If the baby in the negative environment faltered while the baby in the positive environment thrived, then his theory would be supported. Nurture over nature. Our genetics could be overcome."

"But it didn't work, did it?" I said.

"Not at all. A failed human experiment. Given the constraints of my life, I excelled. Maybe my environs limited my ability to become a doctor, which frankly I never considered, but it didn't prohibit me from rising to the top of my profession."

"Both you and Teddy succeeded because essentially you have the same makeup, and that must be some wonderful DNA. You have both led lives packed with achievement."

"Thank you, CeCe," DeRosa said, and I detected a soft blush.

"Why did my father —" I quickly corrected myself. "I mean, Dr. Prentice. Why did Dr. Prentice request you for the case?"

"Because he knew I'd find the answer. He realized that despite my childhood, which he orchestrated, I grew up to be as smart as Teddy. Ultimately he wanted the truth to come out, and I was his best bet." Then he added, "I also think he thought my life could be in danger. Dacks might have come after me next, but if I hadn't been involved in the case, I would have been caught off-guard. I have to assume that your father wanted to prevent more killing."

"How so?"

"Remember when my personal files were stolen from my condo in Freeport? It was mostly medical information from my police work-up. I think someone else was trying to confirm my identity so they could use me as leverage against Dr. Prentice."

"Peter Dacks," I said. "Peter Dacks helped him get access to you and Teddy. According to the FBI, his primary business was falsified paperwork, hence your immigration to the United States as well as your parents. But maybe at some point he lost track of you."

"Yes, and I think Dr. Prentice wanted Peter Dacks stopped. But if he tipped us off to Dacks, his knowledge would have tied him back to the case. He seemed pleased when we uncovered the Relativity.com link to Dacks. If he let me uncover the truth, there was still a possibility he could come off clean. As it stands, we may have only figured out Dacks was pushing Teddy, leaving Dr. Prentice innocent. That's why he needed me to solve the case without his assistance. As I mentioned to you earlier, I also suspect that Dacks has been blackmailing him for years. I believe Dr. Prentice set him up in business not expecting he would actually build a legitimate concern and then turn on the labs."

"That makes sense," I added. "Peter Dacks was a low-level con artist in Eastern Europe. After helping arrange your illegal adoption, he probably tracked my father's rise and then decided it was time for a bigger payoff," I said, letting the facts accumulate.

DeRosa took to pacing again, a sure sign his wheels were turning. I was hoping his cathartic outpouring would loosen him, but he was still wound tight.

"Frank, come sit next to me," I urged. "What you're telling me is life-altering; you can't just walk it off."

He picked up speed, rounding my easel at full stride before stopping in front of me. With his bottom lip shoved forward, he looked as if he were preparing to physically wrestle the unwieldy mound of information into submission. "I think Dr. Prentice's crimes may have involved more than an illegal adoption," he asserted, "I think the adoption was a sidebar to a more serious crime."

"Don't tell me you found something else

in Italy," I said, wondering if my head could find a spare corner for more bad news. "Can we take a break?" I pleaded, as the stress of the investigation enveloped me like a thick fog. For a split second, I felt that if I didn't stand immediately, I wouldn't be able to. Before DeRosa had a chance to answer, I got up from my painting stool and walked toward him, placing my hands on either side of his unshaven face. I pulled him closer until I could feel his breath on my cheek. "Please," I whispered softly in his ear, "Do me a favor," I let my lip rest gently on his earlobe, "don't eat any macadamia nuts before this is over."

"I promise," DeRosa laughed softly. Then it was his turn. "Will you do me a favor too?"

"Certainly."

"Kiss me."

I did. And it was wonderful until he grasped my shoulders and pushed me back, leaving an awkward gap between us. "Is this weird?" he asked, swallowing hard.

"Completely, but I'm willing to ignore it if you are."

"You're *sure* we're not related?" he begged.

"Not a chance in hell."

We stared at each other for quite some

time. I looked hard into his eyes, so hard I could count the flecks of amber gold highlighting his dark brown orbs. I accepted that if it didn't happen soon, it never would and just as I was about to give up hope, he kissed me again. But this time he embraced me like I wasn't the sister of his twin brother, or anyone's sister for that matter. He kissed me like a man who had been harboring a deep and passionate crush on a woman who was equally entranced.

We held each other, forcing time to stand still and wait for us while we lingered in a kiss so deep I felt as if I was falling through the floor. I could have held that pose for an eternity, knowing with unwavering conviction that I was meant to be in his arms. I felt his hand rise along my neck and grasp the back of my head. In one swift movement, he shoved me to the floor.

THIRTY-FIVE

"Stay down," DeRosa yelled as he rolled my body behind the folded futon.

"What the hell?" I screamed, but my protests were drowned out by the shattering blast of glass exploding across the attic floor.

He darted for the light switch, but not before another round of fire shot through the broken window. The room went dark and I reached my hand out, searching frantically for DeRosa. Without making a sound, he grabbed my wrist and slid me across the floor about five feet from the door. His hand was sticky and warm, and I started to feel faint.

"What's the layout of the roof?" his voice low and hushed.

"Uh, there's a short catwalk that leads to the lookout tower." I cried when I realized that the shooter was mere feet from my attic studio. "We can't stay here," I croaked.

DeRosa stuck out his leg, making contact

with a half-gallon can of paint. "Listen closely. I'm going to heave this paint can through the window. The second the can passes the glass, you head for the door. I'll be right behind you." I nodded and filled my lungs with enough air to fuel my impending sprint.

DeRosa bowed his head as he silently counted to three. The paint can arched through the darkness, the thick liquid causing it to wobble unevenly. I watched as the moon lit up the silvery label and then I took off like a rabbit on a racetrack. With DeRosa hot on my heels, I covered my head as another spray of bullets riddled the wall behind me.

The stairs from the attic to the second floor were built for people who died almost two centuries ago. DeRosa's oversized frame took a beating as we tumbled down the steps with me in the lead. With his hand on my shoulder, he forced me to keep up the speed and within seconds I spotted the hinges on the solid oak door at the bottom of the staircase, which unfortunately was closed. I reached for the wrought-iron knob, but the door unexpectedly flung open.

I screamed at the top of my lungs, expecting to see a killer. I fell back onto DeRosa, who took the full force of the fall on his tailbone. I heard a pained huff behind me as I was tossed into the air and over the door's threshold, straight into Charlie.

"What the fuck?" Charlie had one hand on the door and the other gripping a hockey stick. "Igor is on our fucking roof with a shotgun!"

DeRosa stumbled to a standing position, a trickle of blood oozing from a wound on his shoulder. He slammed the door behind him, cutting off the only access to the attic. "Is that a positive ID, Charlie?"

"Damn straight," Charlie said, swinging his stick in hopes that he'd connect with Igor's head. "I just caught him on the security camera. I ran up here right when he pulled off his first round."

DeRosa grabbed the hockey stick from Charlie and shoved it through the door handle as a makeshift bolt.

"What's the fastest way to the roof?" The urgency was spurred by the sound of a heavy footstep on the floor above us.

Charlie grabbed DeRosa's good arm and hustled him into a linen closet two doors down from the attic entry. At the far end of the linen closet was a window. Charlie yanked hard on the old-fashioned sash and pointed to a fire escape about four feet to the left of the window.

"It's a bit of a leap," he said as the detective swung his leg over the paint-chipped sill.

"Get Jonathan and grab some tools," DeRosa directed. "Once I'm safely on the ladder, you need to dismantle the lower half of the fire escape so Igor can't get back down."

"But Frank," I said, "you'll be trapped in the attic with Igor."

He swung his other leg over the window. "Too bad for him."

THIRTY-SIX

DeRosa's hand was slick with blood, and I could see he was having trouble gripping the metal fire escape. I quickly tossed him a towel to sop up the blood, which had left a trail across the brick exterior of the building. He heaved himself up the ladder, his muscular thighs working overtime to compensate for the wound in his shoulder. His torso disappeared into the darkness above, but not before I caught a glimpse of the revolver strapped to his leg. I heard movement below and prayed that Igor was still in the attic and not climbing up after DeRosa. I looked down and watched as Jonathan and Charlie began methodically unscrewing the ladder bolts, effectively trimming fifteen feet off the fire escape from the ground up.

Before I had chance to imagine a scuffle between DeRosa and Igor, a single shot popped like a firecracker, followed by an ungodly wail. I covered my ears as if I were a child wishing away the boogey man, but the screaming continued. The thought of Frank writhing in agony was more than I could take. Losing Teddy had been beyond my control, but no one, including Igor, would take Frank away from me.

I ran back to the attic stairs. With one quick jerk, I removed the hockey stick from the door handle and opened the attic door. I stood at the landing, my legs spaced firmly below me. I gave myself sixty seconds to take stock of my life. This was not the first time Igor and I had crossed paths; by my count, I was winning simply because I was still alive. That was all the encouragement I needed. Let Igor be afraid this time.

My steps were nimble and practiced, having climbed this route repeatedly over the last ten years. Without a doubt, I knew I could make it to the top without disturbing even one cranky floorboard. I managed each step with care. The door at the top of the stairs was slightly ajar, providing a sliver of a sightline. The attic room was long and narrow, covering the entire length of the house. From my vantage point, I spotted four legs splayed prone on the ground in the farthest corner of the room. I poked my head through the door to get a better view and didn't like what I saw.

DeRosa's and Igor's bodies were wrapped so tightly I had difficulty determining where one began and the other ended. Their physical strength was so evenly matched that neither could move the other an inch. Despite the difference in their sizes — Igor short and stocky and DeRosa with his beef and brawn — they were deadlocked in an inextricable hug. The only variable left to consider was endurance. At some point, one of them would break.

I was discreet in my movements, making the most of each step. Working in my favor was the position of Igor's head. If I approached from the left and remained on a course aligned perfectly with the top of his crown, I'd avoid any chances of being caught in his peripheral view. An art table stocked with painting paraphernalia was located about ten feet from me. If I was careful, I could nab something on the table and brandish it as a weapon. In this case, my choices were limited to a handful of paintbrushes with very pointy tips.

Working against me was DeRosa, who had at this point spotted me. He was careful not to look up and alert Igor, but I grasped his message in one quick glance. He wanted me out of the room and fast. But he already knew I didn't take orders well.

Against his wishes, I moved forward, reaching tentatively for the art table and sliding the nearest paintbrush through my fingers. I ran my palm along the tip, putting pressure on the brush to feel its sharpness. DeRosa shook his head as my steps came even closer. When I was no more than three feet away, I saw the reason for his warning. Igor's wrist was pinned down by DeRosa's bursting, bloody forearm. Clenched in Igor's fist was a gun, and his finger was securely around the trigger. DeRosa's arm was shaking furiously and although I had been prepared to see the wound in his arm I could see that the shot I'd heard had torn into his other arm. I drew the paintbrush high into the air, as if swinging an axe and then, with all my might, pierced the fleshy part of Igor's forearm just above his wrist.

Igor screamed bloody murder. His painful grunts were raw and throaty, with an animalistic quality that tore at my ears. My action had caught him so off-guard that he couldn't mimic a human sob. The stabbing was swift, causing his reflexes to respond against his will. As a result, his palm opened like a flower blooming in fast forward. I watched as his hand released and the gun slid a few inches from his grip. If there was a time to strike, it was now.

I pounced on the weapon, grabbing it like a hot potato. It was warm from his touch, the way a metallic necklace feels mere minutes after taking it off. It was also wet with sweat, causing me to fumble. I slapped my hands together in one last desperate attempt to calm the weapon, but my index finger caught the trigger and the gun let out a round of fire that lit up the room like the Fourth of July. I screeched like the audience at a horror film as the gun kicked back, dove to the ground, and twirled across the floorboards.

I watched it rotate and with my fingers crossed, stuck my foot out at the exact moment the nose of the gun was pointing away from my body. I squatted, picked up the gun, turned, and pointed at Igor, who was frantically trying to dislodge the paintbrush from his forearm.

With the gun directed safely at Igor, DeRosa pulled his elbow back at a ninety-degree angle and slammed his fist directly into the man's jaw. The blow knocked him unconscious and left blood smeared across his mouth.

"Showoff," I muttered as I lowered the gun to my side.

"Amateur," DeRosa said, pretending to catch a weapon in midair.

"You realize I'm still holding a gun," I said as he approached me with a smile so transparent I was almost embarrassed. He peeled my fingers off the gun, checked the barrel, and set the safety. Then he leaned into me and kissed me softly on the cheek. "You're a cop's fantasy," he whispered, sending a warm thrill down my body.

Then he turned and walked back to Igor. He stopped at my art table and dunked a paintbrush into a can of turpentine. He knelt down over Igor, slowly waving the brush under his nose until Igor twitched at the smell. Then he slapped him with an open palm and shook his head until Igor's bleary eyes opened. Before Igor could get his bearings, DeRosa dragged his beaten body across the room, shoving his squat back against the wall. He dug his hand under Igor's chin, pinning him to the wooden slats in a chokehold. As he squeezed Igor's neck harder with the better of his two arms, a small trickle of blood formed on his sleeve.

"Here's how it works," he said as Igor came to, "I'm going to ask you questions. You answer yes or no. If I like your answers, your daughter walks. You fuck up and you'll both spend the rest of your life in a dank, dark, cement block cell in Siberia."

Igor moved his head an inch indicating his agreement.

"Your wife died fifteen years ago in a clinical drug trial in Slovenia," DeRosa asserted.

"Yes," Igor answered although it sounded more like *ja*.

"Your brother-in-law, Peter Dacks, helped recruit patients for the test."

I could see he wanted to confirm Becky's story.

"Yes."

DeRosa tilted his head slightly in my direction before asking his next question. "The doctor who conducted the trial was Dr. William Prentice, head of Sound View Laboratories. The trial subjected healthy people to unapproved drugs that ultimately killed them."

"Yes," Igor answered again.

I gasped at the shocking revelation. It was his eureka moment. Detective Frank DeRosa had discovered Dr. William Prentice's big secret: he had conducted unreported drug trials in a foreign country with disastrous results. Healthy people died due to his greed and negligence. In the medical world, it was the type of black mark no amount of backpedaling could erase.

"Peter Dacks successfully blackmailed Dr. Prentice, threatening to reveal the deadly results of the failed trials in exchange for DNA samples."

"Yes."

"He arranged for your daughter, Becky, to deliver cookies to Dr. Theodore Prentice."

Igor grew agitated at the mention of Becky's name. "She don't know," he pleaded.

"We'll get to that in a minute," DeRosa said. "The doctor had figured out the blackmailing scheme and was prepared to go to the press to put an end to a very old secret."

"Yes."

"After Dr. Theodore Prentice's death, Dacks sent you to threaten his daughter, Constance Prentice, as a message that more killing would occur if he didn't stay in line."

"Yes."

"But threatening Constance Prentice wasn't good enough for you." DeRosa tightened his grip as Igor strained to look away. "Answer," he yelled, while, with his other hand, he banged Igor's head against the wall.

"Yes," Igor responded as he shifted his eyes.

Instead of staring down DeRosa, Igor swung his steely eyes in my direction, and I felt his hatred burn through me like hot wax on my skin.

"You wanted Dr. Prentice's family dead. You were seeking revenge for the death of your wife."

Igor's mouth turned down as his red-rimmed lids filled with water. He tried to push the detective backward, but DeRosa held firm. Igor yelled a name I did not recognize, but I assumed it was the name of his dead wife, Becky's mother. The sheer force of his effort drained his broken soul and he sank back on the wall, his shoulders collapsing.

"You stick to those answers," DeRosa said, "and your daughter's safe. You help me with one more thing, and I may even arrange a plea bargain for you."

The man's eyes filled with hope at the prospect of freedom. I wasn't sure where DeRosa was going, but I was almost certain life would be very difficult for me with Igor on the loose.

I listened intently as DeRosa outlined a way to trap Peter Dacks in his own web of lies. The plan was simple. All Igor had to do was have a scripted conversation with Dacks to capture his guilt firsthand, making Igor the prosecution's silver bullet.

Igor nodded once more and this time, it was clear that he truly meant it.

THIRTY-SEVEN

Choppy waves swirled as the wind kicked up over Long Island Sound, making the marine patrol boat bounce around. I lost my footing a handful of times before taking a seat on a plastic floatation device next to FBI Agent David Swell.

"Ms. Prentice," he said, "you've made a habit of keeping the FBI busy."

"I like to see my tax dollar at work," I responded, grabbing Swell's shoulder as the boat careened over a tsunami-sized white cap before landing with a jolting thud. "Can a boat like this crack?"

"Anything is possible in this case," Swell laughed into the sea breezes, his perfectly combed hair remaining unnaturally in place.

"So what's our job?" I asked.

"We wait," he said and then added, "The truth is that most police work is waiting and watching."

What an understatement. We'd been circling the shore of Connecticut for the last hour and my virgin sea legs had given way to a nasty bout of seasickness. The Relativity .com offices appeared like a small-scale house on a train set, while Dacks's yacht bobbed about at leisure two hundred yards away. DeRosa had instructed Igor to meet with Dacks at Relativity.com's offices Thursday morning as if nothing had happened. Dacks was unaware that both Becky and her father had been picked up by the police the previous day. With Becky detained in a cell, Igor — I still couldn't think of him as Stash Volwitz, despite hearing his entire story multiple times — was highly motivated to follow through on the plan. Unfortunately, Igor was not a natural student and his repeated mistakes in the scripted conversation had frazzled DeRosa, who was jet-lagged and injured, not to mention emotionally paralyzed by his own personal drama.

"Repeat after me," he had said hours earlier in the interrogation room at the station. "Does the doctor know you sent Becky to kill his son?"

"The doctor knows you killed his son," Igor misstated.

"No," DeRosa had said with frustration, growing acutely aware of the man's language deficiencies. "Try it again and get it right this time."

Our boat cut through the waves as smoothly as a baby carriage being shoved through a rock quarry. The constant slapping broke down what little resolve I could muster. Apparently, my inability to control my impulses had banned me from the premium seating section in the parking lot of Relativity.com's corporate offices. De-Rosa, Cheski, and Lamendola were all positioned strategically on solid ground, while I had been relegated to the offshore nosebleed seats under the careful supervision of Agent Swell. Our surveillance did serve a purpose, as Swell reminded me more than once.

"If Dacks leaves land and points his yacht toward international waters, you'll get to see some action," he said. "We are plan B, and that means waiting for plan A to fail."

"Waiting is not one of my talents." I pushed my hair aside and felt a wadded, salty knot forming at the nape of my neck. "How much longer?"

Swell referenced his watch and then dialed DeRosa's cell. "What are we looking at?"

I was sitting close enough to Swell for me to hear Frank's response. "Igor's been inside for about twenty minutes."

Then I heard his tone change, his voice

x

390

get a bit louder.

"Wait a second. We got a live one. Igor is leaving the building and he's giving us the signal." I heard a commotion of slamming doors and footsteps as the police team made its way in.

I grabbed the pair of binoculars Swell promised me and focused the ocular dial on the building. "I can't see a damn thing with the boat bouncing like this," I whined as the binoculars slammed the bridge of my nose. "What's going on?" I turned to Swell, who shook his head at my impatience. "Right, I get it. I have to wait."

I sat back down and was rewarded with a trill of Swell's cell phone. He tapped the screen, peered at it, and handed me the phone. "There's your money shot." Sure enough, there was a photo of Peter Dacks, his hands secured behind his back, being escorted across the parking lot by Detective Frank DeRosa. Underneath the latter's long-sleeved shirt were two thick bandages covering a total of seventeen stitches, wounds he had earned solving his twin brother's murder. The man he strong-armed across the parking lot was not only the mastermind behind the murder but the one who had helped tear him and his brother apart in infancy. Within weeks, my life had been turned upside down, but it wasn't about me any longer. This was Frank's life, and that included all the time stolen from him and Teddy.

Swell's phone rang in my hand. I politely handed the phone to him. He spoke to the caller and then passed it to me.

"Frank?"

"We got him."

"You sure did," I said in congratulations and then lowered my voice. "I'm wondering if you want to see my mother. She's leaving for rehab today."

"It's next on my list."

THIRTY-EIGHT

The drive to my parents' house was somber. Teddy had been gone almost a month, but we knew we were close. With Dacks in police custody, the danger of the investigation downshifted, taking on a more personal tone. DeRosa had a right to hear his own story, uncover his own truth. He had laid out a strategy that bordered on entrapment with elements I felt were unethical and downright mean. However, I vowed to stand by him. On some level I knew he was right, but his plan, unfortunately, had cast my mother as a central figure.

"CeCe, this is a typical police setup. We do it all the time." He checked the main road for traffic before turning down my parents' street. "Your mother is the weak link and in a game of prisoner's dilemma, you need a weak link."

"What the hell is prisoner's dilemma? Is my mother going to prison?!"

"Most likely no, but if she thinks she is then she'll rat out her husband or Peter Dacks or any of the players she has knowledge of. That's the concept of the prisoner's dilemma. The subject asks himself, should I lie or should I pin it on the other guy in order to save my own hide? In almost every case, the weak link breaks and spills the truth, which is ultimately used as evidence against the other players."

"Well, since my mother is already broken, I don't think it will take much to get her talking." I wondered how far I would allow him to push my mother before I intervened.

We pulled up to in the circular drive and I realized my family home was becoming strangely familiar to me again. I had been a no-show for years, but I'd made many visits in the last two weeks. Pointing out the best spot to park on the circular drive, I checked for the light in my father's library. The doctor, it appeared, was out.

DeRosa rang the doorbell.

"Really?" I said, "We can go right in, you know."

"I want your mother to assume this is police business. In that case, I can't enter the home without permission."

"Shit, you're really playing the part."

"I hear footsteps."

Norma opened the door and a welcoming smile filled her face when she saw me. I felt like a turncoat, and I had tremendous remorse knowing I was about to disappoint this kind woman. She cared for my mother, and our visit would be difficult for the maid to understand.

"Miss CeCe, you come back?"

"Yes, Norma. Would you mind bringing my mother to the door?"

With a worried look on her face, Norma scurried away. Eventually my mother appeared at the front door and I could tell she was nursing what was possibly the worst hangover of her life. She squinted, her hand shielding her face from the sun, as if every ray were drilling down on her pounding head.

"May I help you?"

She had not even registered my presence.

"Elizabeth Prentice, you have the right to remain silent." DeRosa did not hesitate in his delivery of Miranda rights even as my mother wilted like a water-deprived plant. The scene was intense and I wanted nothing more than to plead for her innocence, but I needed to hear it from her first.

"Please come in," she croaked.

Finally seeing me next to DeRosa, she searched my blank gaze for an answer. We followed her limp figure back to the atrium, where she gratefully took up her spot on her lounge.

"What is my crime?"

DeRosa remained standing as he addressed her. "Illegal adoption and kidnapping across international waters."

"Just tell me what you want from me without accusing me."

And just like that, she folded. Exactly as DeRosa had anticipated. Given the facts we'd already collected, her story was not remotely far-fetched. He had already deduced most of the twists and turns covering a thirty-year span. However, it was more powerful coming from someone who'd actually lived the story — my mother, my real mother.

"I met your father in Italy by chance, at a café, only to find out we were both from the same area on Long Island, just a few towns apart. Our parents were actually acquaintances. We flirted and drank too much. It was a bit of a fling, and then we parted as friends. I traveled back to Germany, where I was involved with a superb Bauhaus artist."

"My father?"

"Yes, CeCe, your biological father," my mother confirmed. "I'm sorry, but it would never have worked." She reached for my hand, and I struggled to accept that the past was just that. Not to say that I wasn't intrigued by this man, my real father, but twenty-eight years had gone by. Another few minutes in the dark wouldn't make a difference.

"The relationship was tumultuous. We fought constantly, but at times we were very much in love. You were a product of one of those moments. Always remember that."

"But I have a father? Right?" I pleaded. "Somewhere out there, I have a biological father?"

"You do."

"Is he alive?" I asked and then turned to DeRosa. "I'm sorry to get off track, but I need to know."

"Go ahead," he nodded.

"Well, I wasn't sure until recently, but I was curious, just as you are, so Norma showed me how to Google." My mother almost whispered the word as if Googling were code for illicit activities.

"And?" I said literally sitting on the edge of the patio chair.

"He's alive and well, still painting in Berlin."

"Wow," I exhaled with astonishment.

I couldn't believe how a few lies had

snowballed into an interconnected tangle of deception. I let my mother's revelation sit for a second before returning to the task at hand. I had more questions, many more, but a strange calm came over me when I learned my real father was alive. I also felt a kind of relief knowing that my mother had experienced love. It was quietly depressing growing up in a home devoid of passion. At the least, I now knew my mother had felt fulfillment and joy, and that I was somehow a piece of it. I could see in her face that she had been genuinely excited at searching for her past love online. She must have been searching my face for signs of him over the years. In the midst of the craziness, it was a bittersweet thought, but it didn't mask the issue at hand.

"Mom, you have to help Frank now. Can you finish your story?"

"By spring I was pregnant with you, but the relationship was over and I refused to terminate. Your grandmother got involved and put pressure on me. I sought your father out and I thought maybe we could make a go of it. Before I knew it, William and I were married."

"Did Dad know you were pregnant?"

"I'm sure he did, but he chose to ignore it. Talking of pregnancy was a little too gauche for him. He may have told himself you were his," she said. "We never discussed it."

"Why did he marry you?"

"For appearances. A prominent doctor needs an attractive wife." My mother caught her words self-consciously. "At least in those days, I was attractive. Anyway, he needed to be married, but he knew he wasn't programmed for a life-partnering. But I came from the right family and because I was independent, he knew he could leave me alone without complaint."

"What about the other babies? Teddy and me?" DeRosa asked.

"Theodore and Franklin," she corrected. "I believe he chose those names because he had great admiration for the Roosevelt family. You can see his library is filled with books on the Roosevelts."

"I didn't realize Dr. Prentice named me," DeRosa said, clenched teeth holding back his anger. I could see it irked him, like a permanent tattoo he despised. "Mrs. Prentice, I have to ask you," he went on, "what was your involvement in our abduction and separation?"

My mother was visibly offended by Frank's accusation. "I was a mother," she said defensively. "I knew Teddy was not my own, but I loved him dearly. As the years passed, I made no distinction between Teddy and CeCe." She squared her shoulders and addressed DeRosa directly. "I would have done the same had it been you, and it easily could have been." She lowered her head, and I'm sure she was reflecting on her involvement in all of our lives. "I may not have been perfect, but I loved my children and I did my best by them."

"You did, Mom," I reassured her. "Teddy and I loved you." I gave DeRosa an icy stare.

"I'm sorry, Mrs. Prentice," he backpedaled, "and I understand. I know my adopted mother loved me unconditionally, and I'm sure you gave Teddy and CeCe the best possible life. I'll never get back the time with my brother, but I can find some peace knowing he grew up loved." He took a deep breath. "Let me rephrase my question: Can you relate the events that occurred shortly after our birth?"

My mother picked up with her interpretation of the days preceding the twins' immigration to the United States. "We went to Italy in August. It was murderously hot, and I was starting to show. I was uncomfortable and I began to realize that it might be very difficult to remain in a relationship with William. On the trip, I was introduced to a man by the name of Peter Dackow, a business acquaintance of William's. On a beach excursion, Peter brought his twin boys along, and although he was fair-haired, I assumed his wife must have been Italian by the look of the twins. The wife never materialized."

My mother began to choke up at this point, and I began to understand that her substance abuse and depression was a by-product of these happenings. Seeds of sympathy started to sprout and I envisioned my father, domineering and powerful, involving her in a sticky spider's web.

"At the end of the vacation, Peter Dackow met us at the airport." She wiped her eyes delicately with a tissue. "I assumed he was traveling to the United States on business with your father. He got on the airplane and secured these two beautiful babies in their airplane seats . . . and then he got off the aircraft. I screamed frantically for the stewardess while we were taxiing, but it was like no one else spoke English. I assumed Peter had forgotten something in the terminal and the plane took off without him, leaving his children on board. I was hysterical. Your father subdued me with a sleeping pill, assuring me everything would be alright. When we arrived at our house, there was only one baby, Teddy. The other one was gone."

"And you didn't ask Dad what happened?"

My mother's eyes flashed briefly. "Oh, CeCe, please don't underestimate me. I badgered your father incessantly." Her hands started to tremble then, and I could see we were pushing her to the limits of her current condition. "Your father insisted there had been a custody fight between this Peter Dackow and his wife. That he'd accused her of mistreating the boys and this solution would be temporary, and then Peter could resettle and reclaim his sons. He promised me that the other baby was with a friend of Peter's. After a few months, your father came to me and told me that Peter was having trouble with his papers and he was afraid to bring the boys home for fear that his wife's family would kidnap them. Your father told me that we would adopt one of the babies and that he'd found a family for the other child somewhere on Long Island. I was hesitant, but how could I doubt your father? He's a doctor first and foremost, and I couldn't imagine him putting this other baby in harm's way."

My mother wiped tears from her face, and I watched as her head started to twitch along with her hands. I was afraid we'd gone too far into the past, but she kept on talking, as if this were her last chance to tell her story. Her fingers flittered across her face as she spoke. "I was so overwhelmed by the separation of the boys that I began to have trouble functioning. I couldn't bear the thought of twins being separated. They were so adorable, nearly identical. So much so, I wasn't even sure which baby had ended up at our house. As I faltered, your father started hiring more help, so I could rest before you were born, and then after you were born. And, the rest you know, CeCe. You grew up in the house. You remember the bad times."

"I do, Mom," I said as I stroked her hair. "Look, you must realize where this is going. Frank is going to have to bring Dad down to the station. Is he at the labs?"

"Oh no," my mother's words slowed almost to a slur. "He's long gone."

"But I saw him yesterday morning. Where the hell did he go?"

"Gone. Disappeared. He came home from work, emptied the safe, and left."

Instantly, DeRosa pounded on his phone. "Let's hope we can catch him at one of the airports."

My mother dropped her head and studied

her loosely folded hands. Her body went slack, and I was concerned her confession had triggered another emotional attack. I hurried out of the room in search of Norma. I had no idea how she handled my mother in situations like these, but it was as though my mother's body had shifted into an irreparable shutdown. As I rounded the kitchen, I heard a shattering of glass from the atrium.

"Fuck," DeRosa yelled. "Fuck, fuck, fuck." The glass table next to my mother's lounge had splintered into a million pieces from the weight of his fist. My mother appeared oblivious to the upheaval while his hand was dripping in blood, a shard of glass sticking out of the pad by his thumb. He shook the blood from his hand, leaving speckles across my mother's aggrieved face.

"Frank, you have to stop," I yelled as I ran toward my mother, shielding her with my body. "Come on, what are you doing?"

He was at his breaking point, his own personal line in the sand. The details of the case aside, I knew his goal had been to confront my father with enough information to bury him in moral purgatory. There was not a minute from the past thirty years he could retrieve and alter. Though they had lived within a few miles of each other, years had passed while he never met his brother. His only retribution was a showdown with my father. Now it seemed this moment, too, had passed.

"Do you know where Dad is, Mom?"

My mother appeared completely incoherent.

"Mom," I screamed as I shook her shoulders. "Where did Dad go?"

She lifted her head like it weighed a thousand pounds. Her eyes were glassy and loose. They rolled as if the tendons holding her eyes in place were inches too long for their sockets. "A baby," she said in a voice that was almost inaudible, "another baby, Teddy told me." I held her head up with my hands leaning into catch her words. "Find it, CeCe. Bring the baby home." And then her body sunk into itself as her breathing slowed and she sank into a deep slumber.

"Frank," I cried. "It's not over."

THIRTY-NINE

Igor remained true to his word. His gruff voice and thick accent lent an air of drama to the court proceedings, which held spectators spellbound as they heard his damaging portrayal of Peter Dacks as the mastermind behind a scheme of blackmail and death. An up-and-coming assistant district attorney had managed to secure grainy photos of Igor's dead wife, Dacks's sister. The shots, enlarged and mounted on a pair of easels, made a lasting impression on the jury. The photos built Igor's credibility and created sympathy for Becky. Who could resist the story of a young, healthy mother seeking a quick fix to her family's chronic money problems? Wouldn't we all have signed on to what seemed like a legitimate drug trial, especially one organized and endorsed by a family member?

Each time the lawyer motioned to the photos, Becky's eyes would stream freely as some jury members shook their heads in dismay. Enhancing the drama, the lawyer sprinkled his presentation with names of faraway places that seemed to lack a sufficient number of vowels. Even Igor and Becky's hometown had an air of intrigue as the lawyer produced witnesses who described rounds of disastrous medical testing on trusting residents. The lawyer made a point of regularly employing Peter Dacks's real name, Piotr Dackow. Each time the young lawyer crunched through the hard syllables, Dacks sounded guiltier.

Igor's testimony was a crucial piece of the case. To prove Peter Dacks had hired Igor and Becky to kill Teddy and threaten me, the ADA needed to craft a compelling story, casting Dacks as a manipulative sociopath with the singular goal of dominating the scientific world. By presenting Igor and Becky as victims of Dacks's larger plot, the negative emotion of the courtroom shifted away from the father and daughter toward Dacks. A believable story emerged. After moving his widowed brother-in-law and motherless niece to the United States, Peter Dacks revealed to Igor that Dr. William Prentice was solely responsible for his wife's death. He led Igor and Becky to believe that Dr. William Prentice was also hindering his ability to build a profitable scientific research company, the results of which would leave the family wealthy beyond imagining. By promising to expedite their immigration papers, Igor and Becky were easily transformed into Dacks's puppets. He would constantly remind them that Dr. William Prentice was responsible for the death of their loved one, making it easy to coax them into questionable behavior.

On the witness stand, Becky held firm to her innocence. The lawyer posed the same basic question in a variety of formats, and each time she denied any knowledge of Dacks's ulterior motive.

"You assert that you had no idea the cookies contained a potentially lethal ingredient for Dr. Theodore Prentice," the lawyer prompted.

"I did not know," Becky stated.

"Did your uncle at any time lead you to believe that the cookies could cause symptoms of choking?"

"No, he did not."

"Where did you purchase the cookies?"

"I did not purchase the cookies," Becky said, knowing full well her next statement was the case closer. "My uncle gave me the cookies and suggested I bring some to Teddy."

The gasp from the crowd was audible.

Igor's attacks on DeRosa and me were omitted from the trial, since they were considered incidental to the case against Dacks. Unless DeRosa or I pressed charges, technically nothing had occurred in the attic; DeRosa had never filed a report or called in for backup. He and I had discussed it at length as we cleaned up the aftermath of DeRosa's nighttime mêlée with Igor in the attic. I was none too happy with the results.

"CeCe, it happens all the time in police work. You trade a small-time criminal for a shot at the kingpin. Our target is Dacks. Think of it as a trade. We swap two lesser players, Igor and Becky, for the big hitter, Peter Dacks."

"Why do men compare everything to sports?" I'd said with exasperation. "So a man breaks into my house with intent to kill and we let him walk?" I picked through the upended paint cans, avoiding a pool of spilled turpentine on the attic floor.

"Close," he said as he pushed the mop across the ancient floorboards. "We're letting Igor walk but with conditions. These conditions — namely, providing testimony accusing Dacks of orchestrating Teddy's death — will increase the chance that Dacks will go to jail for the rest of his life."

I tossed a garbage bag of debris in the corner and approached one of the half-finished portraits of my mystery man, who DeRosa and I both now knew was him. I dipped a paintbrush in a bowl of black paint and swiped a ridiculous mustache on the portrait. Then I painted a pair of horns on his head and added an air bubble. I filled the bubble with the words, *the devil made me do it,* much to his amusement.

The most sensitive part of the case was how to spin my father's role, which hinged, in part, on actually locating him. In a twist I could barely stomach, it appeared that my father was quite possibly not guilty of anything criminal, making it difficult to have him detained when he was ultimately discovered at JFK boarding an international flight to Brazil. We left my mother in a nearly comatose state under the care of Norma, who dialed 911 as we rushed out of the house. With FBI Agent Swell handling the legwork, DeRosa was able to direct a quick sweep of the area airports. We drove to the airport with the police siren screaming on the roof of the car. As DeRosa explained it to me, we were lucky if we'd be able to hold my father for more than a few minutes. There was no evidence that he had actually tried to steal two infant boys. DeRosa guessed that my father would say that he'd agreed to adopt only one baby through what he believed was a legitimate adoption agency. It was also entirely plausible that my father had agreed to accompany the other baby to the United States en route to the child's adoptive parents. Who wouldn't trust a doctor to supervise an infant on a transatlantic flight?

As far as the deadly drug trials conducted more than twenty years ago, the FDA maintained no regulatory oversight of offshore drug testing, hence its popularity among pharmaceutical companies. My father was a pioneer in offshore trials, but he was clearly not the only doctor to take advantage of the low-cost venue. Today, it was common practice. Drug trial patients are made aware, through the small print, of potential side effects, but the FDA requires no explanation of testing results. In fact, a drug that tests poorly and is ultimately shelved never passes over the desk of an FDA agent. Only drugs seeking their approval based on positive testing results go through the rigor of the FDA process. This loophole, the size of a celestial crater, seemed horribly biased against an uneducated population. Yet it was this crack in the system that Dr. William Prentice had so successfully exploited.

Forcing lines of cars to the shoulder, we'd sped to the airport in under thirty minutes, a miracle by New York standards. Frank double-parked the cruiser in front of the terminal entrance and tossed the keys to a uniformed cop. My father had been pulled from the line of embarking passengers by the Port Authority police and transported to an administrative office, where DeRosa and I found him ranting on about his civil rights.

"I had no idea Dacks would kill Teddy," my father said as we entered the room. "You will never prove it."

"You're right. We'll never prove that you put your son in a position that ultimately cost him his life. We'll never prove that you chose to ignore warnings from your son that something was amiss concerning the unregulated transfer of DNA. Moreover, we will never prove that you called Dacks's bluff, providing him with the motivation to kill your son and threaten your daughter."

My father took a step backward, as if twelve inches of distance would soften the blow.

DeRosa took three long strides forward and stood face to face with him. "We can prove, however, with one hundred percent confidence, that you are not the biological father of Teddy or CeCe."

My father stumbled to regain balance, having had no idea we'd uncovered this familial detail, which he'd kept secret for twenty-eight years. DeRosa's words carried the power of a shotgun, and I watched as my father gripped his chest.

But Frank DeRosa was immune to drama, and he continued without allowing my father to catch his breath. "We can also prove that Teddy and I are twins. These facts, however, should not surprise you," he said as my father searched vainly behind himself for a chair.

The seasoned detective kept the pressure on, pulling up a chair of his own next to my father, who had finally located a seat to rest his broken ego.

"I don't care if your next job is hawking useless vitamins on QVC while you try to repair a reputation that I'm going to shred into pieces so infinitesimal you couldn't glue them back together with a ten-gallon jug of glue." DeRosa was speaking through gritted teeth. "You're going to appear in court and give testimony that ensures a life sentence for Peter Dacks or I'll find evidence to make you guilty of something. You are also going to answer any questions CeCe has concerning her life growing up with a self-centered bastard as a father figure."

DeRosa turned to me and then nodded.

"Dad, what's my real birthday?" I asked. I could see by his head scratching that it was not a date easily retrieved, since my actual birthday had never been celebrated.

"It's the last week of September," he said. "I believe it is the twenty-seventh. You should ask your mother to be certain."

"I would love to, but Mom had another breakdown. She mentioned something disturbing as she faded." I hesitated, hoping my father would voluntarily fill in the blanks, but he remained silent. "Mom said there was another baby. Is it possible that I was a twin, like Frank and Teddy, and you separated us?"

Based on my father's actions with Teddy and Frank, it seemed entirely (though horrifically) possible that my mother had given birth to two babies, and that I too had been separated from my own twin. I clasped my hands tightly not wanting to hear the answer.

"You're not a twin," my father replied. "To my knowledge, you do not have any siblings."

I sighed and released my hands, rubbing

them on the side of my jeans. "So what is Mom talking about? Don't tell me Teddy and Frank were triplets?" I turned to De-Rosa with a worried expression, wondering just how much more he could take.

"No, that was not the case," my father said. Then I watched as he took on a pained expression so aggravated in its intensity that it appeared to cause him physical discomfort. His facial muscles pulled downward, elongating his face like a mirror in a fun house. He rubbed his chin, drawing his hands down the length of jaw. When he spoke, the volume was low and hoarse. "Theodore and Franklin would have lingered in a rundown orphanage abroad. They would have been underfed and unloved. There's a strong possibility that without proper socialization, they would have never developed to their potential. Bringing them to the United States was a wonderful gift and despite their separation, it saved them."

"But you purposely placed me at a disadvantage," DeRosa said.

"I did, but you prevailed, and I retain no guilt for my action. I kept regular tabs on you, and it was apparent within a few years that you would do well despite your surroundings. You'll have to trust me when I say that if I saw a potential for irreparable damage, I would have ended the experiment and removed you from the home."

"So it was an experiment?" DeRosa asked.

"Yes, although I do not expect someone outside the medical field to truly understand the importance of the study."

I rolled my eyes. Despite all that had happened, my father still struggled to fully accept the ethical implications of his actions. He insisted on playing God with people's lives by staging environments, determining family units, and parceling out potentially dangerous drugs. There was more, however, and I could see by his strangled expression that he was weighing how to present his next admission.

"Dad, is there another baby?"

"There was . . . potential for another baby," he replied.

"Go on," DeRosa said.

My father straightened his back and found his voice as he slipped comfortably back into professional mode. He started to speak and I knew we were about to hear a lecture. I prepared myself for an explanation requiring a dictionary as my father began his academic ramble.

"The study of epigenetics is meant to occur over generations," he stated. "I was unable to study Frank's and Teddy's parents, or grandparents, for that matter. This prevented me from investigating the environmental impact of previous generations in order to make inferences on the byproduct, being the boys."

My father cleared his throat, and DeRosa called to an officer outside for a cup of water. After a long sip he continued.

"In a long-term experiment, the researcher's age is limiting. I couldn't project forward, and I couldn't control for things like love. I had no idea when Teddy or Frank would meet the right person and produce offspring within a time frame suitable for actual study. I took it upon myself to accelerate the study by securing fertilized ova."

"I'm lost," I said, propping myself against the wall. "And I'm exhausted. Just say what you have to say."

"Constance, soon after your first ovulation, you had a minor office procedure. You may remember it."

I had a flashback so sharp it forced my eyes closed. I did indeed have a memory of a medical procedure when I was in middle school. I remember being embarrassed by my nakedness under a hospital gown, especially because the doctor in question was my father. He gave me a mild sedative and I remember staying home from school the next day.

"Okay," I folded my arms across my chest.

"I extracted an egg from you," he said, his eyes focused on the floor tiles. "Your mother was furious."

"Dad," I screamed, "you violated me!" I started toward him, fists swinging. DeRosa caught my arm in mid punch as I screeched, "What happened to my egg?"

"I was hoping to fertilize the egg with your brother's sperm," my father responded.

My fists opened and flew to my face in horror. I cried the word *no* over and over until my mouth was dry and caked. The soles of my feet ached as I stamped my legs into the floor. Frank cradled me like a baby, whispering soothing words in my ear until I finally exhausted my rage.

"Where's this baby?" I sobbed.

"I can't say there is a baby," my father said as he rose to leave. He smoothed down the lapel of his sport coat and shook out the wrinkles in his pants. He reached into his pocket for a linen handkerchief, passing it over his face before continuing. "I realized the futility of the study as Frank matured into a successful young man despite his disadvantages. Eventually, I lost track of your genetic material. I have no idea what happened after that."

I was dumbfounded. I looked to Frank, but this strange turn of events was beyond his legal knowledge. A part of me might be stored somewhere in a canister of dry ice, but locating what I assumed was my personal property would be nearly impossible. I wanted to react, but to what? In the momentary lapse, my father made his way freely to the door. He started to leave the room, but DeRosa stopped him.

"You *will* be appearing at the trial as a witness for the prosecution," DeRosa said with his hand on the doorknob. "If your responses are scattered or somehow confusing to the jury, I will make the results of your experiment public. I'd like your word on that."

"You have my word."

FORTY

My father's courtroom cameo was scripted
as tightly as a Shakespearean sonnet. Each
word was chosen for purpose, leaving little
room for tangents. The board of Sound
View Laboratories forced him into retire-
ment but still maintained complete control
over his public discourse. In order to avoid
additional negative exposure, the board
ensured that his statements were reviewed
and approved by a fleet of image-control
experts. On the day of his testimony, my
father's "team" hustled him into the courtroom amid a sea of blue suits, making it
nearly impossible for a reporter or camera
to nab a sound bite.

Dr. William Prentice appeared controlled
on the witness stand, barely flinching when
a professional headshot of Teddy was flashed
on the screen. I found DeRosa in the crowd
and was not surprised to see him fixated on
Teddy's image. He appeared self-conscious,

as if everyone knew the two were actually twin brothers. In fact, this point was not revealed in the trial, since it had no bearing on Peter Dacks's motive to kill my brother. Dacks killed Teddy because he was about to pull the plug on his diabolical plot to compile the world's DNA. DeRosa's association with the case was irrelevant.

Throughout the questioning, my father maintained an airtight story. He had no idea that his son, Dr. Theodore Prentice, was averse to the DNA transfer, and he was completely unaware that Teddy had approached Dacks with the intent to reveal his unethical attempt to package and resell personal medical data. I can't say the courtroom believed my father, but he wasn't the one on trial.

In fact, it was in both my father's and Peter Dacks's interest to act as if they didn't know each other. Both men played as if they were passing acquaintances in the medical industry. Dacks just happened to be hired to recruit patients for one of many tests conducted by the Sound View labs. If the jury had been apprised of their previous relationship, Dacks would have looked guiltier and my father's testimony would have been less believable.

I caught the accused man's eye as Teddy's

image faded in the background. Dacks's demeanor seemed impenetrable. Despite the accusations, he seemed strangely confident, smiling to witnesses and patting his lawyer on the back periodically. He was a complete phony. I had seen footage of my father and Dacks socializing on the beach in Italy, and there was no question that for many years, these men had worked in professional harmony. Dacks had been my father's right-hand man abroad, providing a myriad of services my father would have never been able to accomplish by himself in a foreign country.

But the jury knew none of this. Nor would they ever.

I busied myself during the long weeks of trial in the dead heat of summer by sketching a child who possibly had yet to be born. Strange as it was to think of a child created by myself and my brother, I needed a way to wrap my head around what my father had done. I compiled years of photographs of me and Teddy, attempting to find a combination of features that balanced our strengths and minimized our physical weaknesses. I played with eye shapes and nose alignment. I worked through ratios of facial spacing, even measuring distances from the major features and extrapolating results with my charcoal pencils. I drew young girls and boys in profile, then full-faced, and I mixed the results with straight, curly, and wavy hair. Every few days, I'd pass one to DeRosa with the caption *your niece* or *your nephew.*

The trial ended in late September, with Dacks convicted of premeditated murder. The courtroom cheered. Charlie cried like a baby. Trina and Jonathan embraced as if they had just married, and I climbed across the rows of wooden benches and straight into DeRosa's arms.

"Happy birthday," he said as he lifted me so high in the air that I could observe the courtroom from a bird's eye view. I realized, as I stared at the tops of heads, that this was how my father saw the rest of us, a notch beneath him. I slid down DeRosa's body, resting comfortably in his arms, looking up into the eyes of my new future. A lot had happened, much of it terrible, but there was no doubt I had the best seat in the house.

ABOUT THE AUTHOR

Deirdre Verne (Scarsdale, NY) is a college professor and active blogger. A writer whose target audience is the millennium crowd, Deirdre's interest in green living inspired her to create an off-the-grid character who Dumpster dives her way though a suspense-filled mystery series. A member of Sisters in Crime, Deirdre's short stories have appeared in all three of the New York chapter's anthologies: *Murder New York Style, Murder New York Style: Fresh Slices,* and *Family Matters.*

The employees of Thorndike Press hope you have enjoyed this Large Print book. All our Thorndike, Wheeler, and Kennebec Large Print titles are designed for easy reading, and all our books are made to last. Other Thorndike Press Large Print books are available at your library, through selected bookstores, or directly from us.

For information about titles, please call:
  (800) 223-1244

or visit our Web site at:
  http://gale.cengage.com/thorndike

To share your comments, please write:
  Publisher
  Thorndike Press
  10 Water St., Suite 310
  Waterville, ME 04901